MADE
YOU
LOOK

MADE YOU LOOK

TANYA GRANT

Berkley
New York

BERKLEY
An imprint of Penguin Random House LLC
1745 Broadway, New York, NY 10019
penguinrandomhouse.com

Book design by Jenni Surasky
Title page art: Waterfall © zedspider / Shutterstock

Library of Congress Cataloging-in-Publication Data

Names: Grant, Tanya, author
Title: Made you look / Tanya Grant.
Description: First edition. | New York: Berkley, 2025.
Identifiers: LCCN 2024050161 (print) | LCCN 2024050162 (ebook) |
ISBN 9780593954041 (trade paperback) | ISBN 9780593954058 (ebook)
Subjects: LCGFT: Thrillers (Fiction) | Novels | Fiction
Classification: LCC PS3607.R3658 M33 2025 (print) |
LCC PS3607.R3658 (ebook) | DDC 813/.6—dc23/eng/20250620
LC record available at https://lccn.loc.gov/2024050161
LC ebook record available at https://lccn.loc.gov/2024050162

First Edition: November 2025

Printed in the United States of America
1st Printing

The authorized representative in the EU for product safety and compliance is Penguin Random House Ireland, Morrison Chambers, 32 Nassau Street, Dublin D02 YH68, Ireland, https://eu-contact.penguin.ie.

For Jennifer Skogen and Sheila Masterson, my earliest readers and dearest friends. Rumor has it you're legally entitled to compensation for just how many stories I've made you read. I hope you'll accept this book as payment.

And for everyone who uses social media to make the world a better place, one post at a time.

MADE YOU LOOK

Prologue

LIVESTREAM ●

The spray of blood is so bright it appears shocking on tiny phone screens, but maybe that's the point. Sydney is known for her provocative approach to storytelling, her social media star shining perhaps even brighter than her acting one because of the way she immerses herself in whatever narrative she's selling. Whether it's a couture ball gown flown to a castle in Scotland and photographed high in a stone tower or full-body paint that transforms her into a life-size skeleton for el Día de los Muertos, when Sydney commits to something, she commits.

Right now, there's blood absolutely gushing from a slice in her arm. On-screen, her face twists in agony, but you can't hear her scream. The audio's all wrong—it's just the sound of someone breathing heavily in your ear, so you feel like you're the observer, panting out there in the forest, part of the chase yourself.

At home, people hold their phones closer, nudge nearby friends. Whatever Sydney is selling right now, it's going to be good. Is she announcing a splashy return to the big screen? Or is it a campaign for the lingerie she's wearing, the bustier that makes her breasts look absolutely phenomenal as she runs?

You'll have to wait and see.

Sydney stumbles through the forest, bolting straight toward the camera. Blood keeps gushing, staining the bride-white corset and trickling down the legs she shows off whenever she can.

This is extreme, even for her. How delicious.

The scene is probably against the platform's community guidelines, something so shocking where anyone can see. But it's a livestream, and no one seems to have caught on. At any rate, the chase continues.

Sydney's panic radiates through the screen as she squeezes between two tree trunks. It's not quite spring yet, and the tree bark is bleached of all color. She leaves a red palm print behind as she hauls herself through the narrow gap.

Then something off-screen captures her attention. You can't hear anything other than the heavy breathing, but she twists her head to the side with a wild-eyed stare, and that's when it happens.

Her long, thick hair, rumored to be insured for an obscene sum, catches in a tree branch. Her forward motion halts in a heartbeat, and she's yanked from her feet in midair. As she falls, she kicks up a layer of wet rot from the ground—last season's fallen leaves, packed down under an icy layer of snow.

The debris speckles her bloody legs as she writhes on the ground, the air apparently knocked from her lungs.

A shadow falls over her face. She looks up with terrified eyes, opens her mouth to scream, and—

The camera cuts out.

You sit in dizzying silence for a moment, waiting to see if the feed will resume.

When the screen stays dark, you flick on to the next thing.

1

LUCY

Most people only get a chance to die once. In a car or in bed or on a hike of Mount Everest, death comes to claim them, and that's it.

The first time I died was on an operating room table. A Hail Mary surgery to take my breasts and stop the cancer, when my heart, of all things, blipped out. Since the doctors were already there, they put their expensive educations to good use by both bringing me back to life and finishing the job they started.

Afterward, Nick and my mother stood over my recovery bed and told me how miraculous I was. Since I hadn't participated in the event other than dying in the first place, their praise felt misplaced. Nick looked at me like I was superhuman, when in reality I felt my most vulnerable. Right now, though, I wish he could look at me like he did that day, like he was so glad we had a future to look forward to and the world still held some kindness. Instead, when the honk sounds from downstairs, he looks at me like I'm the biggest disappointment in his life.

He pushes aside the cheap lace curtains that came with the apartment, stained from the previous occupant's cigarette habit, and looks out our third-floor window. "A party bus?" He frowns, part of his view obscured by the awning of the bodega on the first floor. The sound of New York City traffic drifts up from below. "Really?"

I cringe. I had no idea what travel arrangements Sydney secured for the trip, but when he mentions the bus, I'm not at all surprised.

"There are six of us," I mutter.

He lets the curtain drop back into place and sighs, shoving a lock of his dark brown hair out of his eyes. I used to love running my hands through his hair, the way the soft waves were such a contrast to the rough scrape of stubble as I slid my fingers along his jaw. But I won't let myself touch him again.

"You're too old for this shit," he tells me.

I'm twenty-six years old. Too young for breast cancer. Too old to celebrate like the young adult I never got to be.

I may never be the right age for anything again. This, of course, is the crux of our predicament.

Unconsciously, I touch the thumb of my left hand to the indent his ring left on my fourth finger. Just my skin, marked by the memory of better days.

Another honk.

This time, we both wince.

"They're double-parked," Nick says.

I don't know if he means it as a general observation or a hint for me to get out. Before now, I didn't think he wanted me gone, which makes his words sting. I rub the center of my chest, finding it hard to make myself move.

Leaving is the right thing to do, but heartbreak never feels good in the moment.

Oboe pokes his cool, dry nose into the back of my knee. Grateful for the distraction he provides, I bend down and rub his long, silky ears, press a kiss to his velvety snout. He holds my eyes with his liquid, hound dog stare, and I almost can't breathe around the lump in my throat.

"You'll take good care of him?" I ask, not letting myself look up to see the grief on Nick's face.

This trip is a chance for him to clear out of the apartment without me around. After he finishes work today, he and Oboe will head to his parents' house upstate, a hobby farm with a few acres for Oboe to run around on until Nick figures out his next move. Deciding that Nick would get to keep the dog was one of the worst days of my life, but since this whole thing is my fault, I figure it's only fair. I have a feeling Nick's going to need a friend.

"You don't have to do this," Nick says. He's still across the room, the cords on his arms shifting beneath his tanned skin as he worries his hands into and out of fists. On afternoons and weekends, Nick teaches drum lessons to neighborhood kids. I've always loved his arms.

"It's a work trip." We both know it's more than me taking pictures of social media influencers in a pretty place. It's also an escape. "I can't let them down."

"What matters more, Luce: what everyone else thinks of you or what you think of yourself?" I look up in time to meet his gaze, and his familiar brown eyes plead with me. He wants me to stay. The knowledge doesn't ease the sting of the situation as much as I hoped.

It's not just my friends I've committed to this weekend—it's the retreat itself. It's a beautiful location, and the owners deserve beautiful pictures. The kind I know I can deliver. Not to mention, the shoot will help pad my portfolio with the kind of photos I want to be taking more of. But I'm sure to Nick, those would all seem like weak excuses, not nearly as important as trying to fix what's broken between us. The one thing I can't give him.

Before I can answer, someone pounds on the door. I startle at the sound, and Oboe stiffens beneath my touch. He slips from my grasp and trots toward the noise, whuffling his nose into the crack to scent out our visitor.

Nick makes no move toward the door, so I stride across the room to open it.

"Morning, Luce." Sydney barges into my apartment like she enters every room, hair-first, rolling out a red carpet of charm to smooth her path.

Unable to contain himself, Oboe spins in joyful, lovesick circles at her feet.

What a sucker. Just like me.

"We've got to go," Sydney says a little breathlessly, and I suspect she raced up the stairs rather than wait for my ancient elevator to make its way to the lobby to collect her. Sydney Kent waits for no one. In this and every equation, she's the queen.

She glances between me and Nick, lifting an eyebrow as the tension in the room finally reaches her. "Ready?"

Of course I'm not.

I want to apologize to Nick over and over again. I want to feel his arms around me one last time. Here, with someone watching, I can't make myself ask.

Instead, I bend for my camera bag and sling it over my shoulders. I extend the handle of my suitcase and drag it toward the door. "Let's go," I say. The look on Nick's face makes me feel like I'm dying all over again.

I don't let myself think about him emptying his things from the apartment, the way he'll take all the button-down shirts he wears to his marketing agency day job, and how he'll clear out the dog toys I inevitably step on no matter how often I corral them into a bin. Four days from now, I won't be able to recognize my life.

Thinking about it will only immobilize me, and it's too late to change my mind. I straighten my shoulders and follow Syd through the door.

I don't want to leave, but I also don't want to come back.

2

CAITLYN

I post quotes on my social media all the time about not falling into the comparison trap, but my entire life—and my career—are built on looking better than everyone else. *Be your authentic self. Don't measure your struggles against someone else's highlight reel. No one else can be you.* When you live in front of a camera and millions of people drink up your every move, you don't get the luxury of not giving a fuck.

Even though today's a travel day, I'm camera-ready in a hip-skimming skirt and a plunging top. Nash has already applied my makeup, though the swirling blue and purple lights studded in the bus's ceiling cast everything in a garish hue. While we're waiting for Sydney to go collect Lucy—*god, what is taking them so long?*—I figure I might as well show off both my outfit and our transportation. Tag the apparel and party bus companies to give them credit. Nash too.

Cha-ching, cha-ching, cha-ching.

"Brent?" I bat my eyes in the direction of the talent manager I share with Sydney and her boyfriend, Jeff. After Brent caught wind that Syd had booked this gig, he dropped an egregious number of hints about what a great opportunity it would be for him to meet with his star influencers and have an in-person strategy session with the three of us, especially since we collaborate almost exclusively via our phones. That, and he kept going on about how he wants to expand his partnerships with hotel brands, and this retreat is a stepping stone to bigger and better clients for all of us. Ostensibly he's here to work, but I suspect the opportunity to enjoy a mini vacation was a motivating factor. "Can you film a 'cheers' situation for us?"

Brent looks up from where he's hunched over his phone. One day his terrible posture's going to give him a hell of a lot of neck problems, but those who live in glass houses shouldn't cast stones and all that, so I keep my thoughts to myself. "Now?"

I try to tamp down my impatience. "It's as good a time as any."

He shrugs, and I stride across the bus to the bar area. Popping the lid on the ice chest, I pull out a bottle of champagne. "Nash?" I ask, holding the bottle aloft. "Jeff?"

"Hell yeah," Jeff says, pushing his light golden-brown hair out of his face. Though his signature look is to go half-naked, common decency and public hygiene standards have encouraged him to, you know, wear clothing. Today he's donned a T-shirt from his marijuana-themed apparel company, High Standards. He rubs a hand over his chest, rumpling the logo as he climbs to his feet. "Let's get the party started."

Jeff's basically an overgrown frat boy. One who makes a scary-big paycheck and has a social media following small countries would covet.

Nash plucks a champagne flute from the glassware selection beside the bar. "Girl, pop the top," he purrs. He lifts his empty flute elegantly, a pinky finger popped out even though I once watched a video that said it's considered elitist. Nash, unlike Jeff, probably doesn't mean to throw shade.

I glance over my shoulder at Brent. "This setup look good?"

He peers at his cell phone and gestures for us to squeeze in. "A little closer together."

Jeff and Nash press closer to me, Jeff a teenager in the body of a tall Greek god on one side, Nash the gorgeous style tastemaker on the other. It would be better if Lucy were here taking the pictures instead of Brent, but we might as well take advantage of the free time.

I shake the champagne ever so slightly so it'll spray when it pops. The higher the drama, the more stunning the shots.

"On the count of three," Brent says.

I tilt my chin so the light will hit my face just right, then nod my agreement. But before Brent can even start the countdown, the bus door crashes open, welcoming in a blast of chilly March air and the cacophony of city noises and smells, as well as Sydney and Lucy.

Sydney, of course, brings her charismatic energy into play, bounding up the stairs like this free trip to the Catskills is the best thing she could possibly imagine. Personally, I'd prefer to be on a beach right now, but there is something to be said for the exclusivity of the retreat. We're the first people staying on the property, setting the tone for what's to come. Not a bad position to be in.

Behind Sydney, Lucy blinks at the rest of the group. With her shock of short red hair; smooth, creamy skin; and wide blue eyes, she could be a knockout. She even pulls off an artsy vintage aesthetic, though sometimes I suspect it's more of a what-was-cheapest-at-the-thrift-store situation than an intentional style choice. For what it's worth, when she makes online appearances, people usually ask about her clothes. Too bad she always shrinks into herself. No fucking confidence.

Today Lucy looks like she's just cried or is about to cry, even doing a little sniff as she boards the bus. Honestly, she's kind of killing the vibe. I'm not sitting on a party bus right now to watch someone break down.

"Just in time," I say smoothly, handing Syd a flute.

She accepts it with a wide smile, pushing her long dark hair behind her shoulders so it doesn't fall into her glass.

I lift another glass for Lucy, but she shakes her head. She holds her camera bag in front of her to form a barrier between us. "No, thanks, I'm good."

She is most certainly not good.

My shoulders stiffen, and I feel a furrow form between my brows. I'll need to tend to that when I return home. A little baby Botox now will go a long way in the future. "Come on," I say, waving the flute in the air, "live a little."

Lucy freezes like I've just accused her of running over a puppy or something. For someone who's survived cancer, you'd think she'd actually want to enjoy her life.

"Lu-cy, Lu-cy," Jeff chants.

I know Syd keeps him around for a reason, but sometimes I just cannot with him.

"It's fine," Brent says. "If she doesn't want that glass, I do. Lucy can take the pictures instead."

Lucy stops hyperventilating and switches places with Brent. "Which camera should I use? Are we going for a quick story or a still image?"

"Let's start with something polished," I suggest.

She nods and digs into her bag to grab her DSLR camera. While Luce snaps off the lens cap and adjusts the camera settings, Sydney squeezes in beside me, bumping me just off-center.

Nice try, Syd.

Since I'm the one with the damn champagne, I take a step forward, putting myself back into focus.

Lucy watches the exchange with a frown, and I'm sure that to her, my actions seem selfish. Despite what it might look like to run a business that's built on my face, so much of why I landed in this job to begin with is about helping other people. It makes the pressure to perform that much higher.

"Let me know when," I say to Lucy, and she brings the camera to her eye.

I shouldn't have been upset with her before—this setup is so much better. Sydney next to me, the men flanking us, the champagne bottle cool in my hands, and the camera going off with a flash.

It's the natural order anyway.

3

LUCY

It's not until after we're done taking photos—Caitlyn popping the champagne, the cork shooting wildly in the confined space, people clinking glasses, and Cait and Syd posing provocatively with the dance pole that inexplicably stretches from floor to ceiling in the bus's center aisle—that anyone other than Syd actually greets me.

By then our driver, Tony, has eased the party bus off the curb and has nosed it toward the Catskills and our retreat, which promises to be an oasis of relaxation just ninety minutes from the bustle of New York.

"Hi, doll," Nash breathes, separating from the group. He places a hand on each of my shoulders and leans in to air-kiss my cheeks.

His kind gesture prompts a flurry of activity. Not to be outdone, Caitlyn gives me a quick, one-armed squeeze. "So glad you made it, Lucy." With the kind of beauty that smacks you in the face and her toned yet curvy build, she's the blonde bombshell to Sydney's dark-haired ingenue, the glam to Syd's sophisticated street style. Even when something as simple as a thank-you is an afterthought to them, they're still so pretty to shoot that it almost makes up for the social slights.

"Thanks," I tell her. My thoughts flit to Nick and Oboe and the widening distance between us, and I feel a pang of regret in my chest. "Glad to be here too." Maybe if I say it enough, it'll start to feel true.

Jeff grunts and nods in my direction, and Brent gives me a fist bump, acknowledging me with a "LuckyLens."

I try not to frown. My social media handle—selected on a whim one night pre-diagnosis when Syd and I got drunk and dreamed up the possibilities for my future—is, in retrospect, an uncreative play on my name. *Lucy* is just a consonant off from *lucky*, but given my life, maybe I'm not so lucky after all. And delivered by Brent, whose overstyled sandy-blond hair has unironic frosted tips, the reminder grates.

I drop onto one of the leather bench seats and run a palm over its surface. Sydney takes a seat across from me, leveling a crooked grin at me that displays the tiny gap between her front teeth. On anyone else, that gap could look unfinished, but on her, it just complements her wide-eyed beauty. She has the kind of face that the camera loves, one that gets more interesting the longer you look at it. She's versatile in a way that makes people take notice. "Nice ride, right?"

I sweep my gaze through the bus's interior. Nick was right to be skeptical. The bus is big enough to hold thirty people, but it's just the six of us inside. Seven if you count Tony up front. The bus was clearly designed to transport people, but not necessarily their stuff. It doesn't have an undercarriage storage section for luggage, so our suitcases are crammed together at the far end of the bus. Each time Tony stops the bus short, the suitcases threaten to roll down the aisle and crush us.

Along with duffel bags and suitcases, there are buckets of fresh flowers gathered from the morning flower market and an honest-to-goodness rolling rack holding gowns and a huge pink, cropped faux-fur coat. At least I hope it's faux fur.

I glance at Tony to make sure he can't overhear me and find his eyes are on the road. "It's . . . something," I admit. It feels weird not to wear seat belts as we're driving. At the very least, it feels like our stuff should be strapped down.

Sydney barks out a laugh like I've surprised her, delight dancing in her eyes. This is how she does it—she gets you so relaxed you don't realize you're in a trap until it's too late. She leans forward, elbows on her knees, and pins me with an inquisitive stare. "So," she says, "what was that about up in the apartment?"

"What was what?" I mumble, and drop my gaze.

Syd won't let it go that easily. "Luce. You and Nick? I thought the tension would kill me." She takes my hands in hers, and my stomach drops the second her eyes widen.

She's figured it out.

"Luce," she says again, this time so gravely my chest tightens with self-pity. She holds up my left hand and examines the finger where my ring should be. "Oh, honey. What happened?"

I don't want to have this conversation on a party bus that smells like soured wine, where anyone motivated enough can listen in, but once Syd sets her mind on something, she's unshakable. Better to get this over with fast and move on.

I lower my voice to a whisper. "It wasn't going to work out."

"Oh, Luce," she says softly. "He loves you."

My chest feels like someone hollowed it out with one of those scoops you use to carve pumpkins; the serrated teeth have scraped me so raw that there's nothing left but pulp. "And I love him. But that doesn't mean I'm good for him."

Sydney makes the connection in a heartbeat. "So *you* broke up with *him*. Not the other way around."

"If I hadn't," I say defensively, "we probably still would have ended up in the same place."

Her mouth twists, part disappointment, part disbelief. She doesn't understand why I haven't figured out how to live the way she does, like everything's full of wonder. The truth is, it's just a slip from carefree to careless—to *reckless*—and I haven't figured out how to toe that line. "When you get scared, you push people away."

"That's normal." I can hear the defensiveness creep into my voice.

"Maybe, but it isn't healthy." Sydney sighs. "Why do you do this to yourself?"

"I don't know what you're talking about."

"You tell yourself you don't deserve love. That you're going to hurt the people around you or let them down somehow."

"And look, I did hurt him. At least I did it now before he realized I'm not what he signed up for."

She frowns. You'll almost never catch her making this face on social media—you can see her forehead wrinkle, which destroys the illusion that she's ageless. "I think Nick has a pretty good idea of who you are."

But he doesn't. No one except Syd knows the worst of me, and even she doesn't know everything.

"Just leave it alone, Syd."

She grasps my hands again. "Please don't push me away."

But of course I won't. She's the one person I need to keep close.

"I promise." I squeeze her fingers and paste on a smile that I hope says, *Look, I'm perfectly okay. Nothing to see here.* "Now, can we drop this?" I don't say it loudly, but the thing about a strained conversation is, no matter how quietly you speak, everyone seems to hear.

Caitlyn perks up farther down the bus, where she's huddled with Brent, holding her second glass of champagne. "Something wrong?"

Sydney glances guiltily at me, letting me be the one to tell Caitlyn that Nick and I separated.

"Oh no!" Caitlyn echoes, shooting me a sympathetic look. "You guys were so good together."

Frustration ripples through me. I don't need her to tell me that Nick was the best part of me. I knew that much myself.

"It's seriously okay," I say, not sure why I have to be the one comforting them about my breakup. "This trip comes at a perfect time. I'm going to focus on hanging with everyone and getting some shots for my landscape portfolio. It'll be just what I need."

As of three months ago, I'm on Sydney's payroll as her photographer. If she had her way, I would have been hired a few years ago, the second I got diagnosed with cancer. Maybe I should have been, for the amount of money and fans I earned her.

During my battle with cancer, every time Sydney visited me in the hospital, she'd share snaps of me and my photography on social media. To her growing legion of fans, our friendship made her seem more caring and human, giving Syd a cause to champion along with her domestic violence advocacy. In turn, I became Cancer Girl, a supporting character in the film of Sydney's life. It could have been gross, but Sydney never made it feel that way. And when my hospital bills threatened to overwhelm me, Sydney swooped in with a GoFundMe that wiped my debts away.

She's given me a clean slate in more ways than one, and my position should feel like freedom. Working for Sydney is a chance to get paid to do something I love while I figure out how to reenter the world. But it mostly feels like another reason I'm indebted to her.

"Okay," Caitlyn says with a nod, as though she's made a decision. "We'll just have to make this weekend so spectacular you'll—*Shit!*"

Her words cut off suddenly as the bus jerks sideways.

A weightless sensation swoops through my stomach, the feeling of slipping wildly out of control. Around me, a string of curses and shouts of surprise. There's a rushing noise, plastic and fabric and metal rolling over the hardwood floor, and I snap my gaze toward the back of the bus to find all our luggage sliding forward, hurtling toward our seats.

"Fuck!" Jeff swears, jamming his arm into the aisle to block the suitcases before they can hit anyone. A weekender bag falls off the stack with a thump and lands inches from Nash's feet.

He gapes at it, looking as alarmed as I feel. "Was that almost death by Prada?"

"That, and your stupid rolling rack," Jeff says, pushing away the offending equipment with a grunt.

"Y'all okay?" By now Tony has pulled the bus to the side of

the road and has turned around to face us, panting and apologetic. "Black ice. Came out of nowhere."

"Black ice?" Syd wrinkles her nose. "It's not supposed to be that cold. The weather app promised it would be, like, fifty degrees this weekend."

"Clearly they got it wrong," Brent says, flicking spilled champagne from his fingertips. The bus's interior is awash with the scent of booze, making my head spin.

"So sorry for all this, folks," Tony apologizes, but it's not like he can control the weather.

"We're okay," I assure him despite my racing heart. He assesses us one more time before nodding and easing the bus back onto the road.

"Look." Caitlyn holds her glass aloft. "I didn't even spill my drink."

"The mark of a true professional," Brent says.

"Or an alcoholic," Jeff adds.

Sydney whacks his arm. "Oh my god, Jeff, be nice!"

Caitlyn just grins and fixes her gaze on me. "As I was starting to say earlier, we should make this an unforgettable weekend. But"—she lifts her glass in a toast—"it looks like we're already off to quite a start."

4

STORY POST

Reverie Retreat—Day 1

Hello, lovelies!" Sydney shoves her hair out of her face and grins into the camera. Like everything about her, her hair color's multidimensional, a dark brown that ripples with red undertones when the light hits just right. There's no hair dye on earth that can quite match it, though plenty of people have gone to their hairdressers begging for the same shade. "Remember when I told you that I had an exclusive invite to the hottest new retreat?" Sydney's eyes sparkle with excitement. "We're finally here!" Her voice rises in a squeal with the exclamation. This is why people love her. She's a cool girl, but never too cool for you to feel like you could be best friends.

Holding one arm out to highlight the view behind her, she spins in a circle. "Is this not the most amazing?" Bare trees stand in a shivering circle under a patch of stark blue sky. Beneath their branches, in the middle of a long driveway, idles a party bus with the words **BASH BUS** printed on the side. Possibly no one considered how *bash* could imply *crash*, and maybe that's not the mental connection the company would want you to make.

Before you can think on it too deeply, Sydney zooms the camera back in so it's just her face framed by the edges of the phone screen. Her long lashes sweep the tops of her cheeks as she blinks coyly at you.

It's a hypnotic dance, showing you her world, pulling you in beside her.

"Okay, before I give you the tour, let's get into the details. We're at the Reverie retreat here in the Catskills. That's *Reverie* like *daydream*, and I couldn't imagine a more fitting name for this place. It's a super-exclusive vacation rental where you get all the amenities of a hotel but with the privacy of being in your own space. Reverie doesn't open to the public for another few weeks, so we're literally the first people who get to stay here, and we're bringing you along for the ride. There's a big central lodge and all these adorable cabins, which I'll show you in a sec. Perfect for a little together time and then, if you need it, a little alone time too." She laughs. "You know what I mean, right?" There's noise behind her, and Sydney brightens. "Ah! Everyone's here. Let's go say hi."

The next clip shows a time-lapse video of Sydney's friends departing the bus. It feels like when a bridal party gets introduced at a wedding reception, the way everyone's pressured to make a grand entrance. Still, the characters ham it up.

Jeff steps off the bus and immediately strips off his shirt and whips it around his head in a celebratory circle, his taut abs highlighted by a glow that likely came from a spray tan rather than actual sunlight.

Nash struts down the steps, his mischievous eyes a hazel color so light they almost look gold, especially in contrast to his dark lashes. He bows with a flourish before twirling away.

Caitlyn winks and blows a kiss at the camera, her full lips glossed to a rosy shine.

Even Brent is here, striding across the packed ground, wearing loafers with golden pineapples embroidered on the toes, a slightly-too-thin white T-shirt stretched across his barrel chest.

The camera cuts again, and you're back with Syd, closer to the tree line. The stark sky makes her brown eyes pop. With one hand on her chest, she takes in a deep breath. "Can you feel that?" She nods and takes another gulp of air. "This place really is a dream. Calm, peaceful, cleansing for the soul. So freaking magical." She beams at the camera. "Wish you were here. It's gonna be the best."

5

CAITLYN

This place is a mud pit. My high heels—mostly impractical but so pretty on city streets—sink into the earth the second I step away from the clearing where the party bus is parked.

I wobble and almost twist an ankle, pitching against Jeff's rock-hard chest.

"Slow down, CaityCat," Jeff drawls as he sets me on my feet. My social media handle sounds way too provocative coming from his mouth. When I picked the name, I wanted something that was, well, me. Easy to remember and catchy. I don't usually regret the choice, but Syd's boyfriend makes me want to reconsider. "In a rush?"

I slap a smile on my face. "The early bird gets the worm. Or, in this case, the best bed." I gesture at the row of six cabins beside us. They're sleek modern boxes arranged mere yards from the edge of a cliff. We're too early in the season for the trees dotting the hillside below to have leaves, so it's a sea of brown sticks broken by the occasional scrubby green pine tree.

From where I stand, I can only see the vertical wood planks

of the cabin exteriors and a hint of the doors, but I know from the brand email Brent sent me that in each cabin, the far wall overlooking the cliff and the trees is pure glass. If I'm going to be out in the woods, I want the calmest, quietest room possible. I want to feel like I'm the only one in the world. After that bus ride, I've earned it.

I spin on my heel to follow through on finding a place to plunk down my purse but stop short when I realize I have no idea how check-in works.

Across the clearing, Sydney's chatting into her cell phone's camera. I presume she's capturing footage to broadcast later, because cell signal cut out a good thirty minutes before we arrived. I pull my phone out of my purse to confirm. No bars.

I'm not sure if the owners or managers of this place thought things through. It's great to hire influencers to promote your retreat, but you miss out on the real-time audience connection if you can't get cell service.

Ignoring the last text message my phone received before the signal failed, the one that makes my skin itch, I shove my cell back into my purse.

"Brent?" I call. He jogs toward me and Jeff, or at least gets as close to a jog as Brent gets. In his thirties, he's the oldest of our crew, and next to Jeff, he's positively doughy. "Do you have keys?"

"Right here." He holds up an envelope that he's procured from somewhere near the main building.

His response attracts Sydney and the rest of our friends. While Tony dutifully unpacks the party bus behind us, we jockey for position around Brent, whose mud-splattered shoes are so hideous they could almost be cute.

"How are we doing this?" Nash asks.

"First come, first served?" I ask, blinking up at Brent sweetly.

Jeff snorts. "So competitive."

Everyone ignores him.

"I've got Sydney and Jeff in the cabin closest to the Lodge." Brent points it out to us. "Then Lucy, Nash, Cait, me, and the spare cabin. That work for everyone?"

Everyone else nods their agreement, but I frown at Brent. I don't want to be in the middle of the group, or this weekend's going to be more stressful than I want. "Can you and I switch?"

He refrains from rolling his eyes, but I can tell he wants to. "Fine."

I clap my hands and grin at him. At the end of the row, it'll be quieter, and I'll be way more relaxed.

"So we check in," Syd says. "Then what's the plan?"

As our digital talent manager, Brent acts as a liaison between influencers—like me, Syd, and Jeff—and brands, connecting the right people to the right companies to make an impact. In his case, he takes it a step further than just making connections, going so far as to lay out a start-to-finish plan of execution so the influencers can focus on what we do best—creating jaw-dropping, enviable content.

Reverie specifically requested Sydney and Lucy for this trip, and since the facility has so much room, Syd invited the rest of us along. For influencers, getting free trips is one of the perks of the job. It's a chance to create content in a fresh environment and keep our profiles from getting stagnant, so of course Jeff and I said yes. Then Syd tapped Nash to do our styling and makeup for the weekend, giving him a chance to get paid and create content of his own. Brent, of course, invited himself.

When Reverie heard the news that they were getting even more star power than they signed up for, they were beyond thrilled. Of course, that meant their shot list expanded right along with the guest list, and Brent's had to factor that into his grand content plans.

"Reverie wants us to capture some of the key amenities. The cabins, the Lodge, the spa and pool area, and some of the hiking trails." As Brent talks, Lucy frantically types notes into her phone, nodding along with each point. Technically, Reverie wants me and Syd and Jeff highlighting teasers of the place on our socials before the official photos get posted, but that means Lucy needs to be right there with us taking pictures. If she's going to do the work of remembering the list of must-have shots, all the better for me. "Supposedly," Brent continues, "there's a waterfall around here too."

Sydney gives a little gasp of joy. Out of the corner of my eye, I catch her exchanging a secretive glance with Nash. Who knew waterfalls would get her rocks off?

"The waterfall, yes," Brent says, preening as though he created the spectacle himself. "Very aquatic."

Dear god.

"Any reason we can't start shooting this afternoon?" Sydney directs her question to Lucy, and after doing what looks like painful mental math, Lucy shakes her head.

"That's fine."

"Great." I hold out my hand to collect my room key. When Brent places it in my palm, I smile back at him. "Maybe Sydney and I can start getting ready with Nash, and you and Jeff and Tony can bring the luggage to our rooms?"

Lucy clears her throat like she's annoyed I haven't mentioned her. It's not like I've forgotten her, but what? I doubt she wants to carry luggage, and she probably doesn't want me to assign her a task either.

I shrug rather than state the obvious, which is *Lucy, you do you*. Right now, she's the least of my problems. "So we're agreed." I glance at Nash to confirm. "Let's all meet back here in an hour."

"If we're doing this, don't be late," Lucy warns. "Sunset doesn't wait just because you need another round of mascara."

"Okay, it was one time . . ." I start, but Nash places a gentle hand on my shoulder to stop me.

"Not only will we meet expectations," he tells Lucy, "we'll exceed them."

For him, she softens her scowl.

I want to roll my eyes, but it's never a good idea to piss off the person who can make you look like either a star or a troll. "You heard the man," I tell her. "We'll be fine."

The group starts to break, but Brent stops us with one last warning: "As a heads-up, there's no Wi-Fi in the cabins. Any posting you do will have to be from the Lodge."

My mood darkens with the news. Everything this weekend is going to be harder than it needs to be. What the hell kind of place is this?

6

LUCY

I always have to stay one step ahead. People assume that being a photographer means you just show up and take pictures of what you see, but when it comes to photographing locations like hotels, you have to do a delicate dance with all their moving parts. Places, like people, are living, breathing things. They're always changing, and you want to capture them in their best light.

In some ways, traveling to Reverie with other people makes my job harder than it needs to be. The retreat wants us to capture photographs of the facilities. And, yes, I'm sure the fact that they hired influencers means that they want real people in some of the images. But I'm equally sure they'll want pictures of the grounds in a pristine state. With the amount of luggage everyone had in the party bus, I'd guess I have thirty minutes, max, before stuff starts spilling out everywhere. After all, the natural law of the universe is chaos.

My cabin might be the only one that I can guarantee will stay untouched until later, so I plan to photograph it after I get through some of the common spaces. First, though, I need to make sure my stuff makes it inside.

I intercept Tony carrying my suitcase toward the row of cabins. Despite the chill in the air, sweat beads on his forehead, and he looks like he hasn't caught a breath in the last fifteen minutes. There are already piles of gear outside each cabin, though the infamous rolling rack is nowhere to be seen. Brent and Jeff were supposed to help with bags, but they appear to have ditched Tony.

Poor guy.

"I've got it from here," I say, taking my bag from our driver with a smile. I fish in my camera bag and pull out a tip for him.

His warm hands close around mine, holding them for a beat. "Thank you, miss." I wonder if anyone else bothered to tip him. "That's it for me, so I'll be back on Monday to pick y'all up."

I wish him a safe drive back to the city, and he climbs into the party bus and pulls away. The rumble of the bus fades into the distance as he exits the way we came: down miles of long, winding road flanked by dense woods.

The silence of the forest settles in around me.

Alone.

At this elevation, spring seems further away. The black ice wasn't a fluke—it really is freezing out. Crisp air curls around my face, and I'm glad for my turtleneck sweater. In March, winter is still here in the woods, brutal and elemental.

I close my eyes and breathe deeply, aware I'm doing the same stupid thing Sydney was doing on camera. I can't help myself. It feels like a place where you can unwind a little, and maybe, after getting all the pictures I need to take, I can finally do that.

Flicking my eyes open again, I haul my suitcase toward my designated room. Up close, the cabins are pretty—gleaming minimalist boxes perched on short stilts to account for the hillside rolling beneath them. Each building is set just a few feet away from the next, like a row of perfectly placed buttons trailing down the spine of the mountain. All of them run parallel to the edge of a steep cliff, far enough away that if you tripped, you wouldn't plunge off the face of the earth, but close enough to the drop to be dizzying. All the better to see the world from, I suppose.

After unlocking my cabin's silver metal door, I drop my suitcase just past the entryway and gasp. Across from me, at the end of the short wooden building, the wall is made entirely of glass. The window, which on closer inspection is a sliding door, opens out onto nature. Trees stretch as far as I can see, rolling away at my feet. It feels like if it weren't for the discreet safety guard over the sliding door, you could tumble out into the clouds.

They did not undersell the view.

I wish I could flop onto the crisp white bed and stare out at the treetops, or even sit in the afternoon sun.

Unfortunately, there's no time.

Instead I grab my camera bag and head toward Reverie's main building. What did Brent call it? The Lodge.

While a person standing between two cabins could reach out their arms and touch both buildings, the Lodge is set apart from the sleeping spaces. The sleek wooden building hugs the crest of the hill, with a wall made entirely of windows facing out over the view. Wood and glass. Glass and wood. The theme is clear.

Unlike the cabins, which have normal-height ceilings, the Lodge's window wall rises to two stories to capture the beauty of the land. The ceiling slopes down to a single story at the back wall.

I immediately want to capture the reflection of the forest in that shimmering wall of glass. I need to get inside the Lodge to shoot the interior before everyone destroys it, but if I hurry, I can squeeze in this shot too.

Keeping my eyes on the Lodge, I skirt around to the cliff side of the cabins, eager to find an angle where everything clicks and the image in my head matches the one in front of me.

There's beauty in the hunt, and I'm breathless when that moment comes. Wind in my face and a tug of recognition in my stomach. When I'm in the zone like this, I can almost forget the disaster I've created of my life.

Here.

I reach into my camera bag without looking, but I'm in too much of a rush to get the shot before someone ruins it, and my fingers are too cold and stiff to get a good grip.

The camera slips, and momentum carries me a few steps forward as I fumble it, determined not to let it drop. After a breathless second, I've got it.

Thank god.

"Not today, Satan," I whisper, looping the camera strap around my neck, but my triumph is short-lived. When I look up, I realize how close that fumble brought me to the edge of the cliff. Another few steps and I'd be at the bottom.

My stomach turns liquid and I sink to my knees with a gasp, not trusting my legs to hold me. That was far too close.

"Lucy?" Brent's voice startles me, sending my heart into

overdrive. "What are you doing on the ground?" He's closer than I realized, rounding the corner of Sydney's cabin.

"I . . ." I shake my head. He doesn't actually want an explanation, and anything I say is going to make me look careless or like I'm not capable of handling myself on this shoot. "Never mind." I push to my feet and take a few shaky steps toward him, grateful when I can no longer feel the pull of the void at my back.

"Walk with me?"

I look longingly at the Lodge. Sitting down sounds pretty great right about now, and if I can't have that, I want a minute alone to collect myself. "I really should get inside for pictures."

"Sure, sure. In just a sec."

I've shot with the rest of this group many times before, but Brent has only joined us for the occasional event, and never for an overnight trip. I don't know him well enough to say for sure, but based on the length of the emails I've seen him send to Sydney, I'm guessing almost nothing with him takes just a sec.

I resign myself to the fact that I'm not going to get that minute alone. "What's up?" Even with Brent running down the clock on daylight hours, for Syd's sake, I can't say no to him. My performance is a reflection on her, so I'll be as professional as I can.

"You've got the list of pictures we need for this weekend?"

"Working through it now," I grit out. *Trying to anyway.*

"Good, good." He hums thoughtfully. "So the photos you're taking are for official sponsored posts after we get home." I nod. "But while we're here, let's also grab some behind-the-scenes pics and stories we can share live. Teasers, you know?"

He's acting like I haven't done the same thing every time we've worked together. "Of course." I smile tightly.

"And I really want you to get the girls together."

"I usually do, Brent." I'm trying my best to stay patient, but I can't help adding, "Is that all?"

Syd once confessed to me that before Brent became a talent manager, he wanted to be an influencer himself. He was a little too try-hard to find success in front of the camera, but she swears he's good at connecting her with opportunities. He seems to like calling the shots, too, but for someone who wants to be in charge, he's doing a terrible job of understanding what needs to be done—actually beginning the shoot.

Brent rubs a hand over his jaw and hesitates for a moment. "Just make sure you don't let whatever's going on in your personal life affect this weekend. It's a big opportunity for everyone."

"You think I don't know that?" The bright sting of tears in my eyes surprises me, and a surge of anger follows. To drag the thing I'm clearly avoiding into the light is a low blow. "Last I checked, Sydney's my boss. Not you." I step around him and march toward the Lodge, no longer caring if he has more to say.

Sometimes I feel like the Big Bad Wolf, dressed up in Grandma's clothing. From a distance, all you see is my frailty, the vulnerability that Sydney displayed for the world in bite-size pieces. It's easy to doubt poor, weak Cancer Girl, easier to dismiss me than admit you've let a wolf into your bed. But if you get close enough and really look, you might see the forest in my eyes, smell the winter in my hair. See the teeth in my smile. It's just that no one bothers to look.

"Wait, Lucy," Brent calls, trailing after me.

I'm too angry and embarrassed to let him see me like this. If he wants to apologize, he can do it later.

I storm toward the Lodge, and when I get within range of the building, my phone buzzes to life. I reach for it instinctivly, and a message appears on my lock screen before I have the sense to look away.

I read the sender first—Nick—with a sharp ache in my chest. But it's the message that gives me pause. Everything ok? Got a weird message from Jeff.

What could Jeff possibly want to talk to Nick about?

Brent's footsteps echoing at my back snap me to attention. I can't dwell on Nick's text right now; Brent's wasted too much of my time already.

I shove everything away—my phone, Nick's question—and reach for the door. I just want to do my job so I can relax in peace. But when I step inside the Lodge, my mouth drops open at what I find.

Forget the text message; I've got bigger problems.

7

CAITLYN

"What are you guys doing?" Lucy screeches, banging open the door to the Lodge. It's a very dramatic entrance—she's backlit by the afternoon sun casting through the open doorframe, and the light against her hair makes her look like she's wearing a halo of fire.

I look at my phone screen and try not to laugh. Lucy's interrupted my live broadcast of the behind-the-scenes peek at our photo shoot, and I've inadvertently caught her antics over my shoulder. This is priceless material.

"Whoops," I say, playing to the camera. "Looks like not everyone got the memo." I keep the video stream rolling, but flip the view so it's pointed at the mirror Nash has arranged me and Sydney in front of. Nash stands behind me, and you can still see Lucy over my shoulder, as well as Sydney, who's frantically waving at Lucy to calm the fuck down.

"Nash?" I ask, trying to salvage the video. "Lucy wants to know what we're doing. Can you fill us in?"

Lucy narrows her eyes but doesn't move. If she wants to look like a crazy person, let her.

I might never understand what Sydney sees in her. I mean, yes, Lucy's talented, and, yes, she's an adoring audience for Sydney. But, like, what do they talk about when they're alone together?

Without missing a beat, Nash catches my eye in the mirror and says, "We're just about to start contouring your face." He taps a makeup brush against the lid of a compact. "Buuuut," he drags out in a teasing voice, "you'll have to stay tuned for the outfit and hair in the final photos." He winks. "Gotta keep some surprises for you."

He's being nice, protecting Lucy, and I'll let it slide for now. There's no need for me to keep filming anymore. I'll only look like a bitch.

"You heard the man," I say. "Stay tuned for the magic to happen. That's all for now, friends." I blow a kiss toward the mirror and then stop the livestream.

The second I lower my phone, Brent sneaks in the door. Looks like someone wisely chose to stay off-screen. "What's the problem?" he asks, sounding beleaguered.

Lucy storms farther into the Lodge and addresses her complaints to everyone. "I thought you were getting ready in your rooms."

Nash shakes his head. "Sorry, doll. They were too small."

The cabins, despite being clean and pretty, really do make you feel like you're in a shoebox. My room is barely big enough to hold my king bed and a small table and chair. There's not even space to do a morning yoga routine.

Lucy glances despairingly at Brent. "But there's makeup everywhere. And clothes." She spins, taking in a view of the Lodge. In fairness, we have commandeered most of the main room.

The Lodge is a long rectangle, with an open kitchen area at one end. The kitchen transitions to a dining area, and beyond that is a glorified lobby/living room, with carefully crafted oak furniture spaced out just so. A floor-to-ceiling stone fireplace rises in the middle of the room, giving you a chance to enjoy it no matter whether you're on the dining or lounging side. On the wall opposite the windows, a narrow hallway I haven't explored yet runs the length of the Lodge.

Right now, Syd and I sit in the living area facing the long, glass-fronted wall to make the most of the natural light. A few minutes ago, Nash and Jeff dragged one of the two communal dining tables to the middle of the living area to hold Nash's gear. Now it's completely covered in makeup and brushes. A curling iron's plugged in to the kitchen island to heat. And the rolling rack of clothes rests near the back wall, with Jeff digging through some of the other luggage beside it. He's been at it for a good five minutes, which leads me to believe he hasn't found what he's looking for just yet.

"This isn't your first rodeo," I say as gently as possible. The effort makes my jaw ache. "You know that styling requires a lot of tools."

Lucy shakes her head. "I needed you guys to stay out of here until I got my shots of the place. It's part of what the brand wanted."

"We're sorry, Luce," Sydney says. "We didn't realize you didn't have those shots already."

Lucy spins on me then, a spark of anger flaring in her eyes. "And what was that about earlier?" she demands. "You seriously kept filming?"

I shrug, fighting to rein in my temper. "This is the only

building with Wi-Fi, so it's not like I can do my job anywhere else. And I wasn't trying to make you look bad. Believe it or not, that doesn't help anyone."

I'm not like Sydney. I don't want a career as an actress. I don't plan to swan off and do something else. This is it for me. So everything that hurts my reputation hurts my future.

"She's right, Luce." Jeff looks up from the luggage long enough to give a little chuckle of agreement. "You don't need anyone's help to look bad."

Lucy's face goes so red, I'm worried she might pass out. "Thank you for that insight," she spits, her eyes narrowed. "And don't think you're off the hook either. What's this about you sending weird messages to Nick?"

"What in the actual fuck are you talking about?" Jeff rolls his eyes. "Why would I send a message to your ex-fiancé? I have nothing to say to that guy." He glances around and realizes he's the center of attention. "Hey, now that we're all talking, has anyone seen my drone?" He says it to the group, but his hard stare's aimed right at Lucy, who looks offended.

"Seriously? That's why you're tearing apart the room?"

"Uh, yeah. You have a problem with that?"

"You're making an even bigger mess!" She frowns as he dumps out a tote bag full of shoes. "I seriously doubt your drone is hiding with the stilettos."

"Okay, then where the fuck is it?" He looks over at the rest of us. "Am I being punk'd? I swear I packed it. Big-ass black backpack with zippers everywhere." He looks at Sydney. "You saw me with it, right, babe?"

Syd looks guilty. "I was so busy pulling together my own

stuff. I wasn't paying super-close attention." She bites her lower lip, considering. "You sure it made it on the bus?"

"Yeah. I mean, it was with the rest of the stuff getting loaded. And now it's not here." He glances at Lucy again. "Did you take it?"

"Why would I take your drone?" she replies. "I'm the photographer, and I have my own camera."

"Well, it's missing. And it's worth a lot, so . . ."

"Assuming the drone actually made it on the bus—" Lucy starts.

"It *did*."

She glares at him. "Then you would have been able to keep better track of it if you'd unloaded your own gear instead of bailing on Tony."

"Who's Tony?"

Lucy looks like she could murder him. "Our driver." I don't miss the scathing look she shoots at Sydney, and this time, I don't blame her. Why Syd spends so much time with someone so clearly out of touch is something I've struggled to understand myself.

"O-kay," Brent eases in before Jeff can accuse Tony of absconding with the drone himself. He turns to Lucy with an apologetic look. "Maybe you should take a sec," he suggests in a placating tone. It's the kind of thing he says when he's trying to calm down someone who's being a diva. I'm not ashamed to admit he uses that voice on me sometimes. "Go for a walk?"

"I was just out for a walk," she says through gritted teeth. "And look where that got me."

Sydney hops from her chair and glances at me and Nash and

Jeff like we're the bad guys here. I will never understand why she always takes Lucy's side.

"Come on, Luce, I need to borrow your cabin to film a story. In the meantime, let Nash finish up with Cait so we can get out and start shooting." She flashes a rueful smile. "Sunset waits for no one, right?"

Lucy blows out a long breath and says, "Fine."

"Great." Sydney strides across the room. She's dressed in one of the plush robes that were hung in each of our cabins. It swallows her delicate frame, and from far away, she looks like a little kid. Sydney loops an arm through Lucy's and tugs our photographer toward the front door.

Lucy gives us one last scowl and allows herself to be pulled along.

"Ah fuck," Brent mutters under his breath when they're halfway across the room. He rubs a hand over his stomach as if he has indigestion. "Lucy wasn't wrong. We do still need the shots."

"So fix things," I suggest.

"You can try to shoot the interior again tomorrow," he calls after the women. "I'll help clean up."

But the two of them are already gone.

8

LUCY

Sydney has looped her arm through mine, gently tugging me toward the Lodge's exit, but as soon as we're outside, the closeness chafes. I pull my arm from hers and make a show of adjusting my camera against my body so she doesn't take my need for distance as a personal slight.

She and Brent were right; I needed to step away, and when the fresh air slaps me in the face, I feel my heart rate calming. It's so much quieter in the woods than in the city. Out here it's just sky and trees. My breath is loud in my ears and my shoes squelch in the mud. I try to make my body whisper, but with nothing else here to dampen the sound, everything I do feels like a shout.

Sydney doesn't say anything, just lets the silence stretch out between us until I rend it with a sigh. "Let's head to my cabin. You can film your story."

"You're the boss," she says agreeably, and it makes my cheeks heat all over again. This time with embarrassment. In reality, Sydney is the boss of almost everyone here. At the very least, she's the sun we orbit around. The golden one. And I've just cast a raincloud over the mood.

We stride toward the cabins, and Sydney gives me space to organize my thoughts without pressuring me to speak. I'm wrestling with myself more than anything.

"Sorry, Syd," I say at last. "What happened back there isn't me."

She gives me a sideways look. "I know."

"I'm only trying to do my job." I need to tread carefully here. "As much as I'm happy to be with everyone, I'm really looking forward to getting to relax too."

She nods. "It's been a rough few days."

A lump rises in my throat, a shameful sting of tears. My personal life is a dumpster fire, and that's before I nearly tumbled off a cliff. "Yeah," I say. We've reached my door, and I'm grateful for the chance to drop my gaze while I dig the key from my bag. "Anyway, the Lodge is pretty, but I much prefer shooting landscapes. And people."

She grins. "Shooting people *with cameras*."

It's an old joke, one from the first time we discovered how much we had in common. It wasn't the first day we met, of course. That was move-in day in the dorms, when some overly eager RA had scrawled our names on brightly colored construction paper and tacked it to our door. **SYDNEY** with a smiley face next to it. **LUCY** with a heart.

It took almost a month of existing in each other's company before we properly spoke. Strange how you can sleep next to someone without knowing much more than their name and the fact that their side of the room is an absolute disaster.

That night, she came home buzzed from a party, somehow

more focused under the influence of alcohol than she was without. When she slipped into the room, I was in the middle of getting changed, yanking my shirt over my head. Behind me, I'd left open the freestanding wardrobe the college supplied instead of a closet, with photographs I'd taken at home tacked to its door with museum putty.

"Are these yours?" she breathed reverently, crossing the room to examine the pictures more closely. It wasn't the first time I'd opened the wardrobe in front of her, but it was the first time she'd paid attention.

"What's that?" I asked.

She gently touched a finger to a nearby photograph, one of the fields outside the trailer park where I grew up. I wanted to escape home as long as I could remember, but when it came time to pack for college, I was surprised to find I wanted a piece of it near me. "I mean, did you take these?"

I shivered with her so close, the smell of her perfume mixed with sweat. She'd been dancing, probably. "Yeah. Photos. That's my thing."

Her face lit up. "I thought you were a communications major."

"Just to keep my mom off my back. She wants me to have a stable career."

She rolled her eyes in commiseration. "Tell me about it," she said, except she was a theater major, which meant someone probably believed in her talent enough not to warn her away from a riskier path.

Sydney stepped closer and drank up the sight of my photographs. One of the moon over the cemetery in October, equal parts spooky and beautiful. One of my best friends from high school, Via, captured mid-laugh, full of life. "These are really,

really good," Sydney whispered. She caught my eye and smiled. "You're so much more talented than the people the school referred me to for my headshots."

I fell into the glow of her. How could I not?

"I do like shooting people best," I admitted.

Her lips curled in a sly grin. "Shooting people with cameras," she corrected, and I couldn't help but groan. With a self-satisfied smile she added, "So, do you have an Insta, or what? I'm going to start sending my friends to you for headshots. This talent cannot go to waste."

I thought she was all bullshit and that in the morning she'd wake up with a hangover and no recollection of our talk. But a week later, one of the theater kids she hung out with sent me a DM and asked to schedule a photo session. It was the first time I got paid for my work.

Before then, all I knew about Sydney was that she worked part-time at the visitor check-in desk and that she liked to listen to music while she read, which I couldn't fathom. How can you pay attention to the words on a page when there are words piping into your ears? But right then, I knew everything I needed to know about her.

She's always been loyal, always been the one to hype other people up. Even now, she's a person with a thousand things going on, and she could have anyone be her photographer, but she chose me. I should be grateful, and I am, but in a way I'd never admit out loud, I also resent her.

"Alright, the room's all clear," I say, unlocking the door and waving her inside. "Now, what did you want to shoot?"

"Just a little story," she says. But when I step inside behind her, her smile drops. "Um, actually, I need a blank canvas for this one. Maybe you can wait outside?"

My face heats, but I nod. "Yeah, whatever you need."

"Thanks, Luce. You're a lifesaver."

I shuffle outside and she flashes me one last smile. Then she shuts the door in my face without a second glance.

9

STORY POST

Reverie Retreat—Day 1

"Psst. I've got a secret." Sydney flashes the camera a conspiratorial smile, then leans forward and puts a finger to her pouted lips. She's sitting coquettishly on a freshly made bed, wearing a plush white robe with **REVERIE** monogrammed over her left breast. The robe hangs off her right shoulder, revealing smooth, glowing skin, her delicate collarbone, and a flash of lacy lingerie.

The last time she showed up on camera to promote a lingerie set, a campaign for a boutique brand's collection, the entire collection sold out within ten minutes of its launch. This is the power she has, to inspire people en masse. At the best of times, she can wield it to promote change for good, like the time she convinced thousands of strangers to wipe away Lucy's medical debt. Even in everyday moments, a word of her praise can be the difference between a brand's obscurity and its success.

Sydney beams and shakes her head, making her long hair tumble over her shoulder. It doesn't fully block a view of the outline of her nipples through the sheer bra. "I'm working on a project that's going to blow your minds. Seriously, I can't believe I'm finally doing it."

She sits back suddenly with a laugh, her face lit with that effervescent glow people try to replicate with makeup, not realizing its origin is charisma rather than beauty products.

With Syd, the line *women want to be her and men want to be with her* falls a little short. Really, anyone might want to be her or be with her, and she entertains that fantasy without hinting at her preferences or casting judgment on yours. Just look at the pictures she takes with Caitlyn sometimes, the way they curve into each other, the flirtation dancing in Sydney's gaze. The way she looks at other people is so compelling that you truly believe if you could be near her, she might look at you that way too.

"Any guesses what the project might be?" Sydney grins, showcasing the tiny gap between her front teeth and pulling you into her confidence. The sunlight kissing her skin has the warmth of afternoon light, though with her, it seems like it's almost perpetually golden hour. She's radiant on any occasion.

Could the project have something to do with the retreat she's at? Or maybe it's a collaboration for that lingerie, or self-tanner, or something that's uniquely Sydney.

"Drop a comment with your guess," she says, "and if you want to be the first to hear about it, sign up for my mailing list at the link in my bio."

Whatever she's been working on, you want in. You want to sit beside her on that big white bed and soak up her shine.

"Thanks for being on this journey with me, friends. Everything I'm working on is for you and because of you. I couldn't imagine doing this without your support." Sydney smiles wide and then waves goodbye to the camera.

Even after the story ends, you sit for a minute, basking in her glow.

10

CAITLYN

Perfection," Nash declares, stepping back to study my face. I know he's talking about the triumph of makeup artistry he's created on my skin, but part of me can't help feeling a little like I could own that word too: *perfection*. Like maybe he means it about me.

I'm not stupid, and god knows I'm not a perfect person. I've spent too much of my life *trying*—trying to erase the pieces of myself that weren't fit for public consumption, trying to show the world only the shiniest bits of my life, trying to build my brand, trying to reach the top of a mountain that gets taller every day. But if I've fooled everyone—if, from the outside, everything people see about me looks *perfect*—then I've done what I set out to do.

"The credit goes to you," I demur. Flattery can be currency just as much as cash.

"Nonsense," Nash says, but he bats his lashes at me, so I know he's pleased. He's wearing winged eyeliner, drawing out the honey in his eyes. I harbor a secret suspicion that he became a makeup artist and stylist because he knew just how pretty he is and wanted to learn how to highlight his looks to his advantage. Not that I blame him. In this world, you need to sharpen every weapon you have: beauty, intellect, or otherwise. "I'm just enhancing what god gave you."

I grin at him. "Amen."

He squeezes my shoulder. "Go get that fine ass dressed so we're ready to go whenever Lucy and Sydney get back."

"So we're agreed, that whole scene was bullshit, right?" Jeff calls from the couch he's retreated to.

Nash makes a noncommittal hum, keeping his eyes down as he cleans his makeup brushes. He and Jeff know each other from photo shoots, but I wouldn't say they're tight friends outside of them. And as much as I want to agree with Jeff, Nash's silence prompts me to bite my tongue to stay on Nash's good side. Instead of answering, I push out of my chair and stride across the room toward the hanging rack of gowns.

"It's like, yes, the room was messy," Jeff presses on, "so Lucy couldn't shoot it. But we also have this waterfall shoot to do, and if you're worried about losing the light, it's counterproductive to storm off."

"Actually, about the waterfall," Brent says in his *I have an idea* voice. "What do you think about wearing swimsuits? You know, to go with the water theme."

Nash and I exchange worried glances. He and I already selected outfits for me and Syd and coordinated our makeup to match. Changing things up now would not only ruin our vision, but my makeup wouldn't match the swimsuit I brought with me. To borrow from Jeff, pivoting now would be *counterproductive*.

"Nash has a plan," I protest.

Brent shrugs. "Yeah, but, like, we can make a new plan."

Brent likes to think he's in control of things, in large part because Sydney lets him believe it. She goes along with everything he asks, because it's easier to hand off the business part of her job than to think and work hard for herself. I guess that's her right, but it all just reinforces her belief that the world will fall into place around her. And it makes Brent think he's hot shit.

I know I sound like a hypocrite when I bitch about Brent's failings, considering he's my talent manager too. It took Syd forever to convince me that it was worth handing him a portion of my income, but I started to realize I was spending an unacceptable amount of time each week forging and managing partnerships rather than creating content. Time's a finite resource, and if I want to truly grow, I need to manage my time well. When I saw it that way, it was easier for me to say yes. Now I let Brent run the parts of my business that take time—contracts and brand partnerships and opening doors more quickly than I could by myself—but I still refuse to relinquish the long-term business strategy. Brent's business is made of dozens of individual influencer brands, but my business is *me*. I'm going to care for my brand the way no one else will, which is why I will not be wearing a swimsuit at the waterfall. It's not the direction I'm going for.

"You know it's like thirty degrees outside right now," I remind Brent. I turn on the portable steamer Nash brought and let it heat to temperature. "The trees are bare, and that waterfall isn't a hot spring. No one in their right mind would be purposefully swimming right now."

Nash shoots me an approving look.

"But I thought—" Brent starts.

"She's right," Nash counters. "I'm sure we can come up with another use for the swimsuits. It would be a shame to waste the gowns."

"Which ones were you thinking?" Brent asks, and I point to our selection. "You know, those *would* look stunning out in nature." He says it like the idea was all his. "Let's do the gowns."

Nash winks at me behind Brent's back.

I turn away to hide my smile and busy myself steaming the hem of my dress.

"You're a wrinkle-killer, eh?" Jeff teases me.

"Something like that." It's a pleasure to lose myself in the work and to take my time getting things right. Here, on this retreat, I can make sure all the details are flawlessly executed. It might take a minute to get everyone on the same page with the big picture, but once we're aligned, no one's going to push back or complain or get impatient when I pay attention to detail, because they're striving for that elusive perfection as well. They know the business we're in, and they know what it takes to put out the highest-quality content. These are my people. With them, I don't have to soften my demanding nature. They're not going to get weird if I don't have a tolerance for wrinkles. And it feels like such a relief.

"What the shit is this?" Jeff sputters, breaking my flow.

I look up from my dress to find him glaring at his phone. "What do you mean?"

He shakes his head, but it's not me he addresses when he answers. "I just saw a headline about myself," he tells Brent. "Something about my social media going off the rails?"

Ah. Sounds scandalous.

I keep quiet, and Sydney and Lucy choose that moment to barge back into the Lodge.

"You all ready?" Syd asks, hurrying across the room to grab her gown off the rack.

"Yep!" Brent says too quickly. "We can leave as soon as you're dressed."

Jeff shoots him an accusing glare.

"I'll look into that thing when we get back," Brent promises.

Sydney glances between the two of them. "Look into what?"

Jeff presses a kiss to the side of her head. "Nothing, babe," he says, but his smile seems strained. He swats Sydney's butt and nods toward the bathroom. "Let's all go get changed."

11

CAITLYN

When you're a lifestyle and fashion influencer, nearly everything in your life is an opportunity for a brand partnership. From the vitamins you take to the deodorant you wear—not to mention the eyelash serums, skin care products, green drinks, razors, phone cases, hotels, and experiences—there's nothing that can't be monetized if you're creative enough. The key, of course, is to partner with the right brands at the right times and only take on products that you're comfortable putting your name behind. Sponsor one bad product and you lose your audience's trust, which is the single most valuable asset you have.

Out of all the opportunities that influencing has brought me, I never would have expected fashion to be my soft spot. It wasn't why I got into the industry, but having gorgeous clothes is a definite perk of the job. And on days like today, when I'm getting paid to wear a flipping gown and hang out with my friends, it's definitely a pinch-me moment.

I hold the dress's long train in my right hand, balancing myself with my left so I don't slide on the muddy path. My pale silver dress is actually two pieces—an asymmetrical crop top, with one long sleeve balancing a bare shoulder, and a flowing skirt with a dozen layers. Sydney's also in a gown—hers a sheer white with a strapless corset top and an explosion of tulle at the skirt—but Nash is holding her train to keep it from sweeping on the forest floor. The two of them are at the front of the group, leading us toward the waterfall they're so desperate to find, heads bent together as they whisper conspiratorially.

I try not to be offended.

Lucy trots on the trail alongside me, sliding me cautious glances every now and then. "You look fantastic in that," she tells me.

It's her way of saying sorry for being weird earlier, and I brush her off with a simple "Thanks." I'm more concerned with listening in on Syd and Nash. The two of them have been acting strange since we got here—more hyped up and secretive than normal.

What could they possibly be saying to each other?

"Was the gown gifted?" Lucy asks, raising her voice over the roar of the unseen waterfall, so I have no chance of hearing them.

I force myself not to frown in annoyance, then nod. The photo shoot for this particular dress is a big deal, a partnership I've waited years to be able to land. I need her help capturing the full beauty of the gown to impress the brand and also to increase my partner commissions after the campaign goes live.

Up ahead, Nash stops short with a gasp and arranges Sydney in a pose at the side of the trail. Honestly it looks like every other patch of trees we've passed on our walk—bare branches without even a hint of leaves, mud slicking the ground. But whatever he sees makes him take out his phone with a smile.

"Ready?" he asks Sydney, and now it's Lucy's turn to frown. She does, after all, have a professional camera. Is this really the best use of everyone's time?

Sydney nods, and Nash counts down for her to blow a kiss to his camera.

"Are we even going the right way?" I snap, interrupting their cozy moment. We've taken a path along the top of the ridge that Reverie sits on, winding through the woods. We haven't been walking for more than a few minutes, but my skin's already covered with goose bumps from the cold. I'm not unaccustomed to sacrificing comfort in the name of fashion, but there's a big difference between the fifty-degree weather they predicted and the verge-of-freezing territory we're living with. If we stay out here too long, the cold is going to make my nose turn pink. Less than ideal for photos.

Nash and Sydney look over at me, eyes wide. Behind us, even Jeff and Brent have caught up to the group, Jeff carrying a bucket of flowers that Nash insisted we bring.

"Of course the waterfall is this way," Sydney says. She moves to the side, and then I see the sign nailed to the tree beside her, pointing down at a steep path: **WATERFALL →**. Now I just feel stupid, which makes my temper flare.

"Well, then," I say, shouldering past her to lead the way, "let's—"

A terrifying *crack* tears through the forest, and I immediately freeze. My heart pounds, and it's hard to catch my breath.

You only need to hear a sound like that once to know it means danger. And out here with no protection, the threat feels visceral, real. Like a warning.

"Was that—?" Sydney whispers, eyes wide. She's jumped

closer to me, one hand pressed against her chest. Her face is pale beneath her makeup, but instead of looking washed out, she's somehow even more alluring, her hair a dramatic contrast to her skin.

It's unfair how pretty she is when she's afraid.

"A gunshot," Brent confirms with a grimace.

"It's not hunting season," Lucy says ominously, and we all spin to face her. An uneasy ripple goes through the group at the idea that someone's here in these woods with us, out of season, with a gun.

"How do you know that?" Jeff asks.

"There's a guidebook in my cabin." We stare blankly at her and she shrugs. "You probably have one in your rooms too. Places to eat, things to see, safety facts."

"So, should we . . . turn back?" Nash asks.

"You don't have to worry," Jeff assures him. "I know you don't like camping and all, but we *are* in the woods. Guns are totally normal out here."

Nash glares at him with a curl of disgust on his lips. "I don't have anything against camping. But I do have something against casual gun violence."

Jeff shifts uncomfortably. "There are plenty of responsible gun owners out there."

"All the same, I'd rather not run into any of them in the woods. Getting shot is not on my bingo card today." Nash winks at Lucy and adds, "Except getting shot with cameras."

Jesus Christ. What a stupid fucking joke. Sydney says it all the time too.

"We'll be fine," Brent says, stepping in as the voice of reason. "Noise carries out here, but that sounded pretty far away. It could've even been a tree falling." He glances at Lucy for backup. "We're wasting the light, right?"

"Yeah." She frowns, clutching her camera against her chest like a shield.

"You heard the woman." Brent waves the rest of us forward. "Let's do this. Everyone just stick together."

So we do, climbing down the steep, muddy path to the base of the crashing waterfall. But as we walk, scrabbling over rocks and tree roots, a thought niggles at the back of my mind. Lucy said she knew about hunting season because of what she read in a guidebook. But if she's been so busy taking pictures and bitching about us wasting time, when would she have managed that?

12

LUCY

Everyone's on edge as we climb down the narrow path beside the waterfall, but once we reach the base, we're all overcome by the awe-inspiring sight of it. Without trees blocking the view, you can see all the way from the top of the falls—which start at the crest of the ridge—down to where the water smashes into a gorgeous pool. The whole rock wall is broken off, making a dozen points for the water to stream over, and the roar is so deafening it feels like my entire chest is vibrating. The air feels colder here too, all the mist in the air damp against my skin.

"This is . . . wow," Nash says, shouting to be heard as we gather on the shore.

I have to agree. There's nothing like the vastness of nature to make all your problems feel small. "Let's get started, shall we?"

I spin toward the spot I want to shoot from and nearly bump into Brent, who stands beside the water checking his phone.

"Is there even a signal?" I ask.

He shrugs and pockets the phone. "Still nothing."

It might have upset me before, being this disconnected from the rest of my life. But I revel in the idea that nothing can touch me. Even if Nick wanted to talk, nature's enforcing boundaries between us. That's good for me. Right?

If I think too hard about him, my chest starts to ache, so I buckle down and step into position. It's hard to keep my mind off him, though. He's the one who bought me this camera, a gift right before my surgery.

Something to look forward to, he said. *For after.*

Just like the ring.

He probably meant for me to photograph happier moments, but as I went through recovery, I also used the camera to take pictures of my fellow patients, haunting and beautiful. Not everyone I captured is still alive today, and I can't bring myself to ever look at those pictures again.

Unlike these.

I photograph the waterfall first, and it's nice to know that no matter how much I'll be shooting for other people today, I'm also doing something for me. I take a few long exposures, loving the way the water turns ghostly when I slow it down, the soft, streaming effect of it against the dark rocks.

Then I ask Sydney and Caitlyn to pose beside the base of the falls, where the mist curls in around them. Sunlight crests over the top of the falls, lighting up the mist and casting a stunning glow on the scene. It feels like standing in a dream.

"Gorgeous!" I shout, snapping pictures as quickly as I can. "Okay, now look over at the falls."

They respond to my direction without hesitation, and I burn with pride.

Power is like water, always flowing and changing. Sydney

and Caitlyn and, yes, even Jeff may have power in so many ways. But the moment I step behind the camera, I'm the one in charge. Admittedly, there's a level of trust built in. They trust me to make them look their best, and I trust they'll follow directions. The photographs are a collaboration, sure. But even if Sydney pays the bills, at the end of the day, the creative direction is my call.

I shoot a few more pictures, then do solo shots of the women.

When it's her turn to step in front of my lens, Caitlyn's face lights up. "I want pictures that are just beyond." She smiles at me, trying to get on my good side. "Everyone who looks at these pictures should want to be me." Her ego normally comes across as arrogance, but right now, we're speaking the same language.

I glance up the length of the waterfall, weighing the memory of my earlier scare against the creative opportunity in front of us. "I have some ideas. But only if you feel comfortable."

I tell Caitlyn what I'm thinking, and in a move of surprising dexterity, she scales a set of slick rocks right beside the waterfall. "My brothers taught me how to climb just about anything!" she calls with a grin when Nash cheers her on. Then she leans in, her face catching the sunlight and the train of her dress dangling out into the water. The mist rises up against the silver fabric, so it's hard to tell where the water ends and where the dress begins. It makes her look ethereal. While she's usually commercial-looking, today she's transformed into high fashion.

Still, I need a better angle. The riverbank where I'm standing feels too far away from her to get the shots I want, so I call for a pause and hand Jeff my camera. Once my hands are free, I kick off my sneakers and roll up the hem of my jeans.

"You're going in?" Jeff asks, looking impressed.

"Anything for the shot," I deadpan. The temperature must be dangerous, but I can't let that get in my way. If Caitlyn's taking a risk, so am I.

Jeff hands back my camera, and I step into the water. The first bite of cold steals the breath from my lungs, and my bare feet slide as I make forward progress. But soon I'm right where I want to be, up to my knees a few yards into the natural pool that's formed at the base of the waterfall. Working quickly, I take shot after shot, and I already know these are going to be some of the best I've ever taken. In any other format, these photos could make someone's career. But on tiny phone screens, they'll only ever look so good. Is my talent being wasted?

I'm not sure if it makes me an asshole that I care.

"Oh shit!" Brent's hoarse cry rings out from somewhere overhead, shot through with fear.

I yank my face away from my camera in time to see a softball-size rock hurtle over the edge of the cliff and plunge toward where Caitlyn's posing halfway up the rock wall.

"Caitlyn, look out!" I yell.

It happens so fast—the rock falls, and Caitlyn scrambles to pull herself in closer to the wall to dodge it. Her free hand, the one she was positioning by her face, swings for purchase but doesn't connect with the slick cliff face. She dangles by a single hand, her scream shattering the forest.

All anyone can do is watch in horror.

My knees lock, and I'm too far away to help. Even if I could get to Caitlyn, if she fell on me from this height, we'd probably both be killed.

"No!" Jeff chokes out, having scrambled a safe distance away.

My breath catches in my chest as the rock whooshes through

the air mere feet from Caitlyn's head and lands at the base of the waterfall with a sickening *crack*.

That sound . . . like something breaking open.

My stomach wrenches with nausea.

For a moment, everything goes silent, save for the roar of the waterfall and my heart. Then Nash cries, "Caitlyn!" and my body lets me move again.

Nash and Syd and Jeff and I race toward Caitlyn, who by some miracle has gotten both hands on the rock again.

"Oh my god, Cait!" Syd calls up at her.

"What the fuck, what the fuck," Jeff keeps repeating, raking his hands through his hair.

Brent's blood-drained face appears at the rim of the waterfall. "Everyone okay?"

"Get down here!" Syd shouts.

Brent disappears while Caitlyn mercifully climbs back down to solid ground, her face deathly pale. Syd throws her arms around Caitlyn, and we stand in a shaking huddle until Brent joins us.

That was far too close.

"Oh my god," Brent says when he arrives, mud streaked up his legs and on the seat of his pants, a bloody gash on his left forearm. "I'm so sorry."

"You could have killed me!" Caitlyn spits at him, but her words are undercut by her trembling.

"I slipped." He points at his suede pineapple shoes. "No traction."

"What the hell were you doing up there?"

"I was taking pictures from another perspective," he mumbles. "Trying to get everyone together."

"We didn't need those pictures," Caitlyn says, stabbing a hand through the air. "We already have a photographer."

"I'm so sorry," he repeats again uselessly.

Syd looks at me with heartbreak on her face. "We should head back to the cabins. Make sure everyone's okay."

"No," Caitlyn says, surprising me. "I'm okay. We're here." She looks toward the rapidly setting sun. "Let's just finish whatever we started."

"Are you—?"

"I'm sure."

And I'm impressed. "At least take a quick breather," I tell Caitlyn. "I can shoot Syd for a few."

When Caitlyn nods her agreement, I signal for Sydney to join me in the water. There's a rock almost perfectly centered in the pool for her to pose on, and now that we've gotten dry shots, I'm ready for something more adventurous.

Without hesitation, Sydney walks into the water like a nymph, the billowing fabric of her gown swirling gently around her legs in the current. There's no hint on her face of how rattled she was just minutes ago or that her feet are going as numb as mine. This is what makes her the best in the business—her unwavering dedication to creating content. People call what she and Caitlyn and Jeff do influencing, and that's certainly part of it. But more importantly, she's a content creator, breathing life into ideas.

Today she doesn't disappoint. She climbs onto the rock like she was born to pose there, so natural in front of my lens that I can't take pictures fast enough.

No matter how I feel about her being my boss, she's always been my favorite thing to shoot.

After a few minutes, I ask Jeff to join Sydney in the water. Even though it's much colder than I expected for March, he strips off his shirt like he's got a fever and plunges into the water. When he reaches Sydney, she climbs into his arms and arches her back, pressing her forehead to his. The two of them make magic together, his physicality a contrast to the delicate lines of her body, their chemistry together giving me endless possibilities to shoot. In real life, Jeff is a beige kind of human. He's . . . just Jeff. Literally, that's his social media handle: JustJeff. But in front of the camera with Syd, he comes alive. It's impossible to look away.

My body breaks down before I'm fully ready to stop taking pictures, the cold spreading to my hands and making my fingertips feel numb. "Should we head back to dry land?" I ask reluctantly.

"Actually," Nash calls from the shore behind me, and I whirl, surprised that he's the one responding. "There's one more thing you need to shoot."

13

CAITLYN

My stomach sinks as soon as Nash asks Lucy to take another set of photos. I'm standing on the riverbank beside him, my teeth chattering from the cold and the aftershocks of my earlier scare. Despite how close that goddamned rock came to my head, I'm less afraid of what happened ten minutes ago than of what Nash might say next. I have no idea what other photos he wants Lucy to take, but from how secretive he and Sydney were being earlier, I suspect I'm not in them. And if they had to be so hush-hush about them, they're likely a big deal.

"Lucy's freezing," I protest. It's not that Nash and Syd can't have some fun ideas or whatever, but I'd like to know if this is a situation I need to manage. I've got some very specific ways I want to use the photos of my gown, assuming Lucy and I got some good shots before everything went to shit and my life flashed before my eyes.

"I'm okay," Lucy calls. As she and Sydney and Jeff wade to shore to reconvene, a visible shudder goes through her.

Liar.

My eyes flick to Brent, and he half shrugs, half nods.

A little stung and a lot exposed, I wrap my arms around myself. First Brent nearly kills me, now he's telling me to let this go? "Whatever you want," I call. What else can I do?

Sydney, Jeff, and Lucy arrive on the riverbank, soaking wet from the waist down.

"What's the plan?" Lucy asks. She has the decency to add, "There's not a lot of light left."

Nash gestures to the bucket of flowers at his feet. "I want to work a little magic with these. Let's get the girls floating on their backs in the water. Once they're in, I'll add flowers to their hair."

A chill goes through me at the idea of getting into the water. "Are you sure—?" I ask, but Sydney's already going off about how she wants the photos to look dreamy and aspirational.

"Okay," Lucy agrees. "But I'm clearly not shooting from the top of the cliff."

"Too bad we don't have a drone right now," Jeff says pointedly. "That would make things a hell of a lot easier."

"No one took your drone," Lucy grits out.

"So you claim."

She sighs. "We can make this work either way. I just need to stick to the edge of the water where I can stand." She turns to scout the location, then points to where she's thinking.

Guess we're doing this.

It's too late for me to protest, and at the end of the day, I'd rather be in the spotlight even if I have to share it. So I follow the women to a spot where the water slows from its frantic rush to a gentle swirl.

"Maybe Sydney alone first?" Nash says, and Sydney lies

down gracefully at the edge of the water, where it's only a few inches deep. Nash works quickly, plucking fresh flowers from his bucket to arrange in her hair, which has spread out around her head.

When he's finished, Lucy steps in to take pictures. Standing here, I can see the world the way Lucy does, and I understand why she might want to live behind her lens. Sometimes the person who watches is in the true position of power. It's safe to stare at Sydney this way, an excuse to drink her in without anyone noticing how long my gaze lingers.

The last of the afternoon glow softens the scene, making it look like it's warmer than it really is, and the flowers pop against Sydney's dark hair. Scarlet roses, pastel ranunculus, orchids, and other flowers I can't name. Her gown is practically see-through at this point, and she's disgustingly beautiful. All I want to do is be near her.

Back when Syd and I met, she asked if I'd seen the movie she filmed in college, and I told her no.

It was a lie.

I didn't want to admit the way I sat in the dark of my apartment and watched her movie play out on my crappy projector, how captivated I was. It's hard to start a relationship on level ground if you tell someone you're a fan. I couldn't give her the power.

It was a small role, but Sydney glowed every time she came on-screen. You couldn't look away. I didn't yet realize how frustrating and inspiring it would be to take photos with someone who has that much innate talent, especially since I work so hard for everything I get. That competition's still there between us—or between myself and the specter of her, I guess, because she's the one who's set the bar, the example I need to live up to—but in moments like this, I'm back to being awed by her, and the frustration slides away. It's just me, watching her pose like she's lying on a bed waiting for me. Like if I'm lucky, I'll be able to undress her with more than my eyes.

Lucy's still shooting when Sydney catches my gaze, making my heart thump hard in my chest.

"Come in with me?" she asks. "Please?"

It's my turn to shiver. "I don't—" I say, but she reaches her hands out for me.

"You will absolutely make these shots." She holds my eyes in an exchange so intimate I'm forced to look away. Sometimes when she gets like this, it feels like I can see all the way inside her, and she can see inside me. Even the things I'm afraid to show anyone. "I can't do it without you."

There's no way I can resist.

I brace myself against the cold, then step into the water. I'm extremely pleased to find I can rest my butt on the bottom of the pool and still feel anchored, even though I look like I'm floating in the water.

I rest my head beside Sydney's, and Nash's deft fingers make quick work of styling my hair. My ears slip under the waterline, and all I can hear is the thunder of the waterfall smashing down from up above. All I can feel is the cold and Sydney's hair drifting gently over my shoulders. The air smells like flowers and earth.

The scene would be peaceful if I could ignore the water around me and the way it could so easily flood my lungs. If I were just on the riverbank, I'd be fine.

Thinking about it makes the pressure build inside my chest, an itch of anxiety below my skin.

Overhead, Lucy makes a waving motion at me, and I tilt my head ever so slightly to hear her.

"Relax your face, Caitlyn," she coaxes, which has the opposite of the intended effect. I feel my face pinch into a frown before I correct myself. Embarrassment heats my chest, quickly transforming into anger, and then resolve. Sometimes this job is exhausting. "Better," Lucy says.

She shoots a few photos of us in the dying light. Finally, Jeff joins us in the water to pose for a few shots, forming an awkward triangle. Honestly, without cell service, I'm surprised he hasn't gotten antsier by now.

At last Lucy calls that it's a wrap. Brent reaches a hand down to haul me from the water, while Jeff launches to his feet and grabs Sydney. None of us thought to bring towels despite visiting a waterfall, and I shiver in earnest as we pack our things and head for the path back to Reverie.

I turn to Sydney and Nash as we start the climb, my feet properly numb. "So are you going to tell us what the extra pictures are for?"

Despite the darkening sky, Sydney's grin is as blinding as sunlight. "Actually, yes. I'm starting a hair care line, with Nash as an advisor. We're going to use these photos for our launch campaign."

Nash grins and wraps Syd in a sideways hug. "Can you believe it?" he asks, looking for me to add my excitement, my unbridled enthusiasm in support of their endeavor. But I know exactly what this means for me, and I can't give him what he wants.

My heart's already plunging in my chest.

14

CAITLYN

I should be happy for Sydney and Nash. I'm supposed to be happy for them. Instead, my smile feels plastered on my face, and I have to drop my gaze to the muddy path so no one can see how fake my expression is.

"A hair care line?" I say numbly, repeating things back like an idiot.

"Plentifol. Pronounced like 'plentiful' but spelled with an *o* like in 'hair follicle.' I've been working on it for a year," Sydney says.

Nash bats his eyelashes at us. "Ahem."

"Right," Sydney corrects. "*We've* been working on it for a year."

A full fucking year. Despite how close we've been these past—what, six? Eight months?—she still kept me out of the loop.

I wish it didn't sting so much.

Syd doesn't seem to notice my pain. She just smiles at me, dollar signs or whatever flashing in her eyes. "We're hoping to launch next month. And you're now a starring model in the campaign!"

The words slip out before I can stop them. "Why didn't you tell me sooner?" I hate how hurt I sound.

Sydney pulls me to the side of the path, letting the rest of the group go in front of us. "I wanted it to be a surprise." She looks wounded and vulnerable, her lower lip pursed and her dress sheer from the water. My own dress clings to my legs, soaking wet and freezing. It makes me feel like I'm carrying around an extra ten pounds. Possibly that's the weight of my dread. "Why do you sound so upset? Are you not happy for me?"

I roll my eyes. "Of course I am." I'm not. "But I just wasted this dress." I should have called off the photo shoot when I had the chance.

Syd frowns, a pesky wrinkle forming between her brows. "You didn't waste it. Like I said, you'll be in this shoot."

She probably expects me to do it for free too.

"I need to use this dress in exclusive shots for the designer." I shake my head. "It's in my contract."

Her face falls. Always the dreamer, she doesn't think about what her actions mean for everyone else. Now she's making me into the bad guy, and I have to choose between keeping my dream sponsorship and supporting her. Because that's what it comes down to—either I've ruined my shot with the dress brand or I've ruined her launch campaign.

There's no right answer.

Back before I met her, when I only knew what other people told me about her, Sydney loomed larger than life in my eyes. She was—and still is—the It Girl. The more I've gotten to know her, though, the more I see all her flaws. Some of them are as charming as the gap between her front teeth, but others are uglier than she'd ever want the world to know.

"Maybe you can renegotiate the contract," Sydney suggests,

but not everyone can just snap their fingers and make the world bend to their will. I know that better than anyone.

"I'm supposed to deliver the campaign in the next few weeks." I look down the path for backup from Brent, but the rest of the group is gone. I can't hear anyone from here, and the fading light makes it hard to see the path. In less than half an hour, the darkness will swallow us.

I shake off a creeping sensation and steel myself against Syd's attempt to assuage me. I know I should drop it, but then it would be like every other time someone's swept one of her offenses under the rug. Actions have consequences. If I don't say something, she'll never learn. "Anyway, your timing leaves a lot to be desired. And didn't you think other people needed to know what you were planning for today? Like Jeff. Or Lucy." God, I'm swinging for the fences now. "Like, didn't you think that your shoot would be more successful if your photographer knew what the fuck she was shooting for?"

Sydney jams a lock of wet hair behind her ear, causing flower petals to shower on the ground. It's obnoxiously cinematic. "I'm sure the photos will be fine."

I cross my arms over my chest. "Even if you didn't want to tell me what the big deal was, you should have respected me enough to tell me how you wanted to use the pictures."

"I do respect you, Cait." Sydney wraps her arms around me and buries her face in my neck, but her hug only presses the wet and cold deeper into my skin. I need a hot shower and a fluffy robe and some space to figure out what I'm going to do.

I glance over Syd's shoulder at the hillside of dark, imposing trees. The memory of that gunshot sneaks back to me, and suddenly I have no desire to be out in the woods. “If you really care about me, then show me.”

I turn and stomp up the path toward my cabin, gripping the hem of my dress so hard I leave puddles behind me.

“Wait!” Sydney calls, but I’m already moving on.

If she wants to apologize so badly, she can catch up.

15

LUCY

Despite the thin, dry sweater I've pulled on post-shoot, my teeth chatter as I trail Jeff and Nash toward the Lodge. The temperature's dropped in the hour since we were out by the waterfall, but it's more than just the weather making my body vibrate uncontrollably—fresh pain plows through me, from my stiff fingers to my aching neck and shoulders to my pounding head.

In retrospect, I pushed myself too far today. People underestimate how physical it can be to run a photo shoot, especially one that requires hiking, hauling heavy gear, and plunging yourself into near-freezing waters. In the moment, today's session felt like an escape, but now I'm paying for my stubborn refusal to accept reality with the kind of agony that gives me flashbacks of my surgery.

So much for coming here to relax.

I've already taken medicine tonight—three ibuprofen shaken into my palm rather than the good stuff, the pills I stashed one at a time from the days when my cancer was at its worst—but it hasn't fully kicked in yet. When the pain gets like this, all I want to do is sleep until it goes away, but I'm not going to waste this trip in bed.

"Catch up, sweet pea," Nash says, looping his arm through mine to tug me along. He's wearing a black T-shirt with **PLENTIFOL** stretched across his chest in light pink, which is a bold move after the way that news of his and Syd's hair care line was received today. Jeff, unsurprisingly, wears a button-down shirt, unbuttoned deeper than is decent.

In the darkness, the Lodge glows like a beacon, the wall of windows blazing light out over the ridge. Reverie's isolation didn't bother me in the daylight, but now I can't shake the sensation that we're a million miles away from everything. That if something goes wrong, there's no one nearby who can help.

Music drifts under the Lodge's heavy door as we approach, a sharp contrast to the quiet outside. It's like the building has a heartbeat. A pulse. When Jeff swings the door open, the noise spills out into the night, squeezing around me like a hand around a throat.

My cell phone dings in my pocket as I step inside the Lodge, and I'm shamefully relieved. It's more than just Wi-Fi—it's proof of a connection.

You okay? reads the text message from Nick. The time stamp shows he sent it hours ago, back when we must have been out at the waterfall. I thought you were going to text me when you got there.

An ache blooms inside my chest at his kindness, his unwarranted worry. There he is again, looking out for me when he doesn't need to. We never agreed to check in with each other, at least not that I can remember, though, admittedly, this morning was clouded with the kind of grief that makes things fuzzy at the edges.

I let his message go unanswered and slip my phone into my pocket. I don't deserve him, and dragging this out is only going to give him false hope.

All I want is to relax and let the medicine seep into my bloodstream. To unwind and forget everything I've left behind. So I follow Jeff to the kitchen and plop onto a backless metal stool, which was clearly designed for looks and not comfort.

"Yo, B," Jeff calls to Brent, who's rummaging around the kitchen, swaying his head to the music as he opens cabinets and drawers. Clothes and makeup are still strewn across the cavernous room, making my anxiety rise. So much for Brent cleaning up. "Did you get a chance to look into that headline I mentioned?" I don't know what headline he's referring to, but there's an edge to his voice. He sounds almost . . . anxious about something.

Brent acknowledges us with a put-upon sigh. "No, Jeff, we've got bigger fish to fry right now."

"What's that supposed to mean?"

"There's a situation." Brent grimaces. "With the food."

"Clarify," Jeff bites out.

Brent throws open another set of cabinet doors like a magician making a grand reveal after a trick. Only inside there's . . . nothing.

"Sooo," he says, and that single syllable, drawn out glumly and edged with guilt, sets the tone for everything to come. "Reverie said they were providing food."

I steel myself for the *but*. Reverie did ask us about food preferences and dietary restrictions. I specifically remember Brent collecting the information to send back to Reverie's contact, the email from him to our group marked *urgent* even though I'm sure he already had at least Syd's and Cait's info on file.

"And?" Jeff asks.

"They provided . . . breakfast." Brent gestures to a welcome basket of pastries on the counter behind him. Wedged into the basket between a double-chocolate muffin and a croissant are about three of those laughably tiny jars of single-use jam. As if anyone who wants jam only wants a teaspoon of flavor.

"That's it?" Jeff asks.

Brent sighs and pokes his head into the freezer as if to make a point, though I suspect there's nothing in there either. Caitlyn enters the room while Brent's head is buried in a cloud of mist, and we all try to pretend we're not dying to know what she and Sydney fought about. At least, I assume they were fighting, given the pinched expression on Caitlyn's face the last time I saw her with Syd. In fairness, Sydney's surprise reveal could have been done with more tact—I would have been better prepared for the shoot if I'd known I was supposed to focus on hair, and I'm sure Caitlyn could have worked her model magic too. But Caitlyn's always trying to be a star right alongside Syd, so you'd think she'd be supportive.

"Can confirm," Brent says, emerging from the freezer with nothing to show for his efforts. "There's no other food."

"You're shitting me," Jeff says, unamused.

Brent raises his hands in a placating gesture. "I'm sorry, guys. It's on me."

"Wait, seriously?" I ask as it sinks in. I never should have let him be in charge of communicating with Reverie—I was the one who was hired from the start, and Brent's just an add-on guest. Syd convinced me he could handle it and that letting him organize the trip would take stress away from me, but she clearly overestimated his attention to detail.

"I must have misread the email."

The scope of the situation strikes me in an instant, and I burst into strangled laughter, which draws a sideways look from Jeff. "C'mon, it's funny," I say. Either I laugh about it or I cry about it. I'm relieved this wasn't Reverie's mistake, but the food mix-up is still a total mess. This wouldn't have happened if I'd taken care of it myself. "We're stuck out here in the woods with no car and a basket of muffins for the next four days. For six adults. With one meat-a-tarian and"—I glance at Caitlyn, who's now sprawled like a starlet across one of the couches—"one gluten-free princess. That's clearly not going to work."

"Jeff brought protein powder too," Nash calls from the window, where he's been staring out at the woods.

So we won't starve, but we won't be happy either.

"Okay," I say, pushing off my stool. This is not how I envisioned a retreat that touted I could leave my cares behind, but it's a problem we can fix. At least, I hope we can. Otherwise, this trip's about to get a whole lot uglier. "Time for plan B."

16

CAITLYN

I pretend it doesn't bother me that everyone's sneaking glances at me when they think I'm not looking. This isn't the first time people have looked at me and wondered what I'm thinking, and it won't be the last. Instead of acknowledging the mess across the room—Lucy trying to place a dinner order because this shitty place didn't supply the food they promised—I keep my legs kicked up on the couch and open my phone. The lines between work and play blur so frequently, but this is a work trip, after all. And the only place with Wi-Fi is this room.

First I check everyone's statuses for the day, even though we've been more or less together. It's important to know where you stand at all times, to understand the competitive landscape. That's the thing people want to ignore when they say to stay in your lane and keep your eyes on your own paper—social media is *social.* It's an ecosystem with a social hierarchy, and if you want to be at the top, knowledge is power. Yet another reason Syd's slight today stings.

Syd's *I've got a secret* story from earlier today—*barf*—makes my chest burn. I flip past it before I need to borrow one of the

Tums Brent's always popping like candy. There are no hints as to where she currently is—and it's been ages since the shoot, so she's definitely hiding—and right now, I don't care. Lucy hasn't posted anything, and Nash's stories are filled with the makeup products he was using on me in conjunction with our livestream.

"You sure you've got it under control?" Jeff asks, and I look up to see Lucy waving him off. Satisfied with her reply, he pulls out his phone and taps away. It's only because I'm looking that I catch the moment his face goes from smooth and unbothered to shocked and furious.

"What the fuck is this?" he bellows. Even Lucy jerks away from her phone at the murder in his voice.

Brent rushes to Jeff's side, already in crisis-aversion mode. "What's what?"

"My fucking profile," Jeff spits. I can see the vein pulsing in his temple even from here. Another few minutes like this and he might require medical assistance. "You told me you had it covered, and this isn't. Fucking. Covered."

Definite scandal.

My fingers fly as I pull up Jeff's profile, greedy for information. He's posted a thirst-trap shot of himself climbing half-naked out of the pool at the base of the waterfall. His thin pants are plastered to his body, showing off *ev-er-ee-thing* below the belt. If a woman posts a breastfeeding shot of herself, she gets her account banned for a week, but here he is with his floppy dongle, racking up likes. Such a double standard. Though it turns my stomach, I don't see anything out of the ordinary for Jeff.

I flip to Brent's profile. He must have been the one to post the shot for Jeff, because on Brent's page there's another wide view of the waterfall with everyone working. Similar lighting, similar angle.

"I don't get it," I tell Jeff. "Though you could have spared us all the view of your schlong, it's business as usual for you, Jeffrey."

He shoots me a glare that would pin a weaker person in place. Maybe I should stop calling him Jeffrey, though usually the constipated look he gives me in return pleases me endlessly.

"Not on my home page," he snaps. "In my DMs." All the blood that rushed to his face when he shouted at Brent seems to drain. "It looks like I sent dick pics to half my followers."

My jaw drops. "What the hell?"

"Exactly." He wheels on Brent. "Did I get hacked? I must have gotten hacked." He starts pacing. "Someone must have gotten into my private photos and . . . and shared them. Who the fuck would do that?"

"I told you Nick got a weird message from you," Lucy says, crossing her arms. "Now do you believe me?"

"You," Jeff says, ignoring Lucy to glare at Brent. "Get your ass in gear and fix this. Now!"

"Oh my god," I butt in as a realization strikes me. A while ago, a bunch of hackers leaked nude photos of dozens of celebrities online, an incident that caused a huge uproar and that the FBI was called in to handle. If more people than just Jeff are affected by today's hack, this could be like Celebgate 2.0. Seriously violating. "Are there leaked pictures of Sydney too?"

"I don't fucking know yet," Jeff snaps. "But not a word of this to her. This is supposed to be her moment."

Internally, I roll my eyes hard enough to sprain them. Jeff might be using Syd's announcement about Plentifol as an excuse to keep us all quiet, but she'd be devastated to learn the truth, especially because she wants to maintain this air of exclusivity, like Jeff is all hers. Jeff's purposefully keeping this leak or hack or whatever from Syd to avoid her disappointment, her anger. And if there are naked pictures of her out there . . . god.

I shudder at the idea while Nash assures Jeff, "Our lips are zipped." Still, he looks uneasy about lying to Sydney.

Brent and Jeff retreat to a table in the corner to confer, and Lucy lifts her phone again, ostensibly to figure out the food situation. My heart's still racing with adrenaline, but I need to make sure that my account's secure. My home page looks as expected, thank god.

I update my password to be safe, then release a shaky breath and let my finger hover over the inbox for my direct messages. The number of messages in there is staggering, which is where Brent usually comes in. He has the passwords to his clients' social media accounts so he can monitor stats and help respond to DMs when our inboxes explode. Once I get Brent my new password, I'll need him to handle my messy inbox, but right now he's busy figuring out what the fuck to do after Jeff's bombshell—not to mention what to do about the hints Syd's dropped online about her own secrets.

I delete a DM from Jeff without opening it—*no fucking thank you*—and reply to a few other quick messages before I realize I should probably post something while I can. Maybe work will help me settle my nerves.

I glance up from my phone and assess my options. The room is still trashed from earlier, so it's not the best backdrop for what I want. I need to stay away from the loose cannon that is Jeff—and with everything going on, it would be stupid to have him in my photos, anyway—so the fireplace is my best bet. Framed just right, I'm sure it can make a romantic backdrop to a story, and I freshened my makeup after the shoot, so I know I look good.

I slide off the couch and circle the floor-to-ceiling fireplace twice looking for a switch to turn it on.

Nash's smooth voice interrupts, making me jump. "Your account okay?"

I nod. "Yours?"

"Wavy gravy."

"Great." Now that we've temporarily moved past Jeff's drama, I wait for the excuses Nash has probably come to deliver after Sydney's grand reveal. I may have had it out with Syd today, but he's just as complicit in keeping their secret. "You see a switch for this thing?" I ask, gesturing at the fireplace.

"I think it's an actual wood-burning one."

"Eww," I say. "I'm allergic to woodsmoke."

"About earlier. Don't be mad at Sydney," Nash says quietly as the woman in question slides through the front door with an oversize tote bag slung over her shoulder. "She just wanted to make everyone proud."

"Can you imagine how bad the smoke smells?" I answer, shutting down that conversation faster than a Kardashian drops a husband.

He's not taking ownership, I see, and he really believes what he's saying about Syd. The truth is, she doesn't mean to hurt people. She just does it by accident. And maybe that's worse, in a way, because it means she never looks beyond herself. She never learns.

Across the room, Lucy hangs up her phone with a sigh.

"What's the problem?" I call.

"We're in the middle of nowhere," she says. "None of the restaurants will deliver out this way."

I still can't believe what a fuckup it was for Brent not to have confirmed that all our meals were included in our stay. In the grand scheme, if he let Jeff's account get hacked, the food might have been the tip of the iceberg.

"Did you offer them extra money?" Syd asks, dropping onto the stool Lucy abandoned earlier, and everyone's attention snaps to her. "What?" She looks dumbfounded, like she can't believe we're all this dense. "Tell them you'll give the driver an extra fee to deliver out here. Just name their price." She says it like it's so easy, like money's unlimited, but I see the way Lucy blanches.

Admittedly, the comment doesn't sit well with me either. My mind flashes to the text message from my dad that I ignored earlier, the one that makes my skin prickle to even think about now. Treatment for my stepmom doesn't come cheap, and I've been sending my dad whatever cash I can to help pay the bills. But as he reminded me, this month's payment is due.

All the more reason to not give in to Syd.

I want the achievement of having landed the gown partnership, yes, but I need the cash from it even more. Much of my lifestyle is supplied by other people, but therapists and inpatient treatment facilities don't accept payment in the form of free clothes. Or *hair care products.* And so far, Sydney hasn't said a word to me about paying me for my work on her hair care campaign.

"Sounds like dinner's on Sydney," I say with a pointed glance at our fearless leader.

She gives me a wounded look—always the victim, isn't she?—but she nods.

Good.

If she's the one making the suggestion about tonight's dinner delivery, she'd better damn well foot the bill.

17

LUCY

Sydney was right, money talks. She paid for our dinner in advance, and now the stoop-shouldered delivery driver is more than happy to exchange two heavy bags of food for a tip in the form of five crisp twenties pressed into his hand. Syd goes into the bank specifically to get fresh bills, a touch I'm not sure the driver has time to appreciate. Crisp or wrinkled, money spends the same.

The temperature's dropped even further, and my breath comes out in frozen puffs against the dark sky as I carry the food from the driveway toward the Lodge. I'm nearly back to the building when I hear a noise over the crunch of gravel—the tinny, mechanical shutter sound of a phone camera.

No one else came with me to get the food. So who's taking pictures?

I glance up from the gravel path, and a flash of light catches my eye—the door to the Lodge is winking shut as if someone walked inside just before me.

A chill that has nothing to do with the cold spreads through my body. I bang into the Lodge, startling the group gathered in the kitchen. "Did anyone come outside?" I pant, my heart tripping. "Just now. The door was open like . . ."

Brent shoves something into his pocket, and my eyes snag on the motion.

"Brent? What was that?"

His face pinches, stains red. "My phone."

"Did you just take a picture of me?"

"Why would I—"

"Brent," Nash interrupts. "I saw you walk inside just now."

Brent crosses his arms in front of his chest sullenly. "Whatever, yeah. I took pictures. I'm documenting what's happening."

I draw in a sharp breath as suspicion seeps into my chest, stinging like acid. "Did you set us up? With the food thing? Did you create this fake mix-up just so you would have"—I can't say the words without disdain—"fresh content?"

"What? No!" Brent cries. "How could you say that?" He searches the room for solidarity. "It was a genuine mistake." He rubs his gut like his stomach has soured. "But, yes, Lucy, I saw a dramatic moment and seized the opportunity to capture it. So sue me."

"Brent," Nash says. "It's violating to take pictures of people without their consent." Do I imagine the way his gaze twitches toward Jeff?

"Well, if Lucy knew anything about creating full stories instead of just pretty pictures, she'd know—"

"Can everyone just stop?" Sydney shouts.

Sydney never shouts.

The room falls silent, and her cheeks flush. "I know it's been a long day, but we said we were going to stick together. That doesn't just mean, like, staying with the group. It means making this trip good for everyone." She glares at Brent. "So, Brent, delete those pictures. And, Lucy, bring the food over here so we can eat. My blood sugar has flatlined, and I'm sure I'm not the only one."

I feel chastened even though I didn't do anything wrong. If Brent was going to sneak away, he should have been using that time to deal with Jeff's scandal instead of taking questionable pictures of me.

As the group jumps into action, Brent wisely stays where he is and deletes the images under Nash's watchful eye while I slink toward Syd.

"Pretty," I say as a peace offering. I nod toward the huge wooden dining table as I set down the bags of takeout food on the kitchen island. Everything's a production with Syd, and while we waited for the food delivery, she insisted on setting the table with what look like hand-thrown ceramic platters, their dark blue glaze speckled with white flecks to look like a starry sky. She's also wrapped silverware in dove-gray cloth napkins and placed flickering tea light candles between the plates.

"Thanks," she breathes. "But taper candles would have been better." She shakes her head and lets out a frustrated huff. "I swear I saw some tapers in one of the closets earlier, but now it's locked."

A prickle of unease runs down my spine, but I force myself to ignore it. Guess we're not acknowledging how shitty Brent was being. "The tea lights are great," I whisper around the lump in my throat.

Sydney nods and peers into one of the bags of food. Now that her outburst is over, she's back to being calm and collected—too calm for me to believe she's caught on to any of Jeff's weirdness.

I'd much rather focus on dinner than accidentally blurt out what she missed while she was gone. As much as it pains me to keep what happened from Syd, I'm also not going to be the one to hurt her with the truth. There's already been enough drama this weekend.

"So how do you want to do this?" I ask. When you're dining with influencers who document every facet of their lives, there's no such thing as simply eating a meal. There's styling and choreography and rounds and rounds of pictures. If you're not careful, your food will be cold before you taste it.

"Let's plate everything in the kitchen so there are no containers on the table."

At Sydney's suggestion, everyone gathers around the island to get to work, the air heavy with the scent of Thai food. My stomach lets out an embarrassing growl as I add a portion of pad see ew to my plate, but I don't allow myself a single bite. Not yet.

First, we all follow an unspoken rule, grabbing our phones so we can photograph the table and the food.

"Is it alright with you if I take pictures of *this*?" Brent aims his question at me like a gun. "Or is it not allowed because it's *content*?"

"You're fine," I grit out. "It's over, okay?"

"Yeah, whatever," he grunts.

I finish my pictures and sit down to find Caitlyn smiling at me from across the table. "Aww, Luce, tonight you're just like the rest of us." When I shoot her a skeptical glance she explains, "No fancy camera."

She says it sweetly, but it's a quiet dig. Every time I deliver photos to her—gorgeous, fully processed images, might I add—

she goes and runs them through her own filters, skewing the colors before posting them to her feed. I'm being paid not to care, but as an artist, I *do* care. Sure, she gives me photo credit, but her photos end up so far from my original images that it feels like a snub. Everyone with access to a phone camera thinks they're a photographer these days, but it's what you do with the pictures that really sets you apart. I have no interest in being credited for crappy editing.

Caitlyn doesn't recognize the value I bring, but maybe at the end of the day, my superpower is my ability to be underestimated. Staying quiet about my strengths doesn't mean they're not there. I know how to use them when it counts.

I smile stiffly. "Figured these pics would likely be on stories rather than a permanent feed." Also, am I supposed to be working constantly? My headache threatens to reappear as I contemplate the idea that I'm here only to serve everyone else's needs. Not such a retreat after all.

When a sufficient amount of posing and picture-taking has concluded and everyone's had a chance to post images to social media, we finally take our seats around the table. I raise my fork, my mouth watering, but Sydney clears her throat. "Can I say something really quick?"

We look at her expectantly—Jeff with a touch of anticipatory dread—while she digs in her tote bag and pulls out a few cosmetic bottles to pass around the table. I lower my fork to accept a set from Nash, rolling them in my hands to read the labels. **Plentifol shampoo and conditioner. Luxury hair care for an abundant life.** Syd's taken a sleek, minimalist approach to the packaging—the pump-top bottles are a brown so dark it's almost black, and the text is written in a peachy pink that matches the color of the peonies Syd wore in her hair at the shoot. It's an understated elegance, just like Syd herself.

"It means the world to me to be able to finally have a brand of my own and to put myself out there for something I'm really proud of. I know I surprised some of you with the announcement"—she glances at Caitlyn, silently asking for forgiveness—"but whether you know it or not, I couldn't have done this without each of you. Thank you for being here with me on this journey." She points at the bottles that each of us now hold. "The shampoo and conditioner are a gift for you. Hopefully they're the start of a very successful line."

Nash grins back at her and raises his water glass in a toast. "To you, Sydney, and to Plentifol. You deserve every bit of success."

Sydney's the picture of blushing humility as we all toast her.

Jeff slides a hand to the nape of her neck and gently rubs her shoulders. It's a small gesture of support, but suddenly I feel achingly lonely. It's not just that I miss Nick, though of course I do. It's also that Sydney's words are starting to have an impact, exposing everything I've done wrong in the last few years. Sydney has her own brand, sure, but as she starts talking about how she plans to use the photos from today's shoot, I'm reminded that my brand is her brand. Everything I've been building since I walked out of the hospital has been for her. Photos of her and her friends. Photos for her hair care line. Even my own social media feeds are like some tribute to the ineffable Sydney Kent. I'm that awkward groupie who doesn't know when it's time to go home. And, yes, Sydney tossed me a lifeline when I needed it, but I haven't been using it to haul myself to freedom. I've been tying myself a noose.

"Cheers," I say, gulping a mouthful of water to calm the burn in my chest. I need to figure out how to do my own thing before I've traded all the integrity that made me pick up my camera in the first place.

When I raise my fork again, my broccoli is as cold as if it had just come from the ground. I find I've lost the desire to eat.

18

CAITLYN

Ugh, why does Sydney have to be so fucking good at everything? It would be one thing if Plentifol were hideous, easier to distance myself because it's not in line with the image I want to project. Except the shampoo and conditioner will look stunning and impactful on a social media feed, they have a sensual gender-neutral scent that you want to keep inhaling, and if Nash is the adviser, I'm sure the products will deliver amazing hair.

You have to hand it to Syd—she's got a vision and she executes. I'll need to pull Brent aside later to strategize how we'll approach the gown brand with an updated proposal. At this point, I know I need to partner with Syd. With an actual viable product and an impassioned speech like that, how can you be against her? You can't.

I catch Brent's eye across the table, and he gives me the tiniest nod. We're both in a shitty position with this, but it's up to us to spin the news the way we want.

". . . so the pool, then?" Sydney's saying when I snap my attention back to the conversation.

My stomach drops. It's not hard to catch up—everyone's planning to put on swimsuits and explore the indoor pool that rests on the lower level of the Lodge. But there are too many times in my life when I've been the last to know something. By then it's too late to do anything other than accept the news you're given, even when it sucks. That panic of not knowing, of being left out, always makes my chest go tight and sends me back to the night everything in my life turned upside down. My stepmom hasn't been the same since that night. None of us have, but understandably, she took things the worst.

I've always stayed driven and made myself hard to protect the soft ball of my heart, the part of me that lost so much so young. But when my dad married Susan and she came into my life, something about her let me finally lay down my armor. She made space for me to be my full self; I could share secrets with her and feel like I belonged. She was a safe, stable place for me until that night, and I didn't realize how much I needed her until after her stroke, when the things I loved most about her were gone. When she got sick, my armor went all the way back on.

"You okay, Cait?" Lucy asks.

"We should clear the table first." It's the world's worst segue, and when she blinks at me like I've said something out of character, it's because I have.

Whatever.

Tamping down a huff of frustration, I start collecting plates from the table. They're hand-wash only, which fucking figures. I dump the plates into the sink. Someone will deal with them later.

"Need help?" Nash asks, but I wave everyone on, making a show of clearing water glasses so I have a second to stay behind.

Jeff grabs the bag of empty food containers to take to the trash outside, and everyone follows him toward the door.

My back is turned when Brent says, "Meet you back here in a few," and then I hear the Lodge door opening and closing.

Alone.

Blowing out a long breath, I lean my hip against the kitchen counter and shut my eyes.

"Are you really okay, though?" Syd's words gust against the back of my neck, and I jump.

When I turn to find her behind me, her huge eyes are fixed on my face, and a worried frown plays on her lips.

I nod slowly. Part of me wants to let her sweat it out, but another part of me knows there's no point in us ruining the weekend by being mad at each other. If anything, Jeff is the one she'll be upset with once the truth comes to light, and that's much better than Syd and me fighting. "If you're asking if I've decided to forgive you, I have."

Syd's lips twitch into a smile, and before I can say anything more, her arms are around me again. "You're the best," she says, but I don't know about that.

Things used to be better back before Syd started turning our hangouts into business opportunities and bringing other people into the picture. Back when our time was just for us. No hidden agendas, no second-guessing why she wanted to see me. I miss how simple things between us used to feel.

Syd and I met, predictably, at an influencer event. A rooftop affair in Los Angeles, where I'd stayed even after I dropped out of UCLA. My grades had started sliding after everything happened, and I'd already decided to make a name for myself online. Though I had no reason to keep living in the city, LA brimmed with possibilities and connections.

The event was for a beachy fashion brand, and I'd worked for months to get an invite, regularly posting pictures in their clothes so they had no choice but to ask me to come. I knew Sydney was going to be there, of course. I'd made it my business to know, and anyway, she was half the draw. But it was one thing knowing she was going to be there and another having her slip her cool hand into mine and level that grin at me—the kind I felt all the way in my stomach.

She was hard not to like, and she saw something in me that she couldn't ignore either. At the end of the night, when she needed a ride back to the airport, I was the one who drove her. By the next week, we were already planning how we could meet up in New York. Becoming her friend was as easy as breathing. It just happened.

I wish things could be that uncomplicated now.

"You know you looked gorgeous today, right?" Sydney whispers, her lips brushing against my ear in a way that makes me shiver. She's so earnest and so eager for my approval that I can't help softening to her.

I roll my eyes. "Flattery will get you everywhere." Her arms are still around me, so she can't see the smile that creeps across my face. I can't see her smile either. But I feel the shape of it against my neck.

"Good," she says. "Let's go get changed."

Sydney and Jeff's cabin is closest to the Lodge, so I drop her off on my way to find a swimsuit. Then I pass the row of glowing boxes, rubbing my arms to keep them warm against the chill.

At first I'm stopped by the splash of deep red on my doorstep, a shadow in the darkness that makes my pulse spike. *Blood. It has to be blood.*

My heart bangs in a desperate rhythm, and I wish I hadn't asked for the cabin the farthest from everyone. I'm aware of just how alone I am out here. With . . . whatever that is.

I dart a glance at Brent's cabin next door and reason that I can scream for help if I need to.

Then I edge forward carefully until a shape emerges on my doormat. It's not blood after all, but roses from Sydney's shoot, arranged in the shape of a heart.

Shaking my head, I take another step forward.

Then I can't help myself.

I smile.

19

LUCY

Determined to get to the pool first, I slide on a swimsuit and make it back to the Lodge with my professional camera in tow. In the hallway that runs along the back wall of the Lodge, I follow a sign that promises me the spa area, though when I slip downstairs and flick on the lights, I find a series of locked doors and only two open rooms—the pool area and a meditation room, which strangely doesn't have a door. I'm not sure how meditative it would be to hear everyone else's noise drift toward you when you're craving silence.

Shrugging off the disparity, I creep past the open doorway and enter the pool area, stopping short with admiration. Like everything at Reverie, the room's impeccably designed. Shimmery white tiles form the pool deck at the near end of the space, leading to a wading pool that looks fairly shallow, though there are no marked depths along the edge. Instead, right past the entrance, the walls of the room hug the pool close, so the only exit to the pool is its entrance. At the far side of the room, the pool butts up against a window that stretches from the lip of the pool all the way up to the ceiling.

The whole effect gives the feeling of being in an aquarium, only whoever's in the pool is the one on display behind the glass, with the forest standing watch over you. I'm sure in the daylight it's beautiful, but there's something about the night that casts an ominous feel over the water. Maybe it's because I'm used to the city, where it never gets truly dark. There's always light from outside spilling in through your blinds, the electric glow of people reminding you that you're not alone. All that light blocks out the stars, and the noise rises like the hum of a fan to wrap you in its fold. Even in the trailer park where I grew up, there was always evidence of people, the warmth and heartbeats of bodies just beyond your walls. Out here, it feels like you're alone, but there's no telling if that's true. You can't know for certain what awaits in the darkness.

Before anyone can ripple the water or drip their way across the pool deck, I take pictures of the room. The lighting's not ideal, but at this point, I want to finish the job—both for the Reverie employees who are counting on us and for Syd. Maybe it's to ease my guilty conscience, but I can't let her down on this, even if part of me knows that being her employee isn't sustainable.

I know I'm always a people pleaser, trying to appease everyone at the cost of my own happiness. Even in the hospital I found myself comforting other people about my illness. But that tendency will have to change if I'm going to do what needs to be done for my business. I just don't know how to move on without hurting Syd. So far, all the defining moments of my life have been about protecting her.

"All clear!" I hear Jeff shout. Before I can protest, he's whiffing past my shoulder to cannonball into the water like an overgrown teenager.

I have the split-second instinct to turn my back before his splash hits me and soaks through the sweatshirt I've pulled on over my suit.

"Seriously?" I ask, spinning to glare at him, but Sydney's laughter's already curling through the room as she runs to follow him. Guess this is his way of distracting her while Brent's left to clean up the hacking mess.

Quickly realizing there's no place to keep my camera safe from the splash zone, I drop it in the meditation room, passing the rest of the crew on my way. Knowing how awkwardly we left things upstairs, I'm worried that Caitlyn's mood might sour the night. But when I shoot a wary glance her way when she's not looking, she has a satisfied half smile on her face that makes me think she and Sydney have smoothed things over. At least for now.

I reenter the pool room with confidence, but a flutter of nerves quickly unravels my charade as Nash calls for us to join him in the water. In this group, Brent's the only other odd man out, so to speak, a normal human with a normal human body. But even he shrugs off his shirt and slips into the pool, leaving me and Caitlyn alone on the sidelines.

Huh. Brent can't possibly have already fixed things with Jeff's account, right? It feels like the kind of thing that would take time, but I can't ask him about it in front of Syd, and I can't even begin to think about who would have wanted to target Jeff. He's such a big online presence—and between his ownership of the High Standards brand and a few questionable social media posts, he's not exactly a poster boy for political correctness—so it could have been anyone. The thought leaves me with a shivery, exposed feeling.

My accounts have always been secure—and I changed my passwords earlier to be safe—but I know how big the ripple effects of hacking can be. A few years back, some influencer had his account hacked, and to the outside world, he seemed to be spewing super-inflammatory comments. He lost a bunch of sponsors and half his audience before they figured out what was happening. It took months of groveling for him to work his way back up, and even then, forgiveness was hard to come by. If this situation is anything like that, I don't understand how Jeff and Brent aren't more freaked out right now. Then again, they're excellent at pretending everything is fine in front of an audience.

"Come on, doll," Nash urges again, and I realize I've been staring. "The water's gorgeous."

The idea of being seen in my bathing suit makes my skin crawl. At the end of the day, I'm not a normal human with a normal human body. Cancer's left me ravaged. The mastectomy didn't just take my breasts, it stole my comfort in my own skin and shattered any illusion that I'd get through life unscathed. Caitlyn and Syd and Jeff walk through the world with the confidence that they're untouchable. Even the potential scandal looming over Jeff hasn't deterred him from enjoying himself in the pool. But I know how tenuous our existence is. They say it's a shame when bad things happen to good people, but honestly, bad things happen to bad people too. None of us are spared.

I glance over at Caitlyn, who's perched on the edge of a lounge chair so sleek it looks like a sculpture. She's still wearing her hotel robe. If I'm the last one in the pool, there'll be no avoiding the group's attention. But if I can make it in before Cait, maybe it'll be the slightest bit easier.

With a sigh, I reach for the hem of my sweatshirt. Stripping off my top to expose my hunter-green halter-neck one-piece feels like peeling off my skin. People can't see my scars because they're hidden by the suit. But I've always harbored a secret suspicion that my early, unexpected cancer might be punishment for my dark deeds of the past. I'm not usually superstitious, but maybe it's my pound of flesh. If you look too closely or squint under a bright light, the truth about me probably glows on my skin like it was written with invisible ink.

I plunge into the pool fast, like ripping off a Band-Aid. Nash cheers as the water cushions me, and I sink into the sensation of weightlessness.

"Get in here, Cait," Syd shouts, her voice echoing off the tiles.

Caitlyn wrinkles her nose and stays put on her chair. "You're the one with the hair care line. You have to know how damaging chlorine can be."

"It's a saltwater pool," I blurt out.

Her eyes snap to mine. "Read that in the hotel guidebook too?"

My cheeks flame.

I dunk my head underwater like a coward, blurring out the world. When I pop back up, everyone in the pool has gone back to swimming and talking. Brent wades to the far end of the pool to peer into the darkness outside, while Jeff slides up in front of Sydney and she wraps her long legs around his waist.

Out of the corner of my eye, I see Caitlyn's face twist. When I follow her gaze, her eyes are locked intently on Syd and Jeff and all the places where their bodies meet. And then it's like she's made a decision.

Caitlyn stands, scraping back the pool chair so loudly every eye jumps to her. With her frown transforming into a sly smile, she trails her fingers along the neckline of her robe. "Sure is hot in here," she purrs seductively. "Don't you think?"

20

CAITLYN

There are three things hidden inside my hotel robe. The first two are mini bottles of champagne, left over from our party bus ride out here. I can't be sober if I'm going to watch Jeff dry hump Sydney. Or is it just regular humping, since they're soaking wet? Either way, I'm not having it.

The third is my swimsuit, the real star of the show. It's a fuchsia cutout one-piece that looks like it's been poured onto me. Starting at my left shoulder, the material wraps in diagonal strips around my body, leaving large swaths of skin exposed and just barely covering all the scandalous areas. Sheer material is so rarely actually sheer, but in this case, it's breathlessly close to looking like bare skin.

I remove the champagne bottles from the robe's deep pockets before I untie its sash and let the coverup pool at my feet.

The reaction in the room is swift and satisfying. Nash immediately catcalls me in a way that makes me preen, while Brent's eyes bulge and Jeff drops his gaze like he's been caught looking at his father's porn. But honestly, they're all superfluous.

The only one in the room I care about is Syd, and she can't keep her big eyes off me.

I set down one of the champagne bottles and pop the other, raising it in a toast to Sydney as an electric look crackles between us. I couldn't ruin the surprise by bringing down a half dozen champagne flutes from upstairs, so instead I drink straight from the bottle.

"None for me?" Jeff calls, finding his voice again. There's a rough edge to it, like he's swallowed knives.

"Aww, don't worry, I'll share." I take a seat at the edge of the pool, dipping my toes into the water and holding out the bottle by the neck. Jeff drops Syd like she's an expired protein shake and wades through the water toward me, the little currents he stirs up lapping against my legs.

I stifle a smile. Jeff's just a silly puppy, distracted by some tits and ass. Admittedly, world-class tits and ass, but still. It's highly predictable. Syd and I have entirely different body types—her lean frame to my curves—and in this realm, I win.

"You sure you're not coming for a swim?" Brent asks. His eyes drop below my belly button, to where the fuchsia material winks from between my upper thighs.

I shake my head and try not to shudder. It's a fine line between someone appreciating you and someone giving you the ick. "Some swimsuits aren't actually made for swimming."

"How about some music, then?" he asks. It's probably an excuse to look at my spectacular ass, but I'll let it slide because I know he won't be the only one watching.

While I'm up to grab my phone and play some music, I snap a few selfies in my suit. This moment absolutely needs to be documented. Then I open the second bottle of champagne and take a long gulp from the fluted glass lip. The champagne hits my blood with a fizz. This feels exactly right—the last of the tension from earlier tonight melting from my body.

Surprisingly, Lucy's the one who reaches for the bottle when I return to the pool. I hand it over, and she takes a hearty swallow that makes me want to cackle. "Glad to see you're as corruptible as the rest of us," I say dryly, and her eyes flare.

"If only you knew," she deadpans, and this time I laugh out loud.

We pass the small bottles from hand to hand, one person's mouth landing where another's has just lifted. It's a strange intimacy to drink from the same bottle as someone else, and there's a feeling of closeness among all of us.

While Beyoncé sings about being a grown woman doing whatever she wants, Syd swims between my legs and blinks up at me from beneath her long lashes. "Got my message?" she asks coyly. Water's sluicing over her skin, and her hair's pushed back to show her face, vulnerable and breathtaking.

I want to capture this moment and live inside it.

"Loud and clear," I whisper. For some reason, there's a lump in my throat. I lean forward to tuck a stray strand of hair behind her ear and hope Jeff isn't adding this image to his spank bank. This moment's just for us.

Much later, when the bottles are drained and the night's winding down, Lucy lets out a yawn that turns into a hiccup, then slaps a hand over her grinning mouth. I like this version of her much better than most.

I haven't gone in the water, but the night has a liquid feeling anyway. Right now, it's easy to forget about the stupid gown contract that gnaws at my conscience, about my stepmom and all her medical bills and what made her body break down in the first place. I can forget all the reasons I need to do things exactly right.

"I'm gonna call it," Lucy says. She wades toward the edge of the pool before stopping sharply. "Does anyone have a towel?"

The realization breaks over all of us—no one has a way to dry off. Jeff just jumped on in and everyone followed him.

"I'll go." I'm in the best position to search the property since I'm dry and have a robe available. But when I peer inside a basket near the door that looks like it should hold towels, I come up empty.

Nash volunteers to join me on a more extensive hunt, pulling himself from the water and shivering across the tile floor. We make for the long hallway that leads back toward the stairs, passing the empty meditation room on our way.

The next door I come to stops me. "Huh," I say, rattling the handle ineffectively. "It's locked."

"Must be one of those housekeeping closets," Nash says. "Filled with bleach and vacuums or some shit."

I shrug it off, but then every other door downstairs is locked too, a fact that both stumps and amuses me. "Am I missing something?" I ask Nash. "Was there a pool towel in my room that I should have brought?"

"I didn't see anything."

"What kind of place with a pool doesn't have pool towels?"

His gaze trails up the walls, falling into the shadows. "The same kind of place that has people shooting guns out in the woods."

A chill that has nothing to do with the cold spills down my back. I smooth a hand over my hair and try to look unfazed even though I'm thoroughly creeped out now. "What do you say we get out of here?"

Nash nods, and we return to the pool.

Everyone looks at us expectantly while I deliver the bad news. "Well, friends, you're on your own."

Brent blinks up at me in disbelief. "No towels?"

I spread my empty arms wide. "I suggest you make a run for it."

21

LUCY

It's snowing. I'm the first one to the door of the Lodge, my sweatshirt yanked over my swimsuit, and I pull up short at the sight of the fat white flakes drifting by my head. For a second, I'm not quite sure if my brain has started playing tricks on me, whether it's an effect of the alcohol, even though I didn't drink that much. The whole night has taken on a fractured feeling, like I'm looking through a kaleidoscope.

Behind me, everyone piles up in the doorframe. It reminds me of the Three Stooges skits I used to watch with my mom in high school, late at night after I came home from the diner where I worked. We'd pop popcorn and turn on old black-and-white movies just to have an excuse to be together, the shows so classic and strange that it almost felt like looking into a different world.

Right now, thick snowflakes are streaking through the night, highlighted in the glow of the sconce by the front door. But that can't be right. It's been cold today, yes, but it's March, and March is spring.

"It's sticking," Caitlyn says flatly. She looks ridiculous in her robe, but she's probably warmer than anyone here.

"No shit," Nash says, full of wonder.

Syd's right there with him, tumbling through the doorway to stick out her tongue, her eyes bright.

The world carries a little magic this way, and even though most of us are dripping wet and badly in need of a towel or a shower, we all pause to absorb the view.

I can't help myself. My hands twitch toward my camera, and I bring it to my face. I always love the way snow looks when you catch it with flash. The world dark and blank in the background, the snow like confetti tossed across a page.

I snap a few pictures of the sky, and then of my friends as they pose outside. There's something wondrous and cleansing about the snowfall, and even though I'm here with all these other people, I wish it were Nick beside me.

The first trip we ever took as a couple was to Vermont during that week between Christmas and New Year's, when everything feels slow and dreamy. There were six inches of snow on the ground, and the little B and B we stayed at had snowshoes you could borrow, so after a morning spent wrapped up in each other in bed, Nick and I made a disastrous attempt at snowshoeing across the landscape.

I spent more time on the ground than I did upright, but it didn't matter because Nick was there, his warm eyes turning my insides molten. Oboe ran between our legs, pushing his nose through the snow and then shaking his head, doing those little dog snorts that made me double over in full-body laughter.

Nick looked at me like I could do no wrong. That night, he said *I love you* for the first time, beneath a sky just like this.

"Talk me out of sending Nick a text," I whisper to Syd. It's not too late; we're still in range of the Lodge's Wi-Fi.

Sydney's face twists with pity. "What do you want?"

She's talking about me and Nick, not me and her, but in this moment, I can let myself believe she won't be mad when I tell her I want to stop working for her. At least officially. I want to go back to being friends who partner together creatively, and I want to shift the power dynamics back into balance. I'm happy to keep taking pictures, but I need to build something of my own—something not tied to my best friend's whims. She's so earnest that I almost let the words slip from my mouth.

Instead I shake my head and say, "Nothing. I'm being stupid." When it comes to me and Nick, I suspect Syd knows my secret truth because she knows *me*. She's been there through all my bad times, and she was there when I fooled myself into believing I could have a relationship with Nick where my past didn't catch up to me.

I can admit it to myself, though: I want to let myself love him and not have it feel like a guilty pleasure. It's not that he's bad for me, but rather that I'm bad for him. That's the rub of it, the stinging burn on my conscience that makes me push him away.

We can pretend all we want, but it's not fair to let him love me. So I can't text him, no matter how much I want to.

I leave my phone in my pocket and replace the lens cap on my camera.

"For what it's worth, I don't think you're being stupid," Sydney says. "Other than standing in the snow soaking wet." She gives me a big lopsided grin, an easy out from the situation, and I gratefully accept.

"Definitely time to head back to my cabin and get changed." My rueful laugh comes out a little scratchy.

Syd loops her arm through mine, ever loyal. "Good. Then, let's go."

Together we head toward our cabins, darting through the falling snow. It's a novelty—a temporary, beautiful turn of weather that romanticizes the evening and heightens the feeling that we exist inside a snow globe. We don't worry about what it will mean; we just squeal as flakes smash against our faces.

It doesn't seem like a mistake at the time.

22

LUCY

I wake in darkness, my heart pounding and my mouth dry, still rattled by my dream of an earthquake shaking down the walls around me. Not a particularly inspired dream, but unsettling nonetheless.

I grope for the water bottle I left beside the bed, only of course Reverie doesn't have standard bedside tables. Instead it's a strangely short three-legged stool hand-carved from mountain oak. Not only do I scrape the back of my hand on its live-edge surface, I also send my water bottle flying.

"Shit," I curse but don't go after it.

Other than a small halo of light cast by a night-light in the bathroom, the room is pitch-black. The better to watch the stars, I guess.

Outside, trees press in close, though I can't see them or the cliff that falls away just a few yards past my window. The idea of all that darkness makes my stomach lurch. It feels like I've been sleeping with the void at my feet.

Trying to orient myself, I keep my eyes open and let my heart settle. Slowly my vision adjusts to the room, and I realize that the claustrophobic feeling that tightens my chest isn't just thanks to sleeping in a shoebox. It's also startlingly hot in here. The shirt I fell asleep in—yes, one of Nick's age-softened concert T-shirts that I stole—is plastered to my skin.

It feels weird to turn on a light and make it easier for people to see inside my cabin while I can't see out, so I locate my cell phone on a slim floating shelf and use its flashlight to guide my way to a thermostat mounted by the front door. Every time I touch a button, the whole machine beeps frantically, spiking my pulse again.

Fresh air it is.

There's no real window in the cabin, just the sliding door taking up the far wall. I wish it were a regular window rather than something that invites anyone to walk inside. But the stifling feeling compels me to open it anyway.

Bang. Bang. Bang.

A low, rhythmic thud drifts in along with a snap of fresh air the moment I crack the door. Now my dream echoes back to me—the cracking sound of the earth rending must have been my brain pulling a fragment of waking life deep into my subconsciousness.

An unexpected sound somewhere between a moan and a scream sends heat straight to my cheeks. It must be Jeff and Syd in bed together. It's not the first time I've accidentally overheard Syd with someone, but I wish I could unhear it.

In college, guys circled Syd like flies, drawn to her sweetness, begging for a taste. She made out with enough of them, but none of them ever lasted more than a month, which made me feel special in comparison. Here we were years into our friendship and she was still choosing me. She had a ton of friends, but no one as close as we were, who she could totally relax with and stop, I don't know, *acting* in front of. Nobody else seemed to have that intimate staying power with her. Until Breaker.

Fall of our senior year, the week before Thanksgiving break started, my professor shared the name of a guy who last year landed the internship at *Bold Photo* magazine that I so badly wanted. Max Price. The second I heard the name, I was intrigued. If I could figure out what set Max apart, maybe I could work some magic too and spend the spring semester walking *Bold Photo*'s hallowed halls.

I mentioned Max to Syd in an offhand comment on a Thursday, and on Friday night, she tugged me along to a house party where she heard he'd be. She delivered the news about our destination with her signature smile, delighted with the gift she was giving me.

It still surprised me sometimes, when I caught sight of us in a mirror or in a picture, that someone so otherworldly would find me worthy. But still, she chose me. And even though I wasn't sure about ambushing Max in a social situation, we went.

The house was claustrophobic, teeming with inebriated students. By the time I found him, Max was passed out in an armchair in the corner, each of his fingers resting on top of a cigarette burn on the chair's moldering fabric. I couldn't tell if he had done it himself, or if someone else had moved him into position after the fact. Either way, he was going to be useless.

Defeated, I slunk back to the kitchen, but some guy had already cornered Syd by the keg. Compact muscles stretched along his tall, lean frame, and his hair was buzzed short enough to make his cheekbones look dangerous. He didn't seem like Syd's type, but sometimes it was hard to tell what her type actually was. Sometimes it felt like she'd entertain the idea of anyone who'd flirt with her.

I brushed by the guy to grab a soda from the fridge, raising my eyebrows behind his back to silently ask Syd, *You okay?*

She lifted her chin ever so slightly in reply. *I'm good.*

I retreated to the corner, out of Syd's sight but close enough that I could still eavesdrop. The party raged at full volume, but between snatches of a pop song, I caught him introducing himself to Syd as Breaker. It couldn't possibly be a real name, but I couldn't begrudge him the chance to call himself whatever he wanted. We're all looking for ways to reinvent ourselves. Some of us take whatever chances we can get.

"Breaker, huh?" Syd asked the guy.

He gestured unselfconsciously toward his face. "I've broken my nose three times."

"Ouch," she purred.

"Trust me, this look is an improvement." He cocked his head, assessing her. "What about you, Sydney? Named after the city?"

She shook her head, a mischievous glint in her eyes. "After the lead character in a movie."

His face lit up. "A *Scream* queen, eh?" It took most people at least a few minutes to make the connection between the Neve Campbell series and Syd's name, especially considering the character's name is spelled differently, but this guy got it without missing a beat. In Syd's eyes, this would be a definite feather in his cap.

She took a long swallow of her beer, licking her lips slowly as she cradled her red Solo cup. "All those movies and they haven't managed to kill her yet."

I never knew if the story about her name was true or just something Sydney said because she liked the way it linked her to a legacy of actresses who came before her. Already she'd landed a starring role in the school's production of *Hamlet* last year, and more importantly, she'd started picking up small modeling jobs around town. She had an audition for a horror movie in just a few weeks. Even then, the camera loved her.

"I like a woman who can go the distance," Breaker said.

Even though the line reeked of sexual innuendo, Syd held out her hand for him to shake. When we got back from Thanksgiving break, Breaker took Syd on a proper date. Even after a few nights out and one very awkward encounter when I caught them in bed together, I still thought (hoped) Syd might drop him. He didn't seem like he was operating at her level—he couldn't match her magic. But we hit New Year's and then Valentine's Day and Breaker was still there, surpassing everyone's record.

It was a giant mistake, but the mistake was all mine. That's what I think about as I lie in bed, the sliding door open but my headphones on to drown out the noise. If I could change anything, I would have faked cramps that first night and begged for Syd to stay home with me. I was the reason she went to the party and met Breaker. Which means everything after was also my fault.

23

CAITLYN

It feels brighter than necessary for 9 a.m. My eye mask—a weighted silk number that just rests on your eyes rather than fastening behind your head so as not to restrict circulation—has fallen off in the night. I blink into the morning, my head fuzzy. I'm dehydrated, in part because of last night's champagne, and in part because my room is hot as fuck.

Reverie is apparently too classy to have mini fridges in each room, so the ice roller that I use for lymphatic drainage and depuffing my face isn't actually icy. I run it under cold water for a temporary chill, then start rolling my face. Up my jaw, over my forehead. It's a calming ritual, part of my morning routine. If you ask me, good skin care is one of the pillars of beauty. When your face glows, the world treats you like a star.

It's not until I've soothed my puffy eyes and turned back to pick an outfit that I realize it seems brighter today because it actually is. Outside, a surprising amount of snow has accumulated on the ground, reflecting the glare of the sun. It might be up to six inches, though I'd have to step outside to be sure.

What the fuck?

We should have placed a grocery order last night along with the Thai delivery. We were so focused on getting dinner—and so distracted by Jeff's hacking scandal—that we didn't think about a longer-term plan for food. I'm realizing now what a mistake that was. Even if, in theory, someone wanted to make the long trek out to this isolated patch of land today, at this point, I can't imagine it's going to be easy to reach us. And if by some miracle someone says yes to accepting an order and making a treacherous drive for shitty pay, who's to say the stores won't be sold out of the basics? Do they even have grocery stores out here, or are they just, like, co-ops? Ew.

My brain can't stop whirling, and I have to make a serious effort not to march next door and scream at Brent. This mistake could have been so easily avoided. It's true that Reverie is normally a bring-your-own-food kind of place, but Brent said they were making an exception for us and that he had it covered. If he's not paying attention to detail on something as critical as food, what else has he missed? Is the bus going to forget about us too?

I'm doubly frustrated because normally I look forward to snow. I might have grown up in LA, but I also spent more than my fair share of time on the slopes of Mount Baldy. My dad hails from Colorado, and even when he was a single dad supporting us on a crappy high school football coach's salary, he always made sure we had season passes to the mountains. It felt like home to him, he said. I understood what he meant, though I've never been homesick for a place. Only a person.

When my dad married Susan, we folded her and Cole into our trips to the mountains too. Our gear got nicer, thanks to

Susan's cushy salary, but the competition to be noticed only got stronger. There were more of us clamoring for attention.

My brothers—three of them now—and I would trade surfboards for snowboards, scrambling for a chance to feel the snow cut just right beneath us. I was good, but my oldest brother, Zach, was better. Early on, it was clear his talent was being squandered on the bunny slopes, so my parents put Zach into private lessons. He was going to be the biggest star among us, or maybe just reach his fame earliest.

He turned pro the day he turned eighteen.

By that point, snowboarding wasn't going to be my ticket to fame, nor would it be for my other brothers. We had to lean in to our other talents. Lately, I've found mine.

In some ways, I've never stopped being that kid begging for attention, the youngest and the only girl in a family of achievers. I'm not afraid of hard work, and I know exactly what I need to do to get to the next stage of my career, which is why I throw on a pair of stretchy faux-leather pants and an off-the-shoulder blouse to show up to breakfast, even though I know I'm overdressed. I might as well look good to do my job, and it's not like I have warmer clothes anyway. Another oversight.

It feels good but cold as I make my way toward the Lodge, and the snap of the air is invigorating against my skin. Maybe I'll leave my ice roller outside overnight for a nice, chilly wake-up call tomorrow. It'll have the same energizing effect as a cold shower—great for endorphins and increased circulation, by the way. It's important to know everything you can about your industry so you're the *influencer*, not the *influenced*.

I'm a quick study.

I've learned all the tricks.

The snow outside Brent's and Lucy's cabins has been stomped through, but it's undisturbed outside the others. Most likely, Syd and Nash and Jeff are still sleeping in, but snow sometimes plays tricks on you. You think you're seeing one thing, but in reality, the snow can hide the truth. It's possible Syd and the others got up early and then fresh snow covered their tracks.

I stifle a laugh as I think about it.

It's possible, sure. But knowing my friends, it's not probable.

I'm freezing my tits off by the time I get close to the Lodge, and I slide my phone inside my bra to keep it warm. I need to keep my phone functional today, and cold can drain phone batteries without you noticing. Your screen might even tell you everything's fine right up until it suddenly goes dead.

No thanks.

I'm adjusting my bra—I never said the phone was comfortable in there—so I'm distracted when the spiky three-inch heel of my unfortunately suede boot sinks into something that's decidedly not snow and not earth.

What the hell?

I look down and realize I've speared a soggy, crumpled-up napkin with my shoe. The glare on the snow made it hard to see until I arrived in the shadow of the building, but now I realize with a twist in my stomach that I'm standing in a minefield of trash.

Instinctively, I freeze. Dart a glance at the area around me. Take a tiny sip of air when I don't see anything else amiss.

I wade through the snow cautiously now, stepping around the grease-covered remains of our Thai takeout containers. A red smear of nam jim gai—sweet and sour chili sauce—decorates the ground like blood.

I'm used to snow, sure. But not this.

A crunch of footsteps around the corner of the building makes my heart rate spike. Brent materializes in a short-sleeve polo shirt, looking disheveled and cold.

"Did someone go through our fucking trash?" He's indignant and confused in the same breath, rubbing at a spot on his chest as he stares at the ground in dismay.

Acid indigestion by proxy.

I sweep a glance over the ground, and then I see it. My blood chills to match the air outside. "Not a person," I tell him. I point grimly to a spot on the ground, where an animal track that dwarfs the size of my hand is a glaring reminder that we're at the mercy of nature out here. "A bear."

24

STORY POST

Reverie Retreat—Day 2

"So, let's talk." Sydney's sitting cross-legged in the middle of a bed, wearing a lightweight sweatshirt that says **HANGRY** in all caps across her chest. The tiny marijuana leaf logo near the collar suggests that it's from High Standards apparel company, a not-so-subtle nod to Jeff.

Speaking of Jeff . . . you can see him in the background, a towel wrapped around his lower half as he gets ready for the morning. The sneak peek of gym-toned abs is both distracting *and* enticing. As delicious as it is to see him this way, it's a bold move for Sydney to feature him in her story at all right now, considering the headlines he's making. Who knows why she's doing it—maybe she's brushing off the rumors and pretending everything is fine, or maybe she's of the any-press-is-good-press mindset. It'll be fun to speculate on the chat boards later.

"You know that I get so cranky when I'm hungry," Syd continues, and your attention snaps back to her, where it belongs. "My blood sugar drops, and then if someone so much as looks at me the wrong way, I get all snippy. It's just"—she swipes a hand through the air—"no bueno. So I wanted to show you what I do when I'm out and about and can't be sure of when I'll be able to eat a solid meal."

She holds up a Hydro Flask that could give those jumbo gas-station Big Gulps a run for their money. It's an ombre pink color, fading from pale peach at the top to deep rose at the bottom. "First up, hydration. Sometimes it's hard to know if you're hungry or just thirsty." She takes a sip from the built-in straw to demonstrate. The water leaves a glossy shine on her lower lip, and when she sets down the bottle, you catch the tiniest glimpse of the letters **P-L-E-N** decorating its side.

Sydney's been known to drop Easter eggs for product launches in her videos, so some of her audience will stop here to freeze the frame and zoom in, looking for clues. The most devoted of her followers will take their theories to the comments section, debating the validity of a dozen acronyms they find online. Still more will argue that it's only a partial reveal, so it's impossible to know.

Guessing is part of the game. Being the one to figure it out gives you bragging rights among the fans.

Sydney smiles back at the camera. "When I know for sure that I'm hungry, my next step is to grab one of these Zyng bars." She holds one up, its package clearly designed with a social media aesthetic in mind. "It's a delicious protein bar that also has caffeine in it, so after I eat one, I stay full *and* energized. And don't worry, it's a green tea caffeine, so you don't feel shaky or jittery after you eat it." She unwraps the bar and takes a small bite. Most people look terrible eating on camera, but Sydney makes it look like a sensual act. "They're also vegan and gluten-free."

Jeff strides into the front of the frame now, that tantalizing flash of abs gluing you to the screen. He sweeps Sydney's hair off her neck and bends down to kiss the flawless skin he's revealed.

The chance to so freely show Sydney casual affection makes a fair portion of the audience sick with envy. What would it be like to taste her skin? Before you sit in that desire too long, Jeff swoops around and takes a giant bite out of her protein bar.

Sydney gasps with a twinkle in her eye, shaking her head good-naturedly while he walks off-screen.

"Did I mention that Jeff loves these too?" Wow, she's really selling him hard. Maybe those headlines were based on lies made up to make Jeff and Syd look bad. It's such a shame when good people get dragged, but that doesn't mean it's not addicting to watch. "My favorite flavor's the key lime pie, and Jeff loves the chocolate brownie. The trick is, I always keep these with me for when I need that energy boost. I've got them stashed in my purse, of course. But when I'm in the middle of the woods, like now, they're the first thing I pack in my suitcase."

There's not much left of the bar after Jeff's attack, but Syd holds it up anyway. "If you take anything out of this, just know that these Zyng bars are more than a protein bar. When you're hungry, they're a lifesaver." She pops the last of the bar into her mouth and smiles. "Sanity restored."

25

STORY POST

Reverie Retreat—Day 2

Poll from Sydney: I'm partnering with Zyng to create a brand-new, limited-edition energy bar flavor coming to you in June! Which would be your top pick?

A. Chocolate Hazelnut

B. Cookies and Cream

C. Red Velvet

D. Peanut Butter Banana

26

LUCY

Someone's arguing. Or, rather, a group of someones is arguing.

The sharp, staccato sounds of a fight reach me as I climb from the Lodge's lower level to the back hallway of the main floor.

". . . not a big deal." This from Jeff's low, smoke-warmed voice.

Fully exasperated, Caitlyn cuts in. "You're fucking kidding me. Of course it's a—"

Some indistinct muffling.

Brent chimes in with "Huge."

I only catch the tail end of Jeff's reply, something that could be *know* or *no*.

Oh god. Did Syd find out about Jeff's leaked photos? The blood drains from my face.

My instincts tell me to stay hidden until I know whether it's safe to enter the room, but people don't take kindly to eavesdroppers. In a situation like this, it's worse to go unannounced. I take a few shaky steps forward until the living room unfolds before me.

The rest of my travel companions stand in a cluster just inside the Lodge's front door, chests heaving. The snow they've kicked in tracks across the wood floor in glistening puddles.

For the most part, everyone's squared off against each other, but Sydney has a hand resting in the center of Jeff's chest. If you weren't paying attention, it could look like a loving gesture, but the muscles in her forearm flex, and her fingers are splayed to add resistance against Jeff's body.

She isn't caressing him—she's holding him back.

From who? Or what?

"Everything okay?" I call out.

Sydney's eyes flash with recognition, and she shoots Jeff a pointed look.

Sit. Stay.

When she breaks from the pack to jog my way, color's flushing her cheeks. "Oh my god, Luce!" Dodging the hard bulk of my camera, she wraps me in a one-armed hug. "Where were you?" She's not as mad as I expected her to be, given what Jeff's been hiding from her.

I'm as awkward as a sixth grader at their first school dance. "Uh. Hi?"

Over Sydney's shoulder, I see Caitlyn's lips twist. "We thought you got eaten by a bear." She doesn't seem too broken up about it.

"No bears today," I say.

"And thank goodness," Syd agrees. I'm not sure anyone here believes that if I had faced a bear, I could have come out of that confrontation unscathed. They don't think of me as a survivor, which is their mistake. Out of all of us, I'm the one who's been pushed to the edge before, who's made the return trip from hell. "We didn't know where you were."

"I was out shooting pictures." I pat my camera to illustrate.

When I woke up this morning—now too cold instead of too hot—I couldn't resist the magic of the snow. No way was I going to let everyone else spoil its pristine beauty.

For some things in life, once they get messed up, they can never be put back. My body's one of them. Snow is another. While I can't ever be the me I was before cancer, I could at least be the first one out the door this morning.

The forest did not disappoint.

Glittering icicles hung from the trees, and everything was a kind of peaceful quiet that felt like the world was holding its breath. Sunrise painted the snow a pale pink, and shadows from the tree trunks striped the forest floor a pale blue. The world looked like cotton candy. I shot until my fingers grew numb, each picture just for me, and it felt like I was exactly where I was supposed to be. Another reminder that pivoting my business will be the right move—once I can gather the courage to tell Sydney.

I'm not oblivious to the reality of the market—shooting people pays the bills. If I stop working for her, I don't know how I'll afford my rent. But if I'm starting over in all these other ways, I might as well start fresh in this way too. It's not that I want to stop shooting with her forever, I just want to go back to things being even between us. No power imbalances. No feeling like I owe her my energy or my time.

There have always been disparities between Syd and me—her wealth; the way she had endless support going to college, while I had to fight my way upstream. Syd never treated me as anything but an equal, so those things never got in the way of our friendship. This job, though, the me-working-for-Syd part, changes everything. It flashes me back to being the trailer park kid who was teased mercilessly, who never knew if I was being invited places out of pity or because someone really wanted me there. Being indebted to her makes me feel poor all over again. If I can remove the obligation between us, maybe I can stop feeling like we're farther apart than we've ever been.

I swear I'll tell her how I feel. Just not yet.

"Which way did you go?" Brent asks brusquely.

I bristle at the sudden inquisition, my skin heating with the discomfort of being the center of attention. I'm not sure how Sydney and Caitlyn and Jeff willingly seek out this feeling. "Does it matter?"

"You made it home alright, so probably not," Caitlyn says.

I'm missing something. A knot of dread tightens in my stomach. "What's going on?" I ask warily.

Nash gives a dramatic little shudder. "The trash got taken out last night, but the lid didn't get sealed correctly, and an animal got into it."

So the fight's not about leaked photos, then. My shoulders drop in relief, and a memory of the plastic takeout bags swinging from Jeff's fingers comes back to me. Nash is protecting him, but judging from the state of the argument, everyone knows exactly who messed up.

"Not just an animal," Caitlyn says. "A bear."

"Oh shit," I say. Guess Caitlyn was being literal when she talked about me getting eaten.

"Oh shit is right," Nash agrees.

"Wait." Jeff cocks his head at me, deflecting attention. "You said you were outside. But you didn't come from the front door."

The scrutiny of all those eyes returns to me, and a prickle of panic races up my spine. I've messed up.

"There's a garage and an exterior door at the end of the hallway downstairs. I saw them on my way back from shooting and gave them a try." When you're lying, you're supposed to keep your story simple. Easy to remember. But I can't stop piling on details. "Figured I might save a few minutes instead of walking around the building. The garage was locked, but the door worked."

"That must be why you didn't see the mess outside," Syd says. "It's a disaster. It even smells oily."

"Someone should probably clean it up," Nash says. "Right? So the bear doesn't come back." He winces. "Or other animals."

Even though what Nash has said is completely logical, the rest of us look to Brent for direction. He's usually the one who steps in to take charge, who plays peacemaker and acts like an adult even if he's not always great at it. But he's distracted right now, his jaw clenched as he pulls his phone out of his pocket.

"Uh, Brent?" Caitlyn waves at him. "All good?"

He glances at us, stress lines bracketing his mouth as he frowns. "It might be temporary, but the Wi-Fi's out."

"I think we'll live if we don't post for a single day," Sydney says breezily. She has no idea the problems Brent's trying to solve online—for Jeff and, therefore, for her. Without Wi-Fi, he won't be able to fix a single thing.

"You're not getting me." Brent glowers at Sydney, and I consider for a moment that I might have underestimated him. "As far as I can tell, there's no emergency landline here. Without cell service, Wi-Fi was the only connection we had with the rest of the world." He barrels on, connecting the dots for us. "We can't call for animal control to check out the bear situation. And if you want food?"—he stabs a finger toward the kitchen, where the lone basket of breakfast pastries sits on the counter—"That basket's it."

The proclamation sucks the air out of the room. Jeff's scandal is the least of our problems. We're in the middle of nowhere with barely enough food for breakfast. Best-case scenario is our party bus shows up to collect us on Monday afternoon as planned. But that's assuming clear roads and good conditions.

In the meantime, we're stuck here for at least three more days.

27

CAITLYN

"Okay, this is bleak." I wave a hand at the kitchen counter, where we've brought together any food we carried individually to assess the situation. No one wanted to go back to their cabins alone, so half an hour ago we ventured outside as a group, making noise to scare off any animals that had decided to hang out nearby in hopes of another pass through the trash buffet. Jeff even pulled a bread knife from a butcher block on the counter to bring with him. Not the sharpest knife, mind you, but it had the longest blade. Now, with our snacks collected, it's clear we all bought into the vision Reverie sold us—a luxury retreat with all the amenities supplied. Including food.

The beautiful quartz counter with its slate-colored veining holds what little we could find:

Eleven protein bars from Sydney.

Two tubs of protein powder from Jeff. (Two tubs! For four days! Technically there are only a few scoops left in one, but still. *Je-sus.*)

A chocolate bar from Lucy. (Is there anything that screams heartbroken ex-fiancée more than that?)

An opened box of almond meal crackers I brought with me, minus one sleeve.

One avocado and three packets of inulin powder from Nash.

Three tiny containers of jam from Reverie, as well as six muffins, four croissants, and four English muffins, all laced with poisonous gluten. It's not my fault my stomach makes me want to shit my brains out if more than a crumb of the stuff passes my lips. I'm just wired that way.

Oh, there's also one bottle of vodka.

What could go wrong?

"We need to figure out where we stand," Brent says. It's great that he's trying to step up to the plate now and be responsible, but we wouldn't be in this scenario if he'd thought to ask a few clarifying questions before we arrived at Reverie. Honestly, the whole vibe of his take-the-lead strategy reads a little desperate and kiss-assy. Too little, too late. "If we really are stuck here . . ."

He doesn't fill in the blanks, but our minds all go there anyway. If we're stuck here, this food has to get us through the next few days. Maybe longer.

"I'm going to say what everyone's thinking," I say. "This isn't going to cut it."

"What the fuck do you want me to do?" Brent snaps back. "There's a crap ton of snow on the ground, and there's no Wi-Fi to call anyone. The getting-groceries ship has sailed."

"Should we divide up what we have?" Sydney asks cautiously. She's wearing one of the High Standards brand shirts, looking deliciously rumpled. It's an approachable look, but as someone trying to land high-end film roles, she doesn't always think about the optics of aligning herself with High Standards. Jeff's not someone I'd blindly support. Especially not right now. "That way it's even for everyone."

"Except for me," I can't help saying a little bitterly. "I can't eat anything in that basket except for the jam."

She shoots me an apologetic look. "Right, yeah." Her cheeks color and she shakes her head in frustration. "This sucks. Maybe we hold off on making any decisions."

"No," Lucy chimes in. "You were right. Dividing things up is a good idea." Of course she'd say that; she's the one who only brought a chocolate bar with her. Not much to survive on if not for the group's kindness.

Nash nudges me with his hip. "We'll make sure you're covered. Because of the gluten thing." He really is one of the good ones.

I nod my thanks, and we miserably get to work dividing the food. Once everyone has their little piles and we've all been told we can have exactly four and a half scoops of protein powder each, it's clear it's going to be a long few days.

I'd never tell the rest of them, but the mix-up with the food has left me unsettled. My dad taught me the rule of threes at an early age: you can survive three minutes without air, three hours without shelter, three days without water, and three weeks without food. Technically, food's the lowest priority on that list, which I guess is good, given that we have air and shelter. But food shouldn't have ever been a question mark. It should have been a given. We put so much trust in Brent that nobody thought to double-check the logistics, and now it's a problem when it didn't need to be one. Especially if we're stuck here an extra day or two.

I don't want to be in a survival situation. And if something actually happens to me . . . god. My family's been through enough tragedy with my stepbrother Cole's death. Losing him sent our lives into a downward spiral, and I can only imagine what the death of another child might do to my parents. They don't deserve to suffer that kind of devastation ever again.

The longer I dwell on it, the more I waver between rage and despair. I wasn't hungry until I was told there was no food, but now I'm starving.

"Anyone actually going to eat?" I ask, eyeing the counter.

It's Sydney's turn to shift uncomfortably. "Jeff and I already shared a protein bar this morning. We filmed a promotion." Her eyes flash to Brent. "Actually, I posted it as we got close to the Lodge. So Wi-Fi must have been working for at least a little while."

Brent folds his lips together and nods. "We'll keep checking it." But his phone stays firmly in his pocket.

It's not a good enough answer. "As soon as internet comes back up, we need to call Reverie and let them know what's going on," I say. "They probably have an emergency protocol for this type of thing. Maybe someone on staff can bring over food and supplies."

"You don't need to micromanage me," Brent huffs.

"Just making sure we're all on the same page. You know what they say about assuming . . ."

"So, hey," Nash blurts out in an obvious attempt to redirect the conversation. "Who's hungry? The avocado's going to spoil. I'll cut that up to go with the pastries."

Those of us who plan to eat stand around the island and grab a few bites of food. There's no styled photo shoot—just the sounds of resigned chewing. We all keep hovering, looking at one another warily. We're friends here, sure, but each of us is an extra mouth to feed.

With a sigh, I arrange a few slices of avocado on six tiny crackers. The texture of the raw avocado makes me gag a little, but this will be the last fresh food I have for a few days, so I might as well make the most of it.

"Okay, this is officially depressing," I say when I've wiped the crumbs from my lips. "I need a distraction."

Sydney's eyes meet mine. "What did you have in mind?"

I sweep a hand toward the living room section of the Lodge, where the racks of clothes wait patiently for us. "We can't post pictures today, but that doesn't mean we can't take them."

"You want to do a photo shoot?" Lucy asks. Sometimes she really does state the obvious.

"Actually, I have an even better idea," Nash purrs, surveying the room with his chin held in one hand. The way he's eyeing Lucy, deep in thought, reminds me of *The Thinker.* I saw the statue last year at the Musée Rodin in Paris when a perfume company flew me to France to create a campaign for the launch of a new scent.

To be honest, it was one of the highlights of my career.

Because I dropped out of college, I never got to have a semester abroad. Instead, my job's given me an informal education, and I soak up knowledge wherever I go. Sometimes people who meet me find it hard to see beyond my looks, but I've always felt it's important to learn as much as you can about the world. You never know when a stray piece of information is going to come in handy.

The week I got to spend in Paris made me realize how much potential I had, not just to make money or to give back to my family, but as a person telling a story about myself. Embodying a fragrance helped me recognize the way people can transform into ideas. Capturing the essence of a scent is tricky, so what you're really doing is making people associate you with a feeling. I wanted to be strength and beauty and glamour and wit. And by the end of the campaign, the perfumers and my followers alike had bought into the idea that I was all those things. The perfumer recommended me to the designer whose gown I wore out at the waterfall, and one thing led to another. If I can keep leveraging these connections to boost my career, there's not much standing between me and the top.

Nash drops his hand from his chin and spins to address the room. "There's only one thing to do when you're snowed in with a dozen designer gowns and enough makeup to get Manhattan through Fashion Week." Nash swings his gaze back to Lucy and smiles so broadly that Lucy's eyes go wide before he's even announced his plans. "We can do the photo shoot. But first we're going to do makeovers. Specifically for you, Lucy doll."

28

LUCY

When I first arrived at Reverie, all I wanted was to relax with my friends, deliver images for Reverie, and take a few photos for my landscape portfolio. It seemed like a beautiful place to unwind and figure out my next move. Now that we're stuck here with a limited amount of food, though, any hope I had of relaxing has fled along with the bear.

Can't forget about him.

At this point, all I'm hoping is that we can get through this weekend quickly and safely. I want to shed the sense of creeping danger that clings to me and makes the back of my mouth taste like bile. There's all this empty space around us, but I can't help feeling claustrophobic. We're trapped here, and there's no escape.

I wouldn't normally say yes to a makeover, but hopefully it can be a distraction for all of us. This is me taking one for the team.

Before I slip into the chair Nash has pulled out for me, I wirelessly tether my camera to my cell phone. I suspect our bear friend is long gone, but I'd rather not have to go back to my cabin to process images. Now any photos I shoot on my camera will appear on my phone, so I can pick favorites and start editing them in the Lightroom app on my cell. Ta-da, no laptop required.

When I'm finally done, Nash smiles at me patiently and pats the chair. "Do you trust me?"

I want to tell him I'm not sure I trust anyone—myself included—but that sounds a little unhinged and ungrateful, so as I sit, I swallow the lump in my throat and nod. "You're a genius at what you do."

That part, at least, is true.

Nash dips his chin to study me, and I fight the instinct to squirm. "I want to give you a haircut. Nothing dramatic, but a more defined shape."

My fingers float to my scalp. Everyone tries to prepare you for the way chemo makes your hair fall out, so you give yourself all these pep talks that it's going to be okay, that it's just hair and it grows back. But the second you lose it, it feels like part of you is stripped away. The first time I looked in the mirror after I lost my hair was the first time I looked at myself and thought I looked sick. It hurt almost worse than losing my breasts.

I trust Nash's judgment, but the idea of losing my hair again makes me want to bawl. It's a visceral, knee-jerk reaction.

"I thought Plentifol was all about long, luscious locks," I say, dropping my hands to twist them in my lap. Isn't healthy hair a symbol of vitality?

"Nah," he says gently. "It's about being plentiful. Living an abundant life."

A lump rises in my throat, sudden and surprising. I'm sitting in a lodge in the woods with a group of people who are mostly indifferent to my existence. Back home in New York, there's nothing waiting for me. Just an empty apartment and a life I don't yet know how to live.

If anyone needs to make over their life, it's me.

"All of us deserve to be pampered," Nash continues. He sweeps an arm around the room, indicating to the group. Brent's stepped outside to clean up the trash from this morning, but Caitlyn and Sydney are examining the gowns, getting ready to dress for our shoot. "Look around. Everyone here treats themselves. You know the reason Syd and Cait and Jeff get so many views online? It's because they take care of themselves and indulge in things that make them feel good. People want to see that, because they want to believe that they, too, are deserving of care. The more you see it, the more you start to understand that a life where you're cherished is within reach."

When I was younger, I used to believe there were good things coming for me, a whole future stretched out for me to enjoy.

I haven't let myself believe that in so long.

That's what guilt will do to you—it'll steal your hope and make you believe you're unworthy. But Nash is giving me permission to want things again, and I find that I do. I'm ready to step into the next version of myself.

"Okay," I whisper. "Do it."

Caitlyn leaves a dress for me hanging in the bathroom, either as a surprise or as a dare. Possibly both. It's a short, gold-sequined number with a plunging V-neckline that I know will expose a huge swath of my skin.

I blow out a deep breath and reach for the hem of the glittery dress. It's not like everyone here didn't see me in a bathing suit just last night, but I feel unreasonably nervous. It's one thing to show up when you're hiding yourself and another thing entirely to show up trying your best to look pretty. There's more to judge when you're trying hard.

Once again, I don't know how Syd and Jeff and Cait do it.

A sharp rap at the door makes me jump. "You're not peeking, are you?" Sydney's voice comes out muffled through the wooden door. She and the others made me promise not to look in the mirror until after my hair, makeup, and outfit were pulled together in a final look. According to Caitlyn, they're hoping for a grand reveal.

"I'll be out in a second," I call back. Without letting myself dwell any longer, I slip the dress over my head. I'm a few inches shorter than Sydney and Caitlyn, so while the dress is still short, it thankfully covers my butt. The material clings to my hips, sliding against my bare legs as I swing open the bathroom door.

Sydney gasps at the sight of me. She does a lot of things in life dramatically, but I can tell her reaction is genuine.

"Nash," she says, not taking her eyes off me. "You are certifiably brilliant."

"Hair, makeup, clothes," Caitlyn agrees with a smile. "Is there anything this man can't do?"

"Find the G-spot," Jeff calls, ruining the moment. *Asshole.*

With the spell broken, I step nervously into the room. "Can I look now?"

Nash swoops over and guides me by the shoulders to a mirror he's propped in front of the window. He's given me the barest of pixie cuts, something that somehow doesn't flash me back to having lost all my hair. It makes my eyes look huge. And instead of making me feel half naked, the gold dress hugs what curves I do have.

I look powerful and fierce and delicate all at once. I look . . . beautiful. What's been broken has somehow been rebuilt that much stronger.

"There you are, gorgeous," Nash says, satisfied with his work. Somehow he's not at all surprised at who I could be, even though I never saw it myself. "Own exactly who you are."

"What if I don't know who that is?" I whisper.

"I think you might. You just need to be honest with yourself about what's important to you. The rest will follow." He squeezes my shoulders as Caitlyn and Sydney join us by the mirror. "You know, recently some photos of me and my boyfriend got posted online without my permission. And at first I was heartbroken. I mean, I try to keep our relationship just between us, and it feels so icky when other people don't respect that. But worse, every time I share a picture of him, haters come out of the woodwork to spew homophobic shit, and they sic their friends on me too."

"Love is love!" Caitlyn chimes in supportively, and Sydney beams at her.

Nash presses a hand to his chest. "Thank you. You know, after this last time with the trolls, though, I thought, fuck 'em. My boyfriend's important to me, and I have to live my life as me, or else why am I living it at all? Might as well celebrate the good things."

"Amen!" Caitlyn agrees.

I wrap Nash in a hug, feeling suddenly shy. "Thank you."

"My pleasure, doll. My pleasure." It's like I'm the one giving him the gift instead of the other way around. He drops his mouth beside my ear and whispers so only I can hear. "And if you're still not sure who you are, then fake it till you make it. All these bitches do."

I stifle a laugh just as Sydney winds her arms around us and pulls Caitlyn in too. "Group hug!" she squeals.

Squeezed in their embrace, a tide of hope rises inside my chest. We're going to get through this weekend, and I'm going to turn things around for myself. Nash is right; I can figure out my next steps. I can make myself proud. Look how far I've already come.

"Ah shit!" Jeff cries from across the room, and we break apart to stare at him. He has his phone pressed against his ear, and he covers the mouthpiece for a second to say, "I've got Reverie's line ringing."

29

LUCY

I'm impressed that Jeff's trying to help the group rather than use the moment of Wi-Fi connection to try to salvage his reputation. The room falls silent save for the wet squeak of his sneakers on the wood floor as he paces. This is what they mean when they say *waiting with bated breath*—we're all poised on our respective pieces of furniture, listening so eagerly, you'd think our lives depend on it.

Maybe they do.

The strained silence amplifies the thrumming of my heartbeat in my ears. To distract myself, I study the muscles of Jeff's back as they tense beneath his shirt. I'm surprised he's even wearing clothes right now. It's not his style to stay covered up when he could show off all the hard work he puts in at the gym.

"Hi, I'm a guest here." For a second, a wave of hope crests in my chest, but it crashes as soon as he tacks on "Call me back as soon as you can."

An answering machine. Jeff didn't get through.

"Fuck," he bites out, yanking the phone from his ear. "No answer."

"What?" I ask stupidly. We all heard him clearly, I just can't make it make sense. Reverie isn't totally operational yet, but they knew they had guests this weekend. So why isn't someone picking up? Did something happen to them too?

A sweaty panic crawls across my chest. Couldn't one thing go right this weekend?

"Dude," Nash says to Jeff, his jaw tight, "that was a useless message. You didn't tell them there was a problem."

"The answering machine said if there's an emergency, we should call 911," Jeff replies defensively.

"So, then, call," Caitlyn says, and my panic flares a little hotter. Everything's spiraling so wildly out of control.

Back from cleaning up outside, Brent groans at Cait's suggestion. "Wait a second. Are we sure this is emergency territory?"

She waves him off. "Let's let the police decide. All I know is we're not going anywhere soon, and we're running out of food. I don't want to find out what happens when it's gone."

"Cait's right." Syd nods nervously at Jeff. "Do it."

Jeff resumes his pacing, and this time, the wait to see if we get through to someone feels even more desperate. My whole body feels leaden, like the floor might give way under me if I stand here too long.

At last he pumps a fist into the air. Relief breaks over me, and I'm in complete agreement with the quiet "thank fuck" Caitlyn mutters.

Jeff stops moving and directs his attention to whoever's on the other end. "Yes, hi," he begins. He explains our plight and then he's back to listening again. "Mm-hmm. Okay." Nash coughs quietly, and Jeff glances up sharply, as though he didn't expect us all to be staring at him. "Yeah." He returns his focus to the phone. "A few days. You're sure there's nothing else you can do?" A long exhale. "Right. Well, thank you." A beat. "Will do."

It's infuriatingly little to go off of, so when he finally hangs up, we all pounce on him.

"Are the police coming to get us?" Caitlyn asks.

"Or sending someone to bring supplies?" Nash adds.

Jeff runs a hand through his hair, a muscle ticking in his jaw. "No."

Sydney's eyes bulge. "What do you mean, 'no'?" She waves a hand toward the window and the snow beyond. "We're not prepared for this."

"Yeah, well, they said they received a lot of calls and they need to prioritize." He informs us that according to the police, there are people in far worse situations than us right now, and the police are focusing on getting emergency services out to the actual emergencies.

"Okay." I blow out a breath. "It makes sense. If people are actually hurt out there, they should be the priority." I don't want to be stuck here like this, but I want to give Reverie—and, at the very least, *us*—the benefit of the doubt. "We can figure out a plan."

"Will the road get plowed, at least?" Nash asks.

Jeff shrugs. "Again, they said they were focusing on high-priority areas."

Caitlyn falls back into a chair with a sigh. "Meaning it'll happen when it happens."

"If it happens," Brent muses.

I shoot a sideways glance at him. "What do you mean? I'm sure it's all going to get taken care of."

"Only if this is a public road. Police are a public service, right? So when they talk about plowing, they're probably thinking about public roads. But if this is a private road, then it's on Reverie to get it plowed. If they even pay for a service."

"So . . ." Syd says, and her regretful eyes flash to mine. "Anyone know if this is a public road?"

My heart drops, and I have to squeeze the word *unlikely* through a throat that's suddenly raw. I take a deep breath, trying to calm myself down. "Okay," I say. "Did they give you any good news?"

It's probably the most serious I've ever seen Jeff look. He shakes his head and folds his arms across his chest. "They had two suggestions. We should stay inside. And we should ration."

30

LUCY

"Oh my god," Caitlyn groans at the police advice Jeff delivers. "This is dire."

"All the more reason to do our photo shoot," Sydney muses. "We could use the distraction."

"Actually," Brent pipes up, "before we do that, let's take advantage of the Wi-Fi while it's up." He turns to me. "Lucy, can you send everyone some teaser pics they can post?"

My face heats. Talk about a pivot. "Oh. Yeah, sure." I'd rather be jumping online too, but the sooner I deliver photos from this weekend, the sooner I can start moving on with my career. Of course, that would mean I need to tell Sydney how I feel, and I'm not quite ready to face that. One step at a time.

"Great," Brent says. He scoops a magazine off a coffee table and heads toward the bathroom. "On that note, I'm going to take a shit."

He exits to a chorus of groans.

Eager to erase Brent's last statement from my mind, I grab my phone and retreat to one of the couches at the far end of the Lodge. My messages appear on my screen first, and I hesitate for a moment. Do I let Nick know that I'm stranded on the mountain? Or do I keep giving him space to start over without pulling him back to me? If I were in his shoes, what would I want?

While I wrestle with indecision, I send a few photos to the group chat.

"Oh my gosh, these pictures are gorgeous," Syd says, dropping onto the couch next to me. While Nash was focused on me earlier, Sydney did her own makeup, and her hair's long and loose around her shoulders. She's beautiful, but it's her happiness that truly makes her glow. "If this is just a handful, I can't imagine how good the rest of the campaign will look."

A pit opens in my stomach. Yesterday's session might have been one of my last shoots with her. Before I can gather the courage to say anything, she leans forward with a widening smile. "Okay, side note: your hair smells amazing right now."

I self-consciously pat the side of my head. "I used Plentifol."

Her smile is positively blinding. "What do you think?" The last time I saw her this radiant with excitement for the future was years ago. She'd just met Breaker and had landed the horror movie role she'd auditioned for. It was hard to say which of those things made her happier. It was nice to see her lit up like that, but Breaker set my teeth on edge for reasons I could never explain. At least, not that early on.

Maybe I was jealous of him, I admit. Sometimes I wonder if all that envy might have buried itself so deep in my cells, it turned into cancer. Or maybe the darkness was already there, moldering below the surface, waiting to be discovered.

Looking at all the hope on Sydney's face now, I know I can't tell her that I want to stop working for her. She's so focused on her products that my confession would blindside her. She'd see it as a betrayal. "It's really good, Syd. Plentifol's going to do well out there."

She claps her hands together and grins. "When we get home and can get you proper studio lighting and all that, would you take product photos for me?"

My chest constricts, and instead of answering, I ask the question that's been nagging at me. "What happens to all your sponsorships when you launch your brand?"

She shrugs a slim shoulder, unbothered. "Brent handles all my contracts, so I gave him a heads-up of what was coming. He's already working on a plan of action, and he'll cancel anything that's a conflict of interest."

Between her hair vitamins and her styling products, that could mean a ton of canceled contracts. I guess it depends on how you define *conflict of interest.* Still, I didn't realize how much of a gamble Sydney was taking by launching Plentifol. To make a product for herself and bring in future revenue, she'll have to turn down a lot of existing income. It's a bold move, and I'm proud of her, but it also puts her at risk.

"Okay," she says, squeezing my knee before bouncing to her feet. "I'm going to film a quick video while I have the chance. Gotta please the boss."

As Sydney steps outside the Lodge, I bend back over my phone. The last time Nick reached out, he asked if I was okay. At the time, things were fine, but now . . . Maybe it would be good to let him know what's happened. If he sees the news about the storm and hasn't heard from me, it'll make him worry worse. That or he'll be indifferent. The thought makes my chest burn too much to contemplate.

I type out a quick message. Made it to the mountains but got snowed in. Give Oboe a kiss for me. I stare at the screen, wondering if I should backtrack and erase the *kiss*. Is it too suggestive? Will he read between the lines and know I miss him too?

I decide to go for it anyway, but before I can hit *send*, the Wi-Fi signal goes out. Looks like technology's made my decision for me.

Even if I wanted to talk to Nick, I can't get through now.

31

STORY POST

Reverie Retreat—Day 2

Want to hear the craziest thing?" Sydney's eyes are wide with scandal. She's flawlessly made up, with winged eyeliner magnifying the impact of her expression, and a pale pink lipstick making her mouth look soft and lush. As she speaks into her phone, all you can see is bare skin from her chest up, so it looks like she could be naked.

Interesting.

You want more.

Sydney shakes her head, and you know it's because of whatever she's about to confess. Maybe she's finally going to address what's happening with Jeff. The tabloids are off to the races with the photos they've turned up, sharing them far more widely than Sydney probably likes. Though some images have been blurred out of respect for Jeff's privacy, the darker corners of Reddit have posted the unedited pictures in all their glory. Photos that make you jealous of Jeff for his unfair blessings and of Syd for getting to enjoy them.

Still, the idea lodges in your mind that if her head shake's not about the photos, she could just as easily be scolding you for the racy direction your thoughts have taken.

Fair point, Sydney. Fair point.

She delivers the news in a breathless rush: "We're snowed in."

Now her camera pans out, sliding to provide a panoramic view of the landscape. The looming wooden lodge behind Sydney gives way to an open area filled with trampled snow. Trees ring the perimeter of the clearing like sentinels, though you can't be sure if they're protecting the forest from Sydney or protecting Sydney from whatever waits in the woods. In the overcast afternoon, the tree trunks have taken on a dull grayish hue.

"I mean, look at this! It's at least half a foot." Sydney directs the camera down the length of her body to show off the hem of an emerald-green gown and the latticed leather of her open-toe heels, which are plunged into a blanket of snow. Then she swings the camera back to her face. The delay allows the impact of her words to sink in.

"We definitely didn't prepare for this," she says. "It could be a couple of days before the snow plows make it our way." Her face is disbelieving and serious, but surely it's a pretend kind of nervousness. She might be standing in a layer of snow, but now you can see the sweetheart neckline of her dress and the glitter of chandelier earrings half hidden by her hair. She's in full makeup and a designer gown, hanging out in luxury accommodations with a group of fabulous friends. What's there to worry about?

Come to think of it, it doesn't sound so bad to be snowed in right along with her.

Sydney gives a shrug. "I guess we're getting the full relaxation we were promised. Wi-Fi's a little spotty too, so I might be quieter than usual." She claps her hands together and her expression brightens. "Oh! I forgot to tell you, yesterday we got to do some shoots for my secret project, and you guys are going to die when you see the photos. Also, I've loved seeing all your guesses about the project. Some of you are right on the money, and some of you have some . . . creative ideas." She grins into the camera. "I've got such good things planned for you. And more surprises to come this weekend, which—"

The feed goes dark, whether from a dropped connection or because she's reached the time limit on her story.

Either way, whatever she was about to say is lost to the world.

32

CAITLYN

Brent, returning from the bathroom, takes one look at our crestfallen faces and frowns. "What did I miss?"

Jeff slings his now-useless phone onto a coffee table and mutters, "Wi-Fi's back down."

"Dammit." Brent rubs his temples with a frustrated sigh. "It's not that I don't love you all, but it would be good to have the option of contacting the outside world."

"You mean it would be good if you fixed this hacking thing," Jeff says, crossing his arms over his chest.

Brent glares at him. "It's a moot point now anyway. I looked for the router this morning, and wherever it is, it's behind a locked door. Nothing we can do to fix it."

The front door of the Lodge swings open, and Sydney hurries inside, stomping circulation back into her feet. The hem of her gown is damp with snow. "It's freezing out there." When no one answers, she gives us all a wary glance. "Everyone okay?"

"Just chatting," I say cheerily. "I think it's high time for our photo shoot. Let's head outside. The snow will make all the colors pop."

"The police said to stay inside," Brent reminds us.

"It'll be fine," I counter. "They just don't want us to get hypothermia or whatever. Anyway, there's no cell service, no TV, and I didn't bring nearly enough reading material. We might as well do something fun and celebrate Lucy's makeover."

"Commemorative pictures," Sydney agrees.

"You know, I'm going to bow out of this one," Jeff says. He exchanges a glance with Nash. "Thought we might celebrate a little differently." *Celebrate? Or escape his impending cancellation?*

Sydney rolls her eyes, already following his train of thought. "Not inside, dude. It's a nonsmoking facility."

"But we can light a fire inside?" Jeff grumbles. "Kind of a double standard." Complaining aside, he slides on his shoes to follow her toward the door.

"Don't want to start a forest fire either," Nash teases. All of us glance out at the snow-covered landscape and burst into laughter.

"We're doing this, then?" Lucy asks.

"We're doing this."

Lucy glances out the window. "Lighting will be better on the back side of the Lodge. We can go out the exit I found earlier, so we won't need to walk outside for long to get great backgrounds."

"See?" I say, looping an arm through hers. "We can totally stay safe about it."

Cold air blasts me in the face the moment we step through the Lodge's back door and out into the snow. Forget ice rolling—I can practically feel my pores shrinking. I know I suggested this, but it feels colder than it did even last night. The weather people did a shit job predicting the temperatures. Still, it feels good to be doing something together instead of stewing inside.

The guys huddle in the shadow of the building while I lead Lucy and Sydney toward some trees. "Pictures of you first, Luce. Can I shoot them?" Photography is a kind of storytelling, which is totally my jam. It's all about selling a narrative. I can already envision the splash of her gold dress and red hair against the crisp white snow.

"You know what to do?"

"I've got this," I assure her, but when she hands over the camera, she looks scared I'm going to drop it, so I loop the strap around my neck while I pose her. "Let's get up against the tree." It's fun to flip roles for once. A new kind of power.

I angle Lucy's body so her hips pop out and her back arches, creating curves for the camera to feast on. Then I step back and take a few shots. The cold makes my eyes water, but I relish how awake I feel.

"What do you think?" I call. "Want to be a model? Or an influencer?"

The sequins cast flecks of light onto her face, making her look ethereal. She's visibly shaking with cold, though she's not letting her discomfort change her expression. Honestly, good for her. It's a challenging thing to do.

Lucy shakes her head with a shivery laugh. "Your job's hard," she replies. "No contest."

A hit of satisfaction makes me smile back at her. "Your job too."

In fairness, I've shot a camera before, so I don't think I'm going to deliver blurry pictures or anything. But I do need to give credit where it's due—Lucy has this ability to capture more than what you can see with your bare eyes, to draw out your best self. It's a rare gift.

"You look stunning," Sydney tells her, watching over my shoulder.

After I'm happy with the first set of pictures, Sydney steps forward to adjust the way Lucy's dress lies against her skin. I glance at the guys to see if they're paying attention and catch Jeff pulling a tin from his back pocket. Since it's branded with **HIGH STANDARDS**, I'd place a sizable bet there's a joint or two in there.

Sure enough, Jeff removes a lighter and a prerolled joint from the case. He offers the joint to Nash to take the first puff.

"Typical boys, not sharing," Sydney says, and I drag my attention away from them.

The three of us move to a new location around the corner of the building, where Sydney takes over staging the shot. Instead of posing Lucy in front of the trees, Syd has her stand just inside the tree line. From between the tree trunks, Lucy glitters like a promise. A gift.

"What do you think about the setup?" Syd asks.

"Beautiful," I say, and frame up a shot.

"Nash!" The hoarse shout, ripped from Jeff's throat, shatters my focus and sends a shard of fear straight to my heart. He's not yelling like they're messing around with each other. It's a shout of desperation, like something's gone terribly wrong.

I yank my gaze from the camera and am running before my brain catches up to my body. The deep snow resists every step I take, and my dress tangles around my legs. Behind me, Lucy and Sydney pound through the snow, but they're farther away from the Lodge than I am.

Jeff keeps calling Nash's name, and there's a flurry of activity that I can't quite make out. The side of the building prevents me from taking in the full picture, but as I turn the corner, what I find makes me stumble the last few steps.

Nash is slumped over in the snow, his lips and skin a sickly gray color.

Jeff and Brent are on their knees beside Nash, Brent slapping his face even though it's clear Nash has slid from consciousness.

Holy shit.

I've been around enough sports injuries that I thought I'd be able to keep calm through anything, but there's something about the way Nash is lying there, just so still, that makes me lose my composure. My heart stutter-stops, and I can't catch my breath. "What happened?" I ask, my voice breaking.

"He took a hit. And then he started shaking," Jeff explains, his words strangled with horror. "His eyes rolled back and . . ." Unable to continue the sentence, he rocks back and forth on his knees, shaking his head.

Lucy and Sydney arrive beside us in a rush of dread. "Oh no, no, no. Nash!" Lucy cries. She dives beside him and checks his pulse. "He's not breathing! Does anyone know CPR?" When no one responds, she presses her lips to his, pumping his chest and giving rescue breaths at intervals.

I can't tear my eyes away.

"What did you give him?" Sydney asks Jeff as Lucy works desperately over Nash's body.

Jeff rockets to his feet and shakes his head. "Just a joint."

"If we don't know the truth, we can't help him," Sydney pleads.

Brent speaks distantly, as if he's in shock. "He looks like he's had an overdose."

"It was just a joint." Jeff's words strike out more firmly this time, laced with anger and defensiveness.

"Not of marijuana." Again that remote, cold tone. It's like Brent's watching a movie play out for someone else instead of seeing it through his own eyes. "Something else."

Jeff runs a hand through his hair and paces through the snow. "There's nothing else it could be," he says. "Everything's legal, aboveboard." But it's clear that whatever happened had to be related to the joint Nash just smoked. Jeff's tin of smoking paraphernalia is tipped open on the ground, the branded lighter and the other contents scattered at our feet.

"Come on, Nash, *please*," Sydney wails, but whatever Lucy's doing isn't working. Nash, normally the life of the party, the truest artist among us, lies stiff and unmoving at my feet.

Lucy sits back on her heels after a few minutes and looks up at us, shaking her head sorrowfully. Whatever glittery magic the makeover brought her has disappeared. She looks cold and scared and heartbroken, and I can't help thinking that even if we could call someone for help, it would be far too late.

"He's . . ." Lucy chokes out, and her entire body crumples in on itself.

The fist of my heart keeps banging, a cold contrast to the way Nash's chest refuses to rise. No one knows what to say anymore, so we sit out in the snow in stunned silence for what feels like forever.

Nash never wakes up.

33

LUCY

Nash lies at my feet, unmoving.

"He's dead," Sydney whispers. The way she says it, with a tear rolling down her gorgeous face, makes it seem like she's delivering a line in one of her horror movies. So beautifully tragic, so macabre.

It's too full circle, and a chilling shock judders through me. My body does this weird thing where I tell it to sit still but it can't stop shaking. Everything in my chest feels like it's collapsed, my heart sunk into a cavity so deep, there's no retrieving it.

"Is this real right now?" Caitlyn asks.

An overwhelming sense of failure crashes over me, and I can't bring myself to look at Nash. Nash, who listened to me and welcomed me and cared. Nash, who gave me the gift of feeling beautiful just minutes ago.

Nash, who I couldn't save.

Gone.

Another unwelcome thought rushes in: my lips were pressed against Nash's cold, lifeless ones. I gave him mouth-to-mouth when he was already dead.

I barely have time to scramble back from his body before I vomit in the snow.

Caitlyn makes a sound like she's stopped herself from gagging.

I'm ashamed of myself and my dramatic reaction, but I couldn't help the sudden surge of nausea. And then I'm furious too, because I've thrown up what little was in my stomach, and we have no food to spare.

"Fuck, fuck, fuck," Brent mutters, pushing to his feet to pace in the snow. "What the hell can do that to someone? That was so fucking quick."

"Heroin?" Caitlyn suggests.

"Fentanyl," Sydney says gravely. Her eyes are huge with shock, her hair a windblown mess from running in the snow. "I saw a documentary on it. Drug dealers cut other drugs with it, and you might not know you're taking it." She lets out a sob. "Just the tiniest bit can kill you."

Shock ricochets through me, freezes me down to the core.

It's ironic that the same thing they give you for the worst of the cancer pain can be a recreational drug that can kill you if you aren't careful. I guess a lot of things in life are like that: fine in reasonable doses, deadly in excess.

I'm more familiar with fentanyl than most people, but not the recreational kind. Except, the stash of painkillers in my suitcase isn't exactly aboveboard, if I'm being honest.

Now I feel like repeating after Brent: *fuck, fuck, fuck.*

Logically, I know no one's going to say, "Oh, Lucy, didn't you bring fentanyl with you on this trip?" They couldn't possibly know. Unless . . . unless someone happened to see the drugs when they were in my room. And everybody was in everybody else's cabins when we gathered our food.

I'm not just ashamed or angry anymore.

I'm terrified.

Even if the fentanyl in Nash's joint wasn't mine, I'd be easy to frame. I can't risk having Nash's death tied to me in any way.

One death on my conscience is bad enough.

I can't have two.

"Fentanyl?" Jeff bursts out. He's been quiet since Nash died, and now his voice explodes over the frozen landscape. "Are you shitting me? That could have been me! I could have died!"

"Way to make it about you," Caitlyn says scathingly, "when your friend is the one dead right now."

"You were the one who gave him the weed," I whisper. I don't mean to say it, but once it's out there, the truth feels like a shield. Like I can hide behind the accusation, like if everyone's looking at Jeff, they won't look at me.

If Jeff's expression wasn't murderous before, it certainly is now. "Yeah, the same weed I was about to smoke. So if you want to accuse me of killing my friend, just come on out and say it, Lucy. Louder for the people in the back."

"Stop it!" Sydney cuts in, her voice raw with tears. "This isn't the time. We have to get help."

"What fucking help?" Jeff demands, pivoting that anger toward her. I might have put up with him because Sydney cares about him, but now I can barely breathe around the knot in my stomach. Anger is one thing. But unpredictable, unstable anger? That's frightening. Who knows what Jeff could do if pushed the wrong way? Syd's been through too much to be with someone whose first instinct is to turn on her rather than protect her. "Our phones don't work," Jeff continues. "And there's not even a fucking landline."

Sydney drops her face into her hands. Silent sobs rack her shoulders, and I can see the column of her spine through the thin material of her gown.

She must be freezing.

I've been too numb to comprehend the cold, but now it rakes over my body like claws and hooks in deep under my skin.

My body keeps shaking and shaking.

"We'll figure out a plan." I say it in part to comfort Sydney and in part because my brain's already whirling to stay ahead of whatever's coming next. I need to get back to my cabin and check my suitcase to know for sure what happened, but now isn't the time.

"First we need to get inside and warm up," Brent says. The police warning flits into my mind. "It's not safe to stay out here anymore."

Caitlyn waves her hands over the general area. I still can't bring myself to look at Nash's body. "Do we just . . . ?"

My heart sinks. "We can't leave Nash out here."

Caitlyn grimaces. "I don't think we should move him."

"Lucy's right," Sydney says, wiping her face and standing. "What if the bear comes back?"

The idea brings a fresh wave of horror, and we all go silent as we contemplate the thought of Nash suffering any more than he already has.

"Okay." Brent blows out a deep breath. "The back door's closest. Maybe we can take him into the meditation room?"

I finally drop my gaze to the ground, and seeing Nash again

is just as awful as the image that's seared into my brain. Shadows creep over the ground, reaching closer and closer to his body. It's like the forest, like *winter,* wants to claim him.

"Jeff," Brent says, and Jeff grunts. "I need your help carrying him."

Jeff looks like he wants to punch a hole in the wall. Or in Brent. He breathes out a short snort through his nose, then nods.

"Wait!" Sydney says. "Before we do this, shouldn't we document the body? So when the police get here they have evidence?"

"There wasn't a fucking crime!" Jeff shouts.

Sydney lays a gentle hand on his chest. "He died under suspicious circumstances."

His body trembles with rage. "I didn't do it. I fucking told you. The only reason I'm alive right now instead of him is because I was being a *gentleman* and offered him the first toke."

As much as he protests, he's the one who gave Nash the joint, and he's the one who procured said joint in the first place. If there was a crime, he'd be the most obvious perpetrator in the group. Other than me, of course.

"No one said you did anything," Sydney says, covering for me because I *did* say it. Or I implied it. But the more she talks, the more I question myself. Maybe she's right—maybe this is all a horrible accident. It would be stupid for Jeff to mar High Standards's brand image by purposefully tampering with the weed. Have I just been projecting because I've been jealous of his role in Sydney's life? Or is threatening his business's reputation the perfect misdirection?

"The police are going to want to know what happened,"

Sydney continues, and I force myself to stop spiraling and pay attention. I can't protect anyone if I don't know all the variables, if I can't see the threats coming.

"You're right," Caitlyn says.

"Alright, then," Syd agrees. "Let's get a few pictures."

And everyone's attention swings to me.

34

LUCY

Anxiety squeezes tight inside my chest. My breath comes out in panicked little bursts. "Why are you all looking at me like that?" I demand, but I know from the sorrow etched on everyone's faces what they're thinking, and I can't handle this right now.

"You're the photographer, Luce," Caitlyn says. She holds my camera out to me, its strap dangling, tossed around in the light breeze that's lifting tiny gusts of snow from the ground.

A fresh wave of horror floods through me. "I can't—"

Please don't turn the one thing I love into something tarnished.

"You know how to use this best. What lens to use . . ."

I put the 85 mm on for this morning's shoot. My other lenses are tucked in my camera bag inside the building, and there's no way I'm going back for anything else right now. This'll do.

Feeling trapped, I reach for the camera, its body still warm from Caitlyn's hands. But I don't feel any of the peace I normally feel when shooting.

Tears stream down my face as I correct the camera settings with numb fingers. I bring the camera to my eyes and position myself near Nash's body. And then I'm forced to take in the details my brain wants so desperately to blur out.

Nash's hands are curled into fists at his sides, the glint of his gold nail polish tucked against his palms. A speckle of froth dots his lips. His face and neck look frozen, and that grayish pallor still clouds his skin.

My vibrant, creative, expressive friend looks . . . he looks dead. And there's no coming back.

I take picture after trembling picture until Sydney sees how much I'm crying and says, "That's enough!"

Brent and Jeff get into position to move Nash, but I can't bear to watch them carry him away. I rush inside the Lodge and slam up the stairs, barely making it in time to dry heave over the toilet. When I catch sight of myself in the mirror, I find my eyes rimmed in red, my face blotchy and swollen. I'm still wearing the ridiculous sequin dress. The feel of it on my skin makes me want to scream.

All Nash's hard work, and for what? It feels like such a waste.

I feel like such a waste.

What's the point of beauty if everything else is falling apart?

I rip off the stupid dress and put my old clothes back on, the familiar sweater and comfortable jeans. Nash might have believed in the best of me, but this version is all I have to give right now.

When I emerge from the bathroom with clammy skin and my tongue tasting like bile, everyone else is back upstairs.

"Still no fucking Wi-Fi," Brent says, checking his phone.

Sydney wraps her arms around herself, looking small and cold and frightened. "There has to be something to help us in here." Her eyes gleam with tears.

Caitlyn sweeps an arm around the cavernous open space of the Lodge. "Like what?"

"Don't you think they'd have an emergency kit of some kind? With, like, a defibrillator or a satellite phone or something?"

Brent's eyes light with recognition at Sydney's words. "Wait!"

We watch as he rushes toward the kitchen and digs around in the cabinets under the sink. He doesn't smile—we're all too destroyed for that—but his voice holds a note of triumph when he sets a zippered case on the island and says, "I knew I saw something earlier."

He unzips the case, which has a red cross printed on its side, and a handful of Band-Aids spills out. My heart tumbles as I catalog the rest of the contents. A few individually packaged pieces of sterile cotton gauze. Some antibiotic ointment. Itch cream. Five tiny two-packs of aspirin.

Despite the promising packaging, it's no better than a first aid kit you'd carry in a purse. A stopgap for minor nuisances.

Band-Aids aren't going to bring Nash back.

"That's it?" Caitlyn asks, dismayed.

Unwilling to give up, Sydney presses on. "What about in the closets? I have to believe places around here get snowed in all the time. Maybe there's a radio or the router in one of those rooms."

"We can't get into them," Jeff says. "They're all locked."

A cry tears out of her. "We have to try!" This is the stubborn streak that built a seven-figure business in only a few years, the determination that makes her unstoppable. She can be flighty and unfocused at times, but when she wants something, she simply doesn't give up. "I swear at least one of those closets was open earlier."

"Okay, yeah," Jeff concedes. "We'll check. And if they're not unlocked, we'll figure something out."

"What are you going to do," Caitlyn asks, "break down the doors?"

Jeff's face is grim. "If I need to." He strides across the room and presses his palms against a door down the hall from the bathroom, testing its strength.

Exchanging wary glances with one another, the rest of us follow him.

"Check the top of the doorframe," I suggest. "Sometimes people keep keys just outside the door in case a kid gets locked in."

Reaching overhead, Jeff sweeps a hand along the trim. When his search doesn't return anything, he rattles the doorknob one last time before taking a few steps back.

Instinctively, the rest of us move to give him room.

"I'm going to ram it," Jeff says. Part of me wonders if he's secretly been waiting his whole life to become the star of a real-life action movie. He certainly has the muscles for it. A less generous part of me suspects this is a convenient way to distract us from what happened outside—a way to get us thinking he's the hero instead of the last person to see Nash alive.

"Are you sure this is a good idea?" Brent asks.

Jeff stares down the door as if looking for its weak spots. "It's the best one we have."

A bad feeling settles into my chest. "Wait, Jeff—" I start, but he's already running full speed toward his target.

His left shoulder crashes into the solid, locked door.

There's an audible *pop* as his arm bone is torn from its socket.

I almost vomit on my feet.

Jeff staggers back from the door, clutching his arm to his body.

Sydney screams and dives for him. She tries to wrap her arms around his waist, but he cringes away in pain. When he turns, there's a visible bulge in his shoulder. *Where his bone is pressing against skin.*

"Holy fuck," Caitlyn says.

"It's dislocated," Jeff groans. Beads of sweat stand out on his forehead, and he's panting with pain. I can't imagine how badly it hurts.

"You need to sit down," Sydney pleads.

My heart is hammering so loudly I almost can't hear him say "I'm okay." He waves Sydney off even though his face is pale with pain. He must be having the worst weekend of his life right now. "I'll try to kick it down this time."

"Jesus Christ," Brent hisses under his breath. "Can you imagine what this is going to do to the insurance?"

Jeff backs up again, his arm flopping uselessly at his side.

I feel lightheaded and nauseous.

Jeff takes another step back, and everything in me screams for this to end. Having someone die before Reverie even opens its doors is going to destroy its reputation. I can't let this beautiful building and Jeff's body get ruined too.

"Stop!" I cry. My chest is heaving with fear and the sickly thrum of adrenaline. I'm one thousand percent going to regret this later, but I open my mouth and force out the words. "I have a key."

35

CAITLYN

What do you mean you have a key?" Brent asks Lucy, scrubbing a hand through his hair. "Last I checked, our room keys don't work anywhere else."

Lucy's eyes are rimmed in red and she's got her hands tucked into the sleeves of her lumpy gray sweater. She shifts nervously, shrinking into herself. I've never seen anyone look as guilty as she does now.

"Don't be mad," she says, shooting a cautious glance just at Sydney.

Realizing she's been singled out, Sydney's face goes pale, those big brown eyes wide with worry. "You're freaking me out, Luce. Just say whatever it is."

Lucy bites her lip. Nods like she's deciding something. Lifts her gaze with a resigned expression. "My cousin owns Reverie. Before we came, she sent me a master key so I could check up on things if I needed to. Lock any rooms that were off-limits for guests."

Holy fucking shit.

This changes things in ways I couldn't have predicted.

"O-kaaaayy." I see the minute the realization hits Sydney, the way shock ripples across her pretty features. "You're saying they didn't choose *me* for this job." Her forehead pinches. "Is that what you're saying? You talked to your cousin and set this whole thing up?"

If it's true, it means everything about this trip is based on a lie.

I mean, it's truly messed up. But inside, I'm cackling with glee.

Tricky, clever Lucy.

"I wanted a trip that felt normal," Lucy explains, pleading with Sydney to trust her. "But now that you're my boss, everything's changed." Her eyes go glassy. "Ever since you hired me, I never know if you invite me places because you want me there or because you feel obligated to bring me." She shrugs. "I had my cousin hire us both so it wasn't a question. We both had a reason to come, and we could hang out as equals. Friends." She drops her gaze. "I asked her to leave me out of the trip coordination so you wouldn't know I was involved."

"Okay, there are so many things wrong with that statement." Sydney wrinkles her nose in disgust. Who knew Lucy was going to be the one to piss off Syd before Jeff did? "You really think I don't want you around?"

"I don't know." Lucy takes a halting step forward. "I just . . . everything's been messed up in my life. With Nick and—" She swipes at her eyes. "I didn't want to focus on all the ways the rest of my life is imploding or worry about you and me. I wanted a guarantee we'd both be here without complications."

"If you needed to get away because of your breakup, you could have just said something. And you could have told me about your connection here. It would have been even more fun. I wouldn't have been weird about you getting me the job." Sydney shakes her head, looking stung. "But you didn't have the confidence to think if I got the invite alone that I'd bring you." She lets out a frustrated huff. "Jesus, Lucy, I wouldn't have hired you if I didn't want to spend time with you. So much for trusting me. You didn't have to make up this whole fake job for us to go on a trip together."

"It's not a fake job. Reverie needed the promotion, so I suggested that my cousin consider influencer marketing." Lucy's shoulders sag. "Except now who knows if they'll even be able to open the doors."

I can't resist making a dig. "Whatever, this place leaves a lot to be desired."

"We're early!" Lucy says. "Not everything's fully set up just yet."

"Whatever you say, Luce. I'm still never coming back here." She sends me a sharp glare, but there's not much she can argue with. Since we got here, there's been one hospitality fuckup after another.

"So that was you earlier," Syd says, still frowning at Lucy. "I told you I saw those stupid taper candles in one of the closets. You had every opportunity to say, 'My bad, Syd, that was me who locked the closet after you opened it. You're not going crazy.' And you said nothing?"

"Wait," I butt in as I realize that Lucy lying about her connection to Reverie means she might also be lying about other things. "Did you have your cousin purposefully give us the wrong amount of food?"

"What? No!" Lucy's face turns scarlet. "Brent was on point

for that. You should ask *him* why he made us starve for click-bait."

"I told you, the food thing was a miscommunication!" Brent sputters. "Yes, I documented our dinner delivery, but that doesn't mean I purposefully put us in danger."

"Is this the most important thing to focus on right now?" Jeff's rough, strained voice makes Lucy step back, blinking hard like she's fighting off tears. "How about we get the goddamned key and see what we can find to help us?"

Lucy nods. "Yeah, that's why I mentioned it in the first place."

"Why the fuck couldn't you have said something before I tried to break down the door?" Jeff bites out.

I make the mistake of looking at his shoulder and want to dry heave. It's not the first dislocated shoulder I've seen—my brothers got plenty of injuries playing chicken with each other on the ski slopes—but it's a pretty gruesome example. Jeff's going to be out of commission for at least a week. Certainly the rest of the time we're here.

"I'm sorry," Lucy squeaks.

"So where is it?"

She swipes her hands over her cheeks to clear a few errant tears. "I'm going to need to go back to my room."

A muscle ticks in Jeff's jaw and he barely holds back a growl. "Then, by all means, let's go."

Lucy looks uncertainly at the rest of us. "Shouldn't we take care of Jeff's shoulder first? I feel like that's the most pressing issue."

"It needs medical attention," I say.

Jeff wheels, turning the force of his anger on me. "Yeah, no shit."

I give a very tiny huff. "What I mean is that we shouldn't try to pop it in ourselves. It can make things worse." I shoot him a sympathetic look, even though he's being a twat. "You should probably take some painkillers, though."

"I don't need painkillers!" he roars. A vein starts pulsing in his forehead. "I need Nash to be alive again. And I need to get the fuck out of here."

"Jeff," Sydney says quietly.

He backs down for her, letting her lead him to the kitchen, where she fishes some medication from the first aid kit and fills a cup with some water. She watches patiently while he swallows the meds and the water, then turns back to us.

"Now we're ready," she says.

None of us actually want to go back outside, but sending Lucy on her own doesn't feel right. For one thing, it's hard to trust her knowing she has a key to any of our cabins. Who knows what she might get up to if she's left to her own devices? For another thing, she's clearly freaked out about being alone in the barren landscape.

Begrudgingly, we all slide on our shoes and make our way to the Lodge's front door. Even Jeff decides to come out with us, though he looks like he'd be much better off sitting down to rest.

When Brent opens the door, a blast of cold air slices through the room. What's more shocking than the temperature is the burst of snow flurrying in on the wind. I don't know when the snow started up again, but it's already filling the footsteps we left outside this morning.

Shit.

I'm not so sure Jeff's going to get out of here as soon as he hoped. And if that's true, it also means our meager food supplies might need to last even longer than we planned.

I cast a wary glance at my companions before I step outside, but everyone's hunched over against the weather, eyes on the ground. The sky continues spitting out messy, wet snow as we trudge toward the cabins. By the time we reach Lucy's place, I'm chilled to the bone.

Lucy starts toward the door, turning back with a hand on the doorknob. "I really am sorry I didn't tell you," she whispers to Sydney, giving off some real desperate vibes.

"I know," Sydney says. Her voice is laced with compassion, and honestly, she's displaying a level of restraint I would not be capable of. "Just go fast, okay?"

Giving us one last glance, Lucy swings open the door and steps inside the cabin. Then she pulls the door shut behind her.

Like she has something to hide.

36

STORY POST

Reverie Retreat—Day 2

You can say a lot of things about Sydney Kent, which is part of the fun, but one thing you can never accuse her of is cursing on her social media. A very rare *shit* might sneak in if she gets surprised during a livestream, but she makes it a point to keep her language PG-13 so her content stays inclusive. That commitment, along with her dedication to body positivity, is what makes parents feel okay letting their kids follow her, even though her lifestyle is a far cry from that of the audience's younger demographic. Syd's not wholesome, exactly, but she knows she's got impressionable kids watching, and friendly language is part of the silent contract she makes with you.

Today, though, the conversation running in the background of the story doesn't have the easygoing tenor Syd normally adopts, and the audio has picked up what sounds like someone muttering a disbelieving "What the fuck" over and over again. It's too muffled to fully make out on the first listen, but your ears perk up anyway.

What the fuck? That can't be right.

You play the story back, listening purposefully this time, and now there's no denying it—someone's definitely dropping F-bombs in the background. The thing is, you can't tell if it's coming from someone off-screen or from Syd and Jeff. It sounds like there are people gathered nearby, but the two of them are the only ones actually in the video, which is shot from afar. They're framed between a pair of wood-paneled cabins, Jeff with his back leaning against the building and Sydney with her face buried in Jeff's shirt. Not far from where they stand in ankle-deep snow is the edge of the cliff. Past that, there's nothing but endless sky.

You can't, for the life of you, figure out what this video is trying to achieve. Maybe Syd's trying something different with this story, like a behind-the-behind-the-scenes. Still, it's strange. Both the audio and the, well, boringness of it. Syd posts a lot, but she doesn't usually toy with your attention. When it comes to her, almost everything has a point.

It makes you wonder what she's getting at. If there's something you're missing. So you watch again.

This time, you zoom in, and now you can see her bare shoulders shaking like she's either laughing or crying. With her face planted on Jeff's chest, you can't see her expression to know which it is. Jeff's rubbing a single hand up her back, and his mouth is moving, so it's possible he's the one muttering the obscenities. Or he could be telling a dirty joke. It's hard to know for sure. All you know is this story *must* mean something. And you can't wait to find out what it is.

37

LUCY

I know everyone's talking about me just outside my cabin door. They must be.

I slump against the wall and curse myself for how I blurted out the truth about this trip without thinking. It was bad enough when everyone thought I was just here because Reverie wanted me to be. Now they know that this whole terrible trip was my doing. And Sydney? God, she looked so betrayed. The sight made my stomach feel split open like rotten fruit.

I did that to her. We're supposed to be in this together, and I hurt her.

In the grand scheme, it's probably better to admit I have a key and figure out how to get help, but it doesn't feel that way. Instead, it feels like I've made an enemy of each of them. It doesn't matter what I wanted or why. All anyone will think about is what I did. The way I lied.

I wipe away the snowflakes that have begun melting on my eyelashes and let myself refocus on the room. The sliding glass doors showcase a view of the ridge, where a flat gray sky winks from between bare tree trunks. Inside the room, my suitcase is splashed open beside the unmade bed.

The master key to Reverie is in my camera bag, of course. I've had it on me the whole time, though I couldn't tell anyone else that. Who knows what kind of questions that would have raised. From now on, the key will remain on my person at all times.

Reassured by the weight of my camera bag at my side, I head toward the suitcase. My reason for coming here is far more selfish than looking for a key. After Nash . . . after Nash died, I needed to get back here to check on my pills, to set my mind at ease that I didn't have anything to do with what happened to my friend. Luckily no one forced their way inside the cabin with me, so I have a second to regroup.

Sinking onto my knees beside the suitcase, I reach for the toiletry bag tucked next to a pair of wool socks. My hands shake as I unzip it and pull out my stash of fentanyl tablets. I tell myself it's because of the cold that's sunk into my bones, but it's pure fear.

I spill out the tiny vial into my cupped palm, my heart sinking. Six pills rest in my palm, but it's the kind of situation where I could have had seven or eight or nine before without knowing an exact count.

I can't tell for sure if any are missing, and even if I could, there's no way to know if someone used them on Nash. Is someone messing with me? And how much fentanyl would it take to kill someone?

Something makes a loud *bang* outside my cabin, and my heart jumps. I might not have the answers I need, but taking too much time is only going to make people more suspicious.

I hastily repack, shoving the pills back into the vial and

sliding it into a side pocket of my suitcase rather than the toiletry bag. Then I strip the pillowcase off one of my pillows and head to the door.

The cabin might be a quiet place to breathe, but everyone out there's waiting for me.

"What's that?" Jeff asks warily after I lock my door behind me. He's leaning against the side of my cabin, his face looking hollowed out with pain.

I follow his gaze to the pillowcase bunched in my hands and try to let the harsh delivery of his question roll off my shoulders. I know how the worst kind of pain can twist you, make you say things you regret.

I raise the fabric like a white flag of surrender, hoping for a truce. I don't trust Jeff, but I don't want to be on his bad side either. "Thought we could make you a sling." Everything I've done up until now has been to try to preserve Reverie's integrity for Meghan's sake, but we've passed the point of staying truly civil. Unexpected dislocated shoulders call for creative measures. I'm sure Reverie can spare a pillowcase or two. "We're still going to try to get help," I say. "But this might help you feel better in the short term."

A flash of guilt flits across his face, followed by resolve. He grunts what could be either a half-hearted attempt at saying thanks or a pointed reminder that he blames me for not stopping him from rushing the door.

I trail the others back to the Lodge, glad I can stare at their backs instead of their stony expressions. Inside the Lodge, Jeff waves off my offer to help tie up his arm. "Let's just open the goddamned doors first."

Chastened, I feel my cheeks heat. "Right." I pull the cold key from my camera bag, letting my skin warm the metal. In keeping with the "back to nature" aesthetic of the building, the key isn't an electronic key card but rather a slim brass skeleton key.

"That's it, huh?" Brent asks, staring at it in my palm.

"A lot of pressure for a little key," Sydney says. She still holds her body stiffly, not willing to look me in the eye. I'm desperate to convince her we can move past this, but it's not the time.

Swallowing hard, I cross the Lodge toward the door Jeff tried to break down. A few footsteps echo behind me as people follow, but I ignore my embarrassment and fit the end of the key into the lock. This better work, or everything I told them will be for nothing.

"Do you know why it's called a skeleton key?" Brent asks.

I glance behind me and find him standing ever so slightly too close, staring over my shoulder. His proximity makes a little shiver go through me, or maybe it's his words.

"Why's that?"

"Because it looks like a skeleton's finger?" Caitlyn guesses. I'm still not sure how she can maintain that bored detachment, but maybe it's her way of coping with this fucked-up day.

Brent gestures at the key, with its long, slim shaft and just a single bit at the end. "Because it's been filed down to its essential parts." The way he says it feels foreboding, but it's hard to judge if that's my imagination twisting things. Right now it's hard not to imagine everyone's anger and disappointment turning into threats.

Even as I turn the key, I halfway believe it's not going to open the lock.

Please work, please work.

Nash's death has already blown up every plan I had for this weekend; I need something to go right.

But the key turns over and the lock gives way with a satisfying *click.*

Relief rushes through me.

"Alright, everyone." I step back from the door to let the others pass by, my knees still a little unsteady. "We're in."

38

CAITLYN

Considering the Lodge's relatively minimal interior, the closet's packed with items. The shelving that stretches to the ceiling in the tiny room holds a few dozen packages of the hand soap that's in each cabin, fresh bed linens, and extra tea light candles, dishes, and silverware to replace anything in the kitchen that might break over time. The scent of laundry detergent fills the space, but otherwise the room is sterile and unused.

"This must be the storage closet for the housekeeping service," Sydney says, stepping into the room behind me. An electric charge goes up my back at her proximity.

"Then where are all the cleaning supplies?"

We find them behind the next door we open: mops and buckets, a vacuum with its cord curled neatly around its base like a snake, a set of dingy cleaning towels, spray bottles filled with liquids in various colors, a stack of Magic Erasers, and enough sponges to build a raft and float us down the river if it ever comes to that.

So many items, and not a single one built to help us escape.

Each time we approach a new door, a little balloon of hope inflates inside my chest. Maybe this will be the door that holds our key to getting rescued, or at least contacting the outside world. Each time Lucy swings open a new door, my lungs crush with disappointment. There's nothing here to aid us, and who the hell knows where the router is. You'd think it would be someplace obvious, but we have yet to find it. With our luck, it's in a locked box or something, to prevent guests from walking away with it.

"We need to check downstairs," Brent mutters darkly, and somehow it feels like there's no air left in this whole godforsaken Lodge.

Downstairs is where we took Nash, where his body waits in the doorless meditation room.

Downstairs feels like a black hole of death.

A shudder runs through me even though I know he's right. It doesn't make it any easier to drag myself downstairs.

"I can do it myself," Brent says, looking at everyone's solemn faces as we hover at the top of the stairs. He reaches out a hand to accept the key from Lucy. Honestly, I'd love to get ahold of that key myself. I'd feel better knowing that anything Reverie has to offer is at my disposal. But Lucy hesitates, clutching the key to her chest.

"It's okay," she says quietly. "I feel responsible."

"Damn straight you are," Jeff says.

Even though her cheeks flush, Lucy manages to flash him a returning scowl. "I didn't say I was responsible for everything. It wasn't *my* joint that killed Nash."

Score one for Lucy.

Jeff's face goes 'roid red, and the only thing saving Lucy from his explosion is the hasty retreat she makes downstairs.

Not wanting to be left out, I follow her, even though my skin crawls with discomfort the farther I descend. It feels colder down here, though I'm sure if we checked, the thermostat would read the same as upstairs. It's the eerie quiet settling over us that makes the chill sink into my skin, the feeling that there should be movement, heartbeats, *life* down here.

There's just a long, dark hallway and silence.

Not yet ready to face the sight of Nash's body, I'm relieved when Lucy stops in front of another locked door close to the stairs. This room holds all the pool towels that somehow never made it to the pool.

I take a cursory glance and then spin on my heel to exit the room. "It's just more towels," I tell the group.

But Sydney's gaze is trained over my shoulder. She's not yet willing to give up, god bless her.

"What's that?" Her eyes gleam with excitement as she points to something behind me. And, there, shoved back behind a stack of fluffy white towels, is a gray rectangle of plastic I didn't see the first time.

"Bingo," Brent says, lunging for the object. He knocks towels to the floor as he pulls the item off the shelf, but no one even blinks. "A radio."

He pushes the power button, which just clicks without engaging.

Brent frowns and tries again.

Another hollow click.

"Does it have batteries?" Jeff asks.

Brent flips over the radio and pops off a panel at the back to reveal an empty battery compartment. "Negative."

A hysterical laugh bubbles up inside me. Of course it wouldn't be that easy.

Everyone except Jeff starts digging through the shelves, searching for batteries. But as I suspected the first time, the only other thing in here is towels. Dozens of them.

"Anyone have batteries on them?" Sydney asks weakly.

We all shake our heads—we have plenty of electronics that need power, of course, but everything uses a cable for charging.

She turns to Lucy. "What about your camera?"

Lucy's forehead furrows. "It's a special kind of battery, so highly unlikely." She gestures for Brent to hand over the radio and then inspects the battery compartment. "It's not a match."

Sydney deflates. I squeeze her hand and allow myself to feel the tiniest bit of relief when she squeezes back. "We're not done searching yet. There's still one more place to check."

I mean it to sound reassuring, but the air in the hallway tightens as we realize what that means: we're down to one last chance. We're running out of luck.

And, somehow worse: the door we haven't opened is the one beside the back exit. The one that may or may not lead to a garage.

To get there, we have to go past Nash.

When I was little, my brothers and I used to hold our breath and lift our feet from the car floor anytime we drove past a graveyard. *So their souls can't enter through your soles,* Cole would say.

The idea of some wayward spirit being trapped inside my

body freaked me out, even though I knew he was only saying it to scare me. There's enough personality in my body with just me here, thank you very much.

His words flit through my mind as I follow Lucy down the hallway with the others at my back. My legs feel as heavy as stone, and I hate the uncomfortable, melancholy feeling that crushes my chest when I think about how Cole is just a soul now, like all those graveyard spirits he warned me about.

Logically, I know what I'm feeling is grief, but I've never learned how to sit with my sadness. As the only daughter in a family of all guys, I didn't exactly get an education in emotional calibration, and by the time Susan came into the picture, so many of my patterns were already established. Instead of letting myself experience anguish, I've spent my life turning sadness into anger and using it to fuel my ambition. It's how I've gotten where I am today.

We're outside the meditation room faster than I imagined we would be. I'm not ready to face what lies inside.

"Okay?" Lucy asks quietly, looking over her shoulder at the rest of us. A few more feet down the hallway, and we'll be in front of the last door.

Jeff croaks out a rough "Yeah," and one by one, we filter past the open meditation room. Holding my breath like Cole taught me is a stupid superstition, but I can't help re-creating a version of it as I rush by. I don't let myself look inside, but goose bumps prickle tight over my skin as if Nash himself is watching me.

Maybe he is. His eyes were open when he died.

Lucy yanks open the far door, and I let out my breath as I step through to what's definitely a garage.

A tarp-covered lump sits in the middle of the chilly room, a vaguely mechanical shape resting underneath the cloth.

Brent's eyebrows rise as he strides toward it. With hands that tremble ever so slightly, he reaches out.

He lifts the tarp.

39

CAITLYN

My heart races and a clammy sweat dampens my armpits even though it's nearly freezing in the garage. I hug my arms around my waist and tell myself it's the adrenaline of anticipation causing my body to react this way. Brent is really dragging out this whole reveal, so it's no wonder my body's gone haywire. It's definitely not the fact that I just sprinted past Nash's corpse.

Seconds later, all the grossness I feel washes away, replaced with an electric buzz. Because when Brent lifts his hand, a headlight peeks out beneath the corner of the tarp. I mean, it's generous to call the cheap plastic fixture a headlight, but nonetheless, that's what it is. Which means we have ourselves a fucking *vehicle.*

Now we're talking.

"What is it?" Sydney asks, her voice trembling with nervous energy.

Brent just smiles. Then he yanks off the tarp, which makes a *whoosh* sound as it slides easily over the hard surfaces of whatever lies beneath.

It's a golf cart.

Sydney lets out an actual squeal as she dives into its front seat. With a proud, wide stance, powder-blue exterior, and two white leather seats, the golf cart gleams with promise. Unlike everything else in this place, it also comes with a key.

Grinning broadly, Sydney holds up one of those black coiled wrist key chains. The gold key dangling from it shines dully in the garage's murky light. Her gaze flicks to mine before landing on Jeff. "We can get out of here," she tells him.

Relief breaks over Jeff's face. "Thank god, babe."

My skin prickles with hurt. Obviously Jeff's the most in need of rescue, and Sydney did look at me first. But I would have hoped she would have included me in her plan first too.

I don't want to be anyone's second thought. Especially when their first thought is Jeff.

"Before we rush off, should we see what else is here?" I ask. I've been so focused on what was under that tarp that I've neglected the rest of the room. And while a golf cart is great, it doesn't negate the fact that there are at least six inches of snow on the ground, with more falling. Driving in these conditions will not be easy, if it comes to that.

But maybe it doesn't have to.

I spin to survey the garage and nearly gasp at what I find. This is clearly where the Reverie owners store all the pointy things. On the back wall, beside a huge stack of firewood, a perfectly organized pegboard holds tools ranging from hedge trimmers to trowels and even a wicked-looking axe, the shapes outlined in neat black paint so you know what belongs where. A wall-mounted rack next to the pegboard holds long-handled tools: rakes, three kinds of shovels, and a long-handled soil aerator that reminds me of the way women carry keys tucked between their knuckles for self-defense, all the blades pointed out, sturdy and sharp. A chainsaw sits on a shelf just above eye level.

"Holy shit," I breathe. "Did you see the rest of this stuff?"

"They must take out the golf cart and tools to keep the trails clear," Lucy says. "Like the path to the waterfall." She's peering at the back of the golf cart, and when she steps away, I notice the cart's storage rack, which I couldn't fully see until now. The rack holds two deep five-gallon buckets, the kind florists use to display flowers at a farmer's market.

When I look inside one of the buckets, I find some dirt and a few pine needles. A curl of bark from the pernicious trees that surround this godforsaken place.

I wrinkle my nose at the damp earthy odor rising from the bucket, but I have to agree with Lucy. "It's like an arborist's wet dream."

We spread out to search the rest of the room, turning up a flashlight with batteries that are a different size than the radio needs, but batteries nonetheless, as well as a plastic safety whistle and a roll of duct tape.

My earlier enthusiasm drains away. The extra supplies could come in handy, but they're not going to connect us with the outside world. "What we really need is the router," I say. "But if it isn't anywhere we looked, then where the hell is it?"

"I don't know, but this was the last room," Sydney reminds us, her chest rising and falling unsteadily, her body humming with a nervous energy. She's always been a free spirit, but right now she looks manic and unpredictable, like a variable I can't control. I'm going to need to keep an eye on her. "We didn't find what we needed. So you know what that means."

Brent rubs wearily at his temples. "We're fucked."

"We're going to need to go for help."

It's the obvious conclusion—without a Wi-Fi connection or access to the router, we don't know if or when we'll be able to get through to the police. As far as we know, we're not on a priority list for them, and things have dramatically changed since this morning. To their knowledge, we've placed a call but are otherwise healthy and whole.

Since then, Jeff's mangled his shoulder in an attempt to prove his manliness. He needs medical attention before he injures himself even worse.

And they have no idea Nash is dead.

"Fuck me." I blow out a breath. "What did you have in mind?"

"We can all go together," Sydney suggests. "Take the road until we reach civilization or cell service and call for some help."

I give her the side-eye and then jab a finger toward the golf cart. "In that thing?" I shake my head. "It'll fit, like, two people. Three if someone light hangs off the back."

Jeff juts out his chest defiantly. "So some people can walk. And we'll trade off who gets to ride." By *some people*, he clearly means the rest of us. With his arm that messed up, there's no way Mr. Macho's about to embark on a jaunt through the woods in freezing weather.

"I'll walk," Sydney hurries to agree. I don't know if she's saying it to make peace with everyone or because she really believes she's capable of a grueling trek. If it's the latter, she might be delusional. Girlfriend sometimes reps a two-piece yoga set in pictures, though it's all for show. She's skinny, but her muscle tone is zero. She's not built for stamina.

"In what shoes, Syd?" Lucy's voice is gentle, like she can tell how close Sydney is to her breaking point and is scared of pushing her too far. "Your photo-shoot stilettos?"

"I'll go barefoot if I need to!"

I like Syd feisty. But she's also being blind to reality, which is dangerous. She lives in a dream world for so much of her life—free clothes, free food and travel, sexy parties—that she forgets that everything has a cost.

Weather like this makes you pay.

Lucy beats me to delivering a reality check. "You won't get far with frostbite."

Sydney's face falls, and she blinks at us incredulously. "Are you saying you *want* to stay here?"

"No," I counter. "Wanting to stay and knowing it would be stupid for all of us to go aren't the same thing."

Lucy steps forward with a look of resolve. "I'll go." She doesn't outright say that she feels guilty—after the last time she claimed responsibility and Jeff came at her with guns blazing, I don't blame her—but remorse is written all over her face.

Jeff lets out a savage laugh. "And leave our future up to you?" Lucy takes a step back as though she's been slapped. "No fucking way."

"Okay, enough." Sydney presses a hand to Jeff's chest, and I see him flinch. That arm has to be killing him. "Shitting on each other isn't going to help." She takes a deep breath. "I might not have shoes to walk in, but I can certainly drive."

Brent and I exchange a look. Living in the city, no one has any reason to drive on the regular. We're all out of practice, but Syd's as good a driver as anyone, especially in a golf cart. The problem is that no one wants to be stuck here with a miserable

Jeff. Sydney's the only one who makes him tolerable to be around.

"God," I say, holding back an eye roll. "Everyone wants to be a hero."

Lucy lifts an eyebrow. "You don't?"

"Only in seasonally appropriate footwear."

Of course I'm deflecting; I'm nervous as hell.

With everyone else ruled out, it's up to me or Brent.

40

LUCY

They don't trust me to go.

Everyone argues around me, but I'm still stinging from the rejection, stuck in the moment when they told me they'd rather risk their own safety than let me help fix things. It hurts more than it should.

I lied, yes, but it's not like I'm the only one hiding things. Just yesterday Sydney and Caitlyn almost had a blowout fight. Over secret *hair care products*. Surely what I've done doesn't warrant being stuck in the dungeon forever. I want a chance to make things right.

"You should go," Caitlyn tells Brent. She looks a little pale beneath her spray tan. "You're the obvious choice." I'm not sure if she's scared or being pragmatic, but her insistence doesn't surprise me.

Brent, though, seems shocked. His eyes bulge, and he looks kind of sweaty, the way you do before you throw up. "This isn't a good idea. We should stick together." He mops his forehead with the hem of his shirt as he pleads with her. "There's safety in numbers."

But Sydney shakes her head. "You'll know what to say to the police, what to do. They'll trust you. And the snow is getting worse. What if the party bus can't get through and we're trapped for longer than we expected?"

It's a possibility no one wants to contemplate.

"So what's the plan, then?" he demands. As someone used to being in charge, he's not taking well to the role reversal. "I just drive out into the unknown?"

"Too bad we don't have a drone we can fly," Jeff says bitterly. "An aerial view would sure come in handy right about now."

My stomach sinks. Jeff's not wrong, and now I can't help feeling like the missing drone is a much more sinister problem than I originally thought. I shouldn't have been so quick to dismiss him.

I speak up despite my fear, determined to help in any way I can. "It's not entirely uncharted territory." When everyone's attention swings to me, I continue. "We took one long road into this place, right? So if that's true, all we need to do is follow it for a few miles. There's a map in the guest book upstairs, so we can take a look and figure out which direction Brent should turn if he does get to a crossroad."

"A few miles?" Caitlyn scoffs. "It's got to be, like, ten."

"Maybe seven," I counter, even though I don't honestly know.

"Whatever," Sydney says. "The point is, driving's our best chance."

Jeff frowns and kicks at one of the golf cart tires. "What kind of mileage do you think this thing can get?"

"A hundred or so miles on a full tank of gas," Caitlyn answers confidently.

Sydney shoots her a questioning glance. "That's . . . oddly specific."

"I golfed a bit in high school." Caitlyn shrugs. "I'm pretty good with a club."

For some reason, that doesn't surprise me at all.

"So is there gas?" Jeff asks. He's starting to get impatient, pacing around the vehicle. If his arm were in better shape, he'd probably be the first one peering into the gas tank, checking it out himself.

Caitlyn strides forward, and in one smooth move that makes my heart leap, she yanks the entire front seat from the golf cart's frame. Is she . . . dismantling . . . the one vehicle we have?

"What the hell, Caitlyn?" Jeff growls.

She flicks her hair over her shoulder and rolls her eyes at him. "Don't shit your pants. The gas tank's usually under here." She nudges the bench seat to the side and points triumphantly to a plastic tank. Then she bends over and cracks it open.

The smell of gas wafts through the room, making my eyes sting.

"It's not a full tank, but it should do the trick," she says.

Brent tugs at his shirt. "I still don't like this."

Caitlyn frowns. "Join the club." She starts to reassemble the cart as I take stock of everything we've found.

"We have to plan for the roads being a mess," I say. "It'll be slow going. Add a few extra hours if you need to dig out the cart."

Sydney winds a lock of hair around a finger, then releases it. "It's still faster than anyone can walk."

I nod and move one of the shovels from the tool rack into the back of the golf cart. "To dig yourself out if you need," I tell

Brent, whose eyebrows rise at the idea. I've been through enough dangerous situations in my life to have learned it's better to prepare for the worst than to underestimate how badly life wants to kill you. "When you find help, you should ask for a police helicopter. Or a snowmobile. I doubt the snow will be melted off by then."

"Ah shit," Brent says. "You're really going to have me do this."

I don't want to be the one to say it, but I have to acknowledge that he could get stuck out there and then have to walk—either back toward Reverie or onward toward help. "You should be ready to travel on foot if something happens to the cart. We need to get you better clothes."

"Disaster-Preparedness Girl has a point." Caitlyn purses her lips and tosses something small at Brent that he catches against his chest. "You should take the rape whistle with you just in case. Maybe the bears around here have a hard-on for city boys."

I freeze at the words, my eyes flicking to Syd to gauge her reaction. Not the line about the bears—although, god, why would you remind Brent?—but the first point.

The rape whistle.

It's a crass name for something meant to protect you, to warn away ill intentions and signal for help. My best friend's face is as pale as the day I walked in on her shaking after a date with Breaker, and her eyes are glazed with remembered fear.

She'd asked for privacy for the two of them that night, though when I came home and found her afterward, her face streaked with tears and her body wrapped up in bedsheets, I kicked myself for having left her. Still, we lived in the dorms, and it was a Wednesday night. Plenty of people had been around to have stopped things if they had heard. If Sydney'd had a *rape whistle* to call for help.

If she'd had one all those years ago, who knows if we'd be here now. Because part of Syd died that night, the trusting, free-spirited part of her that loved quickly and easily and deeply, and then I did everything I could to make sure that the spark inside her had a chance to come back to life.

"We're wasting time," I say to cut through the tension in the room. "Cait and Syd, you should get changed out of your dresses. Then let's find some warm clothes for Brent."

Caitlyn sighs like I've spoiled her fun, eyes narrowing at the way Jeff rubs a hand up Sydney's back. I don't much care for his affections either, but I watch Sydney relax the slightest bit and know that I did the right thing back then. I'd do it again if I had to.

"Let's go," Jeff says roughly, and everyone follows him to the door. I'm the last to leave, hesitating in the doorway at the thought of all those deadly tools just sitting there.

When everyone's turned to head for the stairs, I lock the garage door behind me and pocket the key.

41

CAITLYN

The weather has fucked us over in more ways than one. First is the most obvious: the fact that we're snowed in to begin with. Then there's also the sheer fact of the temperature. It would be one thing for Brent to make this trek for help if he had brought along a coat, or if it were warmer like the forecast originally promised. But with frosty temperatures and an unknown destination, poor Brent's going to freeze his balls off.

I'd sound like a bitch saying it, but I think it nonetheless: *better him than me.*

"You're going to have to wear layers," Lucy suggests when Brent tells us he only brought along one long-sleeve shirt, a button-down that I'm sure is stylish but that will do nothing to actually keep him warm.

"I've got a long-sleeve shirt you can borrow," Jeff announces as we hover in the living room, too anxious to sit but not yet prepared to canvass the cabins unless we need to. It'll be best to minimize our time outside.

"Anyone else have something for Brent?" Sydney asks.

I'm clearly skinnier than Brent, so I don't bother saying anything. Brent may not be ripped, but there's still no way my clothes are going to stretch across his barrel chest.

Lucy shakes her head, and Brent sighs. "Layers it is," he says. "Let's go get Jeff's shirt."

We move as a unit toward the front door, even though retrieving the clothing is, at most, a two-person job. No one wants to be left behind in this huge room with Nash's body cooling downstairs.

Honestly, it's a shame Nash isn't with us right now. I'm sure he'd have a field day piecing together an outfit out of everyone's scraps.

Wind whips my face as I step outside, snow blasting along with it. The forest creaks in the distance like it's as unsettled as we are. Despite the warm, dry clothes I changed into—not as pretty as my photo-shoot dress but definitely a better idea in these conditions—a chill skitters down my spine.

"It's good you're leaving," I tell Brent, and he shoots me a dirty look over his shoulder.

What? It's not like I want anyone to have to go, but the group's decided. The snow is picking up.

Sydney and Jeff's cabin is our first stop, where Sydney scurries inside to grab the famed shirt, since Jeff's earlier stunt has rendered him useless. She hands the Henley shirt over to Brent—of course it wouldn't be a plain long-sleeve shirt but rather something that unbuttons for maximum chest exposure—and Brent takes it with a look of grim resignation.

"Might as well put it on now," he says, sliding it over his head.

The thin cotton-blend material stretches to fit, but it hugs

Brent's stomach in a way that's definitely not flattering. On second thought, I'm not sure how much magic even Nash could work here, given the circumstances.

"I should get some things from my room," Brent says.

"Like what?" The words slip out before I can consider that they sound a little judgmental. He *is* the one braving the outdoors for the rest of us, after all.

Ever the peacekeeper, Sydney flashes me a warning look, and I hurry to amend my statement. "I just meant that you won't need to bring your suitcase with you. You'll be back."

"Right," Sydney agrees, leaving no room for an alternate outcome. Her relentless optimism never makes space for things to go wrong. I've had enough go sideways in my life that I usually believe Sydney's outlook is sweetly naive, but right now, I think it's dangerously naive too. Weather like this will chew up your innocence and claim your life if you aren't careful. There's a reason it's called toxic positivity.

We shuffle down the line toward Brent's cabin, where he pops inside and returns wearing his clothes in new layers. Nash would positively cackle at the sight of Brent's outfit: a long-sleeve blue-pinstripe button-down shirt over top of a short-sleeve button-down in a red plaid—the two stacked collars seeming to squeeze in around his thick neck—with Jeff's Henley shirt now as a base layer. He's still wearing his stupid suede shoes, though the snow has made the color bleed from the pineapples on the toes. It looks like a dog's pissed on his feet.

"Have what you need?" I ask.

Brent pats his pockets and nods.

"Did you actually get anything?" Jeff asks.

Brent refrains from rolling his eyes. "A phone charger, for

when I get wherever I'm going. And a wallet in case anyone needs ID or insurance information." His face clouds at that. "Ah fuck. Sorry to your cousin, Luce, but I'm pretty sure insurance is going to go through the roof on this place."

Lucy looks about ready to borrow one of Brent's antacids at the thought.

"So that's it?" Sydney asks.

"I ripped the map page out of the guidebook."

Syd surveys Brent's poor excuse for a winter uniform. "No other clothes?" He shakes his head, and she frowns.

"What about—?" Jeff gulps in a deep breath, and when he speaks again, his voice is rough and strained. "What if there's something in Nash's room that can help? I mean, he's the fashion guy. Shouldn't we look?"

A prickle of awareness runs down my spine like someone else is out there in the woods watching me, but that's stupid. The only other person here is Nash.

And he's dead.

42

CAITLYN

It's amazing what you can tell about someone just from seeing their room. Some people—ahem, Nash—unpack right away, revealing an organized, thoughtful nature, while others leave piles of dirty clothes strewn about the floor. The five of us cramming into Nash's cabin makes the space feel cramped and claustrophobic, but it also feels remarkably like *Nash*. The fact that his stuff is neatly laid out makes it creepier, his razor and shaving kit left tidily beside the stylish sink as if waiting for him to return.

It hits me again that he's not coming back to this room, to New York, to life.

At this point, all anyone can hope is that what he's left behind will keep Brent comfortable as he goes for help.

Sydney sweeps open the door to the teeny closet, where a row of hangers holds Nash's preplanned outfits, the pants and shirts grouped together.

"Ten bucks said he had a whole lookbook for the week," I say.

Sydney's voice comes out scratchy with tears. "He's been planning this trip for the last month."

Brent grunts and brushes past her to thumb through the options. He wrestles a lightweight knit scarf from one of the hangers and wraps it around his neck.

"What do you think," he asks wryly, "is chartreuse my color?"

"Smashing," I deadpan.

It's not until I turn away from Brent that I catch sight of Lucy bent over Nash's laptop bag.

"What are you doing?" I squeak. My face feels hot with embarrassment on his behalf. Clothes are one thing, but electronics are *personal.*

"Maybe he's got a portable hotspot." Lucy worries her lower lip as she unzips the bag, the skeleton key that gave us access to the room neatly tucked away in the pocket of her jeans.

"If he had one, he would have told us."

She blinks up at me, her face carefully neutral. "Maybe not."

"Are you kidding me?"

She shrugs. "Maybe it was a game to him. You know how he liked to romanticize things." She darts a glance at Sydney, whose entire existence is built on romanticizing things, but Sydney just eyes the laptop that Lucy's pulled out.

I can't say anything else or I'll be the bad guy, but what she's doing feels invasive. Sure, Brent has access to my Instagram inbox so he can help reply to messages, but anything more than that would make my skin crawl.

"Caitlyn's right," Jeff says. I'd feel some solidarity if I didn't believe he was coming to his own defense rather than mine. "I wouldn't want someone going through my digital history."

"Too late!" I cackle before I can stop myself.

Syd stares at me in shock. "What's that supposed to mean?"

Fuck.

"Nothing," Brent cuts in with a glare in my direction. "It's just a shame when private things don't stay private. Like text messages or, uh, OnlyFans accounts, or whatever."

Jeff freezes at the mention of OnlyFans, and Syd doesn't fail to miss the guilty look on his face.

"OnlyFans?" Her eyes narrow, and color stains her cheeks. "Is that what he's saying? That you still have one going?"

"He didn't say anything," Jeff says with a scowl. "He used it as an example."

"Well, your face sure said a whole lot, Jeff." She shoots a betrayed glance at him, and I can't help remembering the arguments that clouded the early days of their relationship. Jeff wanted to keep raking in money by charging fans to see his half-naked (or sometimes fully naked) pictures online, and Sydney, understandably, didn't want those images out in the world. "You told me you shut that down when we got together."

A muscle in Jeff's jaw clenches. I wonder if he thinks this revelation is more or less damning than his dick pic escapades. Now that I think of it, his OnlyFans account is probably the reason he had a slew of naked pictures of himself to begin with. Because Jeff's definitely still posting. Not that *I'm* looking, of course. But people talk. "Is this really what's important right now? We need to see if anything here can help Brent"—he delivers this with a glare at Brent, who's just unloaded this potentially damning secret—"and then we need to get going. It'll be dark before we know it."

A little gasp from Lucy interrupts, and I glance over to see the laptop pried open in her lap.

At least Nash should have a—

"No password," Lucy says.

Oh, Nash, you sweet, trusting idiot.

My heart does a funny sympathy lurch again, but there's no stopping Lucy from her mission.

"No Wi-Fi," Lucy confirms, which, duh. Then she tucks her tongue between her teeth and narrows her eyes in concentration. "Am I reading this right?" Blood drains from her face, and she shakes her head, slamming the laptop lid closed.

"What did you find?" Brent asks.

"You know what, maybe Jeff was right. We shouldn't be doing this."

"Show us," Sydney demands.

Lucy reluctantly pries open the laptop. She turns the device to face the rest of us and opens an email window. "It looks like an email to Nash from someone at a cosmetics manufacturing facility." She looks up at Sydney with wide eyes. "The Personal Care Formulary. Do they manufacture Plentifol?" Her lips part on a disbelieving exhale. "Why would Nash be talking to your suppliers?"

"Like, recently?" Syd asks.

Lucy nods. "Like, *today* recently."

Syd stares incredulously at the screen. "I mean, he consulted on the active ingredients and scents in the development stage. But that was big-picture stuff, never the specific details, and it was ages ago. He had no reason to talk to them now. Something's off."

I push past them to read the line that Lucy's highlighted. "'Attached please see the ingredients list with active ingredient percentages.'" I wrinkle my nose. "They're giving him the formula?" The hot thrill of scandal races through my veins. "Sounds shady."

"Nash is on the advisory board," Sydney says. "Was. But he was never an owner. The formula is proprietary. Sending this violates our NDA. I don't understand . . ."

"What does it look like?" Lucy asks. "Talk it through with me."

Sydney shakes her head. "It sounds like they're sending him a formula. But maybe it's not Plentifol." She clicks open the attachment and her face blanches. "This can't be right," she whispers again. She really, truly seems shocked by the idea that someone would send Nash the exact formula for her shampoo. But she's an actress, so it's hard to know what's real.

Lucy gently nudges Sydney's hands away from the laptop and closes the lid. She looks up at the rest of us with forced cheeriness. "Let's just grab the scarf and go."

Jeff gives a rough grunt of approval and wraps his good arm around Sydney's shoulders to steer her toward the door. The air's gone out of the room, any momentum we were making toward rescue pierced by the news of Nash's possible deception.

Lucy gingerly slides the laptop back into its case like it's contaminated, then wipes her hands on her jeans as she stands. One by one, we filter out the door and into the howling wind. I don't even try to protest when Lucy locks the cabin behind us. Whatever secrets Nash kept can die with him.

But as we trudge back toward the golf cart in the Lodge, my mind can't stop worrying over one damning possibility: Sydney's walking away from some very lucrative partnerships to launch Plentifol. If what Lucy uncovered was evidence of Nash sabotaging her business or cashing in on proprietary information, that's one hell of a motive for her to want him dead.

43

LUCY

I keep watching Sydney, waiting for cracks to appear in her facade. Admittedly, I've spent a lot of my life protecting Sydney, ever since she beamed that smile at me freshman year. But the news about Nash—or the news we think we discovered—had to land like a blow.

Jeff keeps Sydney pressed tightly against his side as we step back into the Lodge, so it's hard to read her. I know how often she pretends everything is okay, only to have the world fall to pieces later. Right now—in these conditions—we can't afford any missteps or meltdowns. The fact that she's letting Jeff stay so close suggests Nash's possible betrayal is hitting her even harder than the OnlyFans thing and the idea that Jeff could have been the one to hurt Nash to begin with.

"Alright, you know the plan?" Jeff calls over his shoulder to Brent.

"Take the golf cart, find help." Brent adds with a grimace, "Try not to freeze."

I shiver at his words. We weren't outside for more than a few minutes, but standing in the Lodge now, my skin still feels tender and pink from the cold. I can't imagine going back out into the snow for who knows how long. "Do you want to eat before you go?" I ask. Maybe the calories will help his body hold on to some extra heat.

Brent opens his mouth, but Caitlyn cuts in. "Not to be a bitch," she says, "but the sooner you leave, the sooner we get help."

With a resigned sigh, Brent gestures toward the kitchen. "I'm good. I'll take some food to go."

Sydney wriggles out of Jeff's clutches to dump the box of protein bars onto the counter. "Here," she says, holding out the empty box to Brent. "You can put your stuff in this."

I try not to flinch when he shoves an English muffin, a croissant, and two squares of chocolate into the box and a protein bar into each pants pocket. With any luck, he'll be back with help before it's even time for dinner. But if not . . .

My stomach turns over.

That's a lot of food gone from our meager stash. If Brent doesn't find help, who knows how much longer we'll be stuck here?

An irrational impulse to snatch the food back from him floods through me.

I don't want to be stuck here.

I don't want to starve.

And I don't want to die.

If Brent takes too much food—if he fails—all of those things could happen. Him piling away supplies has triggered some primal survival instinct deep inside me that's been dormant ever since my cancer diagnosis—or, honestly, back even further to *that* night. I've been coasting through my life, not truly committed to living it. But my fingers twitching at my side prove otherwise. And as bad as it feels to be angry at Brent—because of course he should take food with him—maybe it's a good thing that I feel this way. Maybe it's a sign of progress.

Suddenly, a lump of hot, painful guilt lodges in my throat, and then that guilt transforms into anger at myself.

Self-loathing is a beautiful, devastating spiral.

"I guess that's it, then," Brent says, and we follow him toward the stairs. I pause at the top to gather my courage, because going downstairs to the garage means another horrifying trip past Nash's body.

I pat my pocket, where the skeleton key meets my fingers with reassuring resistance. There'll be no missing Brent's send-off. Unless I'm willing to hand over the key—which I'm not—I don't have a choice but to go downstairs.

"Wait!" Caitlyn calls from across the room. I didn't realize she'd separated from the group until I watch her jog the last steps toward Nash's rolling rack of clothes. "What about this?" A strangled laugh dies in my throat as she reaches for the oversize pink fur coat and holds it up.

"It's like Miss Piggy and Big Bird had a love child," Brent says.

Caitlyn rolls her eyes. "I mean for you to wear. For warmth?"

He gives it a skeptical glance but still shrugs it on over his assorted layers. "I look ridiculous."

"*Phhsst.*" Sydney waves him away, but then her face cracks into a grin, and Caitlyn, who's been tight-lipped too, can't seem to control herself, and then suddenly we're all cackling at the ridiculousness—of Brent's outfit, of the situation, of this life—a manic laughter that cramps my stomach and makes my heart pound and that, if I dwell on it too long, feels scary close to turning into tears.

We finally pull ourselves together and tromp downstairs, Brent in the lead trying to cling to his dignity like an aging showgirl. The mirth from upstairs evaporates quickly, though. The closer to the garage we get, the quieter Brent falls, until we're all as silent as trespassers in a tomb.

The skeleton key permits us access to the garage, and when we tug at the exterior door, it slides open smoothly. I blink into the blinding brightness of sunlight on the afternoon snow, my insides as frozen as the landscape.

Brent's leaving.

This is real.

It might be our only shot.

Brent braces himself against the shock of cold and climbs into the golf cart. When he twists the key, the engine comes to life with a satisfying growl. And when he eases the golf cart into the snow, the wheels spin but finally catch. Some of the drifts come up almost to the bottom of the golf cart, but at least it's temporarily stopped snowing. I can only hope it doesn't start up again after he leaves.

Brent pauses just outside the Lodge so we can say our goodbyes.

"Good luck," Sydney says, squeezing his shoulder.

"Hurry back," Caitlyn adds with a wink.

Fresh shame courses through me as I add a hoarse "Thank you" over the engine's roar. On any other vehicle, the noise would annoy me, but I can't help thinking it's a good thing, that it'll attract help that much sooner.

And then Brent's off, the powder-blue golf cart bumping slowly but steadily through the snow.

It's good he's going, I tell myself over my pounding heart. *He'll find help. It's not like he's leaving us behind.*

But as I wave Brent off and watch him disappear around a bend in the road, I have a terrible feeling that he's not coming back.

44

CAITLYN

Lucy's at the front of the group, waving Brent off like he's heading to war even though he never once turns around to look back at us. It's like she's trying to atone for past sins or something, and it at least makes a very dramatic framing shot for the video I'm filming.

"Alright, let's get the fuck inside," Jeff says.

Lucy drops her arm with a shiver. She turns to head inside, but then catches sight of me and freezes. "What the hell are you doing?"

". . . and cut!" I deadpan, pressing a button to stop recording on my phone. "I can always count on you to deliver a classy ending, Luce."

Her face purples. "Is this some joke to you? Brent's leaving to try to save our asses and you have to *film* it?"

I've been filming all along—I can't help it if she hasn't been paying attention. But the vehemence in her tone is so sharp and surprising, I stumble back a step. "I'm aware of the situation."

"So you just never stop."

My hackles start to rise, the fighter in me always primed to defend myself. “Stop what?”

“First Brent, now you. Can’t you ever set aside your phone and just be human for a second?”

There it is. “Let me get this straight. I’m not human because I’m documenting what’s happening.”

“You know what I mean. There’s a time and a place for it.”

I narrow my eyes at her. “Listen, babe, I’m not some mommy blogger who only posts after my kids have gone to bed. If you think I have boundaries like that, you’re sorely mistaken. Work is my life, and to maintain this lifestyle, I have to work.” Regaining my composure, I straighten my spine and take a step forward. “If I’m offline—being human, as you say—I’m missing out on visibility and exposure, and I’m battling against an ever-changing algorithm. I could lose followers for simply not showing up.” I’ve learned that lesson the hard way, and it’s not a mistake I want to repeat. “You think this is easy? Name another job where you need to be working seven days a week and the entire world feels like they’re entitled to give you performance reviews whenever they want.”

Lucy rolls her eyes. “I get it, your job is tough. But it’s not like you can even post that video right now.”

I glare at her. “Obviously I can’t post without internet or cell service. But at some point, my audience is going to want to see what happened this weekend. Especially since we’re on a job and there’s a client holding us accountable.” I cross my arms over my chest. “Unless you think that because you know the client I should tell them to fuck off? Is that what you want?”

Lucy’s face goes pale. It’s so easy to be high and mighty if you live in a bubble, but I live in the real world, where I have a professional reputation to uphold. Pushing past her toward the garage, I toss a final grenade over my shoulder. "Last I checked, your job is to be the photographer, and I don't see you taking a single damn picture right now."

"She has a point, Lucy," Sydney says, making me pause in the doorway to bask in the moment. Syd's next words make her look like she's just gotten a terrible manicure and doesn't know how to break it to the nail technician, but she blurts them out anyway. "We might need to show the video to the police at some point."

Lucy's eyes go wide as she gets it. "You mean if something happens to Brent."

"Nothing's going to happen to Brent," Syd amends. "But when they get here, and they will because of Nash, they might need help putting the story together. Videos will help them understand. Just like the pictures you took of Nash."

"Fine." Lucy throws up her hands and eyes the garage like it's an escape hatch. "Jeff's right. We should get inside."

She stomps past me, and I send a pointed look Sydney's way. But instead of the commiseration I expect, there's something almost like guilt written across Syd's beautiful face.

It fucking figures.

My cheeks burn, and I turn toward the garage just in time to watch Lucy disappear into the cavernous dark. There has to be more going on than what Lucy's saying. Which leads me to wonder why she's so against documenting things. Is it because she's the reason we're all on this trip and it's become a nightmare? Or does she have something even worse to hide?

45

CAITLYN

Now that Brent's gone, it feels like we're a bunch of schoolkids at a sleepover, staying up late after the parents have gone to bed. I mean, except for the dead body. There's a feeling of giddy recklessness, like anything could happen without supervision. There's also a frisson of tension in the air as no one tells us to get along or include the girl who's made herself an outcast.

Lucy sits in the living room section of the Lodge while Jeff and Sydney and I grab a table in the dining area and otherwise ignore her.

"We gonna do this?" I ask Jeff, running my fingers over the pillowcase Lucy grabbed from her cabin. I'm not overly thrilled about getting super close to a guy with anger issues, but I'd rather be on his good side than receive the brunt of his frustration. Bandaging him up is a gesture of goodwill—a small sacrifice in the grand scheme of things.

Jeff's handsome face twists in a grimace. "What are the odds this makes it worse?"

"Anything's a possibility." I aim a mirthless grin at him. "Do you want to live dangerously?"

Wordlessly he waves me on, and Sydney hands me a pair of pointy scissors that she found in one of the closets, a gleaming silver pair that hopefully is just as much function as form. Otherwise it'll be another useless pretty thing, like the rest of the stuff at Reverie.

Pleased to find the scissors sharp as sin, I slit the pillowcase at the seams to form a long strip of fabric. Then, carefully, I begin wrapping it around Jeff's shoulder, down below his injured arm, and then back around his neck. By the end, I've got a respectable sling keeping his arm immobilized. It's not pretty, but it gets the job done.

"You're not half bad at this," Jeff says when I sit back to admire my handiwork.

"A woman of many skills," Sydney says, wrapping her arms around my neck in a quick hug. "Your brothers teach you that too?"

My chest goes suddenly cold, my muscles tightening beneath Sydney's touch. I've mentioned my family to Sydney before—leaving out the tender, broken parts—and I told Lucy about them out at the waterfall, but it doesn't feel right to talk about family at the same time as Jeff's eyeing Syd's arms around my neck like we're fodder for his fantasies. I can promise him this: I'm definitely not here for his benefit.

I toss my head, forcing Syd to let go, and meet Jeff's eye. "Wiggle your fingertips every now and then to make sure your circulation is okay."

"And if it's not?"

I nod toward his sling. "Then we retie this thing."

He grunts and leans back in his chair, gaze drifting away from me to lock on Lucy. "This is all Lucy's fucking fault."

Fighting a smile, I dart a quick glance at Lucy. It feels deliciously illicit to talk about someone who might overhear us. But Lucy gives no reaction, continuing to stare wordlessly at a Catskills guidebook that's spread out across her lap.

Sydney lays a hand on Jeff's uninjured arm. "I know everyone's feeling a little extra sensitive right now. But Lucy didn't make you hurt yourself, babe."

He flinches away, and hurt dances across Sydney's features. She's trying to play peacemaker, but Jeff's all testosterone and blame.

"Fuck that," he growls. It's an animalistic sound. Predatory. And it strikes me that Jeff's wrong side is not a place anyone should hope to be.

Sydney, though, is undeterred. "Listen, Brent's going to do his thing, and then help is coming. We just need to sit tight and play nice with each other. Fighting is only going to make this worse."

"I'm not fighting with anyone." Jeff looks at me for backup. "Am I? I'm just sitting here, minding my own business while I'm in a world of pain. And, yeah, Lucy's the reason I'm on this fucking trip, so excuse me if I don't want to make friendship bracelets and braid her hair right now."

"I'm the reason you're on this trip." Sydney's voice is soft but firm, a rising fire in her eyes. "Not Lucy." Her voice steadies further as she picks up steam. "Lucy might have coordinated the job, but she and I were the only people specifically requested for it. I'm the one who invited you to join us." She captures me and Jeff in a stare. "Both of you."

Jeff shakes his head, his scowl compounded by his frustration and pain. "You're my girlfriend, Syd. Doesn't that mean anything to you?" His voice cracks at the end, and the tips of my ears start to burn. We're snowballing way past where this conversation started. "I don't get why you're always defending her instead of me. For fuck's sake, she practically accused me of killing Nash."

I shouldn't be here for this. But also, I really, really want to know the answer.

I drop my gaze, but not before I see the way Sydney's eyes go liquid and soft. "She was there for me in my worst moments. And she's always let me be exactly who I am." She means it as praise for Lucy, not an admonishment of me or Jeff, but all I feel is that I've been found lacking.

A protest rises in my throat, that knee-jerk reaction to protect myself and my place in this world. Letting Sydney be herself doesn't mean we can't be mad when she does selfish things. You can embrace who someone is but still hope that they grow.

"Oh come on," Jeff protests before I can open my mouth. If he could cross his arms like a petulant child, I'm sure he would. "I've never stopped you from anything you wanted to do."

I realize then that it's good I haven't spoken, because there's nothing we can say that won't put us in contrast to Lucy. Sydney's always going to keep her on a pedestal.

Sydney rises from her chair, the air around her tightening like a noose. Jeff might be dangerous, but a scorned Sydney is dangerous too. "Maybe not. But if me being your girlfriend really means something to you, then why the hell are you still on OnlyFans?"

"I'm being hacked!" he blurts out. "Someone's messing with

all my stuff. Leaking photos, putting me on OnlyFans, shit like that."

Way to use one disaster to cover up another, Jeff.

"You expect me to believe that?"

"It's the truth. Ask anyone."

Syd darts a glance at me, and I hold up my hands. "No way, I'm not getting in the middle of this." As soon as she hops online, she's going to find out that Jeff never stopped sharing pictures on OnlyFans. I don't need to be the one who breaks the news.

"Screw you, Caitlyn," Jeff hisses.

"Hard pass," I volley back.

"Stop it, both of you!" Syd screeches. "Hacking or not, it still doesn't explain why you had naked pictures to begin with, Jeff. You certainly weren't sending them to me."

"Syd," Jeff starts, but she shakes her head.

"*No.* I'll find out the truth the minute the internet comes back up. But I meant what I said before. Nash is . . ." A tear glistens at the corner of her eye. "Nash is dead. And if the rest of us are going to make it through this, we need to work together. *All of us.*"

Before Jeff can say another word, she glides away toward Lucy on the wings of old grudges. But across the room, Lucy's already gone.

46

LUCY

I want to leave the moment Jeff first mentions my name in that scornful tone of his, but I don't want to give him the satisfaction of knowing he's affected me. My stomach cramping—with hunger, with his derision—I wait until the group is too absorbed in their toxicity to notice my absence before I set my guidebook aside and slink toward the stairs.

So many times, being Sydney's friend has been a buffer for me, softening the edges of any criticism that floats my way, blunting the impact. But I miscalculated today. She might be my best friend, but here in the woods, I'm the odd man out. The only non-influencer in the group. And when I snapped at Caitlyn for taking that video, I insulted everything she and Sydney and Jeff do. With limited food available, it's a mistake I can't afford to make again. Even though I really, really want to tear apart Jeff's character the way he seems to have no qualms doing to mine.

No matter what happens from here, I know that nothing between Jeff and me will ever go back to being the same. He's only ever tolerated me because of Sydney, but this weekend will change that. And if Sydney's boyfriend hates me, assuming they stay together, it'll strain my relationship with her. I just hope it won't be beyond repair. I might have started this trip uncomfortable with our dynamic, but I can't lose her.

Instinct propels me toward the stairs, an escape route that will take me past a dead body but that will let me avoid my judgmental companions. I don't know what I'm going to do in the basement of the Lodge, but in the moment, I can't think of anything but fleeing.

Their voices are a harsh murmur that might as well be barbed.

My feet hit the top step and Sydney's reply floats my way, muffled by the wall between us but still clear enough for me to get the gist. "She was there for me in my worst moments."

Oh, Sydney.

The mention of that night rips open a chasm in my chest, the memory turning into a roaring blackness that swallows me whole.

She was there for me, and as I pound down the stairs, I'm tipped back into senior year and the raw wound of Sydney and Breaker.

She was there for me, and I'm rushing past Nash's body and into the cool expanse of the garage, opening drawers I can't see, searching for something I can't name.

Sydney insisted Breaker never raped her the night I came home and found her shaking and pale in bed, but she still spent weeks nursing the bruise on her cheek, telling everyone it was a mugging outside the dining hall.

"You should see the other guy," she would say, laughing, spinning abuse into a fairy tale and turning herself into an avenging princess.

Other people crowded close to hear the story, and she shone

briefly under the glow of the attention. But back in our dorm room, she fell apart each night. Stopped sleeping, while the bags under her eyes grew as dark as Breaker's scowl.

I'd always been the moth to Sydney's flame, but Breaker had dimmed her light. It made me hover closer, watch more anxiously.

I hated the way she now flinched at loud noises, the way she held herself stiffly and second-guessed the right thing to say. She'd once been lush and vibrant, and now she was as brittle as autumn leaves.

I couldn't ask things like *Are you okay?* because she'd tell me yes, of course, she was fine. By then Syd had landed her first movie role, and Breaker had attached himself to her star. She couldn't leave him; he wouldn't leave her. I had to find the opportunities to help her when I could.

That early spring night, Sydney and Breaker were heading to a bar, walking because it was cheaper and less stressful than hailing a cab. He came to collect her in our room, and Syd looked . . . like she didn't want to be there. Or, at least, not with him. So I grabbed my coat and chose my words carefully. "I'm going that way too."

Breaker looked pissed at my imposition, but Sydney had good manners and a desire to please everyone who asked for something from her.

I'd like to think she was secretly grateful I came.

Certainly afterward, when we clutched each other on the street and cried until our throats went hoarse, I know for a fact she was glad I was there.

The three of us shuffled outside, Syd's hand in Breaker's, the night brushing against our skin as cool and thin as cobwebs. It was maybe a little awkward walking together. But it was fine.

It was fine.

It was fine until an intersection with a car screaming toward us, until Breaker, perched impatiently on the curb, swayed a little too close. I only watched him from the corner of my eye, my gaze fixed on Sydney, her gaze fixed ahead.

"Be careful," I warned, but Breaker just scoffed.

And then, between one breath and the next, he stumbled forward into the street. Just one foot hitting the pavement, but he wasn't fast enough to jump back, and the car sweeping toward him wasn't fast enough to stop.

I couldn't tell you if his grunt of surprise came when he touched the ground or when the car reached his body. My mind can't untangle the truth, and so the sounds are woven together forever in my memory—the metal snapping his bones and smashing through flesh, the air leaving his lungs.

I've been through a lot in my life. I died before I ever had a chance to live. And still, that moment with Breaker was the worst moment of my life.

It was the best moment too, because then Sydney was finally free.

I fight to push down the memory as I comb through the shadowed garage, but it's impossible to stop hearing Sydney's words, to stop living in the haunted place of Breaker's death. The past feels written into everything I do.

Focus, Lucy.

We've all searched the garage, but I can't help looking again. For food, maybe. Or for hope.

The tools are as we left them, the golf cart's plastic tarp tossed haphazardly in a pile.

I find nothing useful until I slide open one of the drawers on the workbench and reach into the shadows at the back. My fingers brush against something hard and cool, a shape that instinctively sends a wave of dread through my body.

"Lucy?"

My heart leaps in my chest, and I whirl to face Sydney, positioning my body to block her view of the drawer. I'm not yet ready to trust her with what I've discovered inside. "What are you doing here?"

"Looking for you." She cocks her head to the side. A flush paints her cheeks in the dim light. Embarrassment or anger, I'm not sure. But she's here, and I'm so grateful for it.

Right now she's chosen me.

"I came back," I explain, "to see what else I could find." She nods and scans the room behind me, but I shake my head. "There's nothing here."

Her lips twist to the side, and she shoves a handful of hair over her shoulder. "This place is creeping me out." She doesn't say anything about what I overheard upstairs, and I don't mention it either. Maybe it's a cop-out, but there's a fragile truce in this moment that I don't want to shatter with a confrontation. With her in front of me, the image of blood pooling under Breaker's broken body starts to fade from my mind.

"Syd?" It's the first time we've been alone since this afternoon, and the hush of the basement makes me brave enough to ask: "Are you sure you want to spend the night with Jeff after everything that happened?"

Her expression tightens. "I'll be fine. You don't have to worry about me." She shakes her head. "Jeff wouldn't . . . I'll be okay."

"Right," I whisper, the word scratching the back of my throat. She probably thinks I overstepped, but how could I not say something? For years, all I've done is try to protect her. I'm fine with giving people the benefit of the doubt, but sometimes Syd trusts too much. Sometimes she forgets that she needs to protect herself. "Forget I said anything. Let's go up."

When Sydney turns her back, I slide the flare gun from the drawer into the waistband of my jeans and cover it with my sweater. It rests against my skin, as cold as broken promises. I don't like keeping secrets from Syd, but this one might just save my life.

"Coming?" Sydney calls over her shoulder.

I barely recognize my voice as it rasps into the night. "Right behind you."

47

CAITLYN

I hear Lucy and Sydney coming before I see them—Sydney's light, purposeful footsteps and Lucy's almost reluctant march up the stairs. They're not talking, though. It's all held breath and fraught silence. Either because of something that happened between them downstairs or because neither of them knows what to say to me and Jeff.

I shouldn't be surprised that Sydney went to find Lucy. Even though everyone's at odds with one another and there's a pit in my stomach, it still feels like there's safety in numbers, like if you let someone out of your sight, something terrible could happen to them. Or to you, I guess. There's always that unsettling thought.

I continue browsing through the makeup table Nash set up yesterday, trying to ignore the prickle of eyes on my back. The surface is a disaster of eyeshadow palettes and concealer tubes, the disorderly array of an artist interrupted before he could clean up. A little extra riffling on my part isn't going to make things worse. Either way, Lucy's never going to get her photographs of the room now.

I still stand by what I said about accountability, but we're so far past the point that this job even matters. People will hear about Nash's death, about Brent's golf cart ride for help, and Reverie will sink faster than the *Titanic*. That, or it will become so immensely popular that you won't be able to book a reservation. People love to gawk at the scene of a crime, so I guess it could go either way.

"Really, Cait?" Sydney asks, and I finally turn to face her.

Lucy's gone back to being a shadow at Sydney's side, wisely holding her tongue even though she watches me through narrowed, judgmental eyes.

No doubt she's still reeling from the argument she overheard earlier. How embarrassing it must be to be the center of Jeff and Sydney's fight and know it wasn't the first time they'd battled about you. Like divorced parents arguing over custody, but in this case, custody of a kid no one wants.

I let my fingers linger over the table, then pluck a pink tube from the chaos. "It's emotional support lipstick, okay? Nash isn't going to use this stuff anymore."

Lucy blanches, but surprisingly, Jeff's the one who speaks up from his spot on the couch. "Give it a rest, Cait." His face goes blotchy, his voice rough. "The guy's not even in the ground yet." He's undoubtedly a little twitchy about his own prospects now that he's trussed up like a roast pig. A sling's not so great for mobility.

"Whatever," I mutter under my breath. I let the lipstick fall with a clatter. I can always come back for it later.

"Any luck on the Wi-Fi situation?" Before anyone can answer, Lucy's stomach growls so loudly that even Jeff looks up across the room.

"Alright there, Luce?" Jeff asks mockingly.

She ignores his sneer and drops her hands to her stomach. "Guess I'm hungrier than I wanted to admit. I never ate lunch."

For a second, I want to throttle her. All her need does is expose my own, and I don't want to be here, starving on a mountain. I want the rich food and lush amenities I was promised.

"Me neither," Sydney says, which feels like a low-stakes way to align herself with Lucy. None of us ate lunch. We were too busy watching Nash die.

That thought's enough to quiet the ache in my stomach, but the reprieve won't last long.

I glance through the window to the sky, where soft fingers of pink have begun to comb through the blue. It's getting late. Somehow, when we were focused on other things, time slipped away. That's the thing about time: there's always either too much of it or not enough. Right now, I'm caught between today's extremes—the dragging horror of watching Nash die and the quicksilver way we've blinked and jumped to dusk.

I'd feel better if Brent were here, but I keep the thought to myself. No point calling attention to his absence when we have no idea what to expect tonight.

Lucy glances at me and Jeff, the wild cards in this equation. "We don't all have to eat together if you're not ready to." She's giving us an out if we decide we're going to be assholes, but I'll bite my tongue and leave the assholery to Jeff.

"No," I say, "let's do it. It'll be a good distraction." And if there's additional drama between Syd and Jeff and Lucy? All the more fun.

We make our way to the kitchen, where the food supplies are a grim reminder of our situation. Everyone else at least gets an opportunity to eat some of the welcome-basket pastries, but my only options are packaged goods. Protein bars or protein powder or crackers. Not a speck of fiber in sight.

Eenie, meenie, miney, mo.

I reach for the protein powder, and my spirits tumble when I scan the label. "Seriously, Jeff?" I spin the package to face him. "When we divided up the food, we agreed that we could each have some protein powder."

"And you can." He taps the lid of each tub. "Chocolate or vanilla?"

Is he really that dense?

"Neither," I say flatly.

"What's the problem?" Syd wraps an arm around my waist, a gentle way to quiet me. But I'm too hungry to keep playing nice.

"This has glutamine in it."

"It's a whey protein," Jeff says, scowling at every place Syd's body touches mine. "Whey is milk."

"Well, glutamine comes from wheat protein." I shove the tubs back at him. "I can't eat this."

"We'll find you something else," Sydney promises.

"There are those almond meal crackers," Lucy pipes up.

Sydney's face lights. "And protein bars! They're certified gluten-free. The marketing text says it and everything."

I stifle a retort about marketing materials and accept the protein bar she presses into my palm. "Aren't you sick of these by now?"

She grabs a bar of her own in solidarity and rips into it. While I appreciate the gesture, all she's doing is eating her way through my possible stash. We need to redivide the food before all those good intentions get chewed up. Literally.

"Cheers," she says, and touches her bar to mine.

48

STORY POST

Reverie Retreat—Day 2

"Okay, I might have lied."

The camera catches Sydney from below and to the left, an unusual angle for someone whose magnetic eye contact you've come to expect. Even when she's doing a "get ready with me" video or vlogging "a day in the life," she's always looking at you, talking to you, throwing glances over her shoulder to bring you in on her jokes.

Tonight she seems unaware of the camera, stripped down and raw. The luster from earlier today has worn off, like something's been lost in the hours since she posted about being snowed in at her fancy retreat. Syd's always captivating, sure, but now dark circles hang under her eyes as if she hasn't slept for days, and a frown mars her perfect face. The effect is a little off-putting; there's a new distance between you and her that you don't quite trust. Still, you want to give her the benefit of the doubt. Maybe this is like that behind-the-behind-the-scenes shot, another new thing she's trying. Aren't people always talking about authenticity as a conduit for human connection?

Sydney takes another bite of whatever's in her hand, her jaw working as if she's chewing on a dried-out Airhead or a piece of that vintage Bazooka gum. The kind that has quaint little comics wrapped around the candy, gum that's technically edible but not advisable.

She rubs at her cheeks when she finishes chewing and cringes. "Definitely lied." She rolls the wrapper back over her food, and that's when you see a flash of the distinctive branding, the bold *Z* for *Zyng.*

Ummmm . . .

"I can't believe I have to eat these for the rest of the weekend. All my body wants is real food, and this"—she tosses what's left of the bar onto the counter—"just sits in my stomach like a brick."

Holy shit. Does Zyng know that Sydney's trashing their bars right now? Something doesn't feel right about this. The uneven lighting, the way she won't look the camera in the eye. What Syd's saying could cause a scandal, but it would also be scandalous for you to look away.

You keep watching.

Someone says something indistinct off-camera. A voice that's too muffled for you to tell if it's male or female. Who's with her on this trip again? You flash back to the party bus emptying itself of passengers, their dazzling march down the stairs and onto the brittle earth outside. But Sydney was always the center of the narrative, and it's hard to say quite who was there.

Sydney rolls her eyes at whoever's talking. "Yes, I know I have to do it." With a sigh, she grabs the protein bar again and shoves the rest into her mouth in two unflattering bites. She speaks around the food in her mouth. "Well, they're definitely not going to help my anxiety." Swallowing hard, she balls up the wrapper with a little silvery crunch. "So jittery. I hope I can sleep."

Good point. Why's she eating something with caffeine at this hour? It's not ridiculously late or anything, but she's the same person who taught you that caffeine stimulates your adrenals to produce more cortisol, which can create hormone imbalances. Who says influencers never taught you anything?

"And key lime pie?" Sydney continues, sending a withering look at the crumpled wrapper. "One at a time is doable. Key lime pie for a whole weekend . . ." She looks a little green at the thought.

What the hell is happening? This isn't the Sydney Kent you know.

A jolt of unease tightens your chest, and then you remember: she still hasn't announced her secret project. Maybe she's creating a competitor product, an SK-branded protein bar built for impeccable tastes. It could even be a collaboration with Jeff! He's always been about the "if it fits your macros" lifestyle. What if this whole scandal with him is just a way to get press before a launch announcement? Holy shit, you'll have to add your guess to the comment boards online. If you get this correct, bragging rights are yours. You knew there had to be a reason for Sydney to talk this way.

With a wry smile, Syd flicks the wrapper off the counter. It wings off-screen, but she doesn't bother to watch it fall.

"It's good for me?" she snorts, her pretty face a contrast to her ugly words. "No. What would be really good for me is if—"

She never gets to finish her thought, her words lost somewhere in the static of the internet, so you'll just have to imagine what she might have said.

You scroll to the comments to see what other people are saying about this fiasco.

Then you sit back and wait for Syd's next post.

49

LUCY

No one wants to say it, but Jeff finally does. "Something's wrong." We've all been so absorbed in our own bubbles that his words take the rest of us aback. Not that the message is so surprising, but the way it shatters the illusion that our long wait will be worth our while.

After our bleak dinner, eaten standing around the kitchen island, we retreated to various chairs and sofas around the Lodge to stare at our disconnected phones and zone out. We stayed close enough together to give the effect of solidarity, the feeling that we weren't quite alone, though we sat far enough apart that no one had to address the tension in the room—both between one another and from the situation.

This whole time, I've studiously avoided looking at the clock, pretending that if I can't see the numbers changing, time's not really passing. But it is. It's been hours since Brent drove away. The sunset is long gone, blotted out by an inky black that will brighten again in just a few hours. This far past midnight, the Lodge has gone back to feeling claustrophobic, like the darkness has thrown a blanket over the windows and smothered all the air inside.

I should have been the one to call Reverie when we had the chance, not Jeff. I was so worried about hiding my connection to this place, but if I'd only done the right thing, maybe Meghan would have realized we truly needed help. Maybe she would have sent someone for us long ago and we wouldn't be stuck in this desperate, endless waiting.

"We should have heard something by now," Jeff says.

Caitlyn, legs kicked up over the arm of a sofa, looks like she wants to roll her eyes. "It takes how long it takes. It's not like you could have gotten to help any faster."

The air ripples around Jeff as he surges to his feet and starts pacing. "It's not that." The floor groans quietly under his steps, his body held stiffly to minimize jostling of his arm. "I've just been doing the math."

"You can add?" Caitlyn quips.

Jeff ignores her. "We've been waiting way longer than it should have taken to find help. Even if Brent had to ditch the golf cart, either he or emergency services should have made it here by now."

It's hard to disagree with him, and my brain keeps spiraling through a list of things that could have gone wrong. We know someone with a gun was close enough for us to hear them yesterday. What if Brent surprised that person and they happened to have a twitchy trigger finger? Or maybe Brent offended them somehow, causing an altercation that led to his demise.

A knot twists in my stomach, and that's before I count the possibility of wild animals attacking Brent or the more mundane but equally deadly chance that he had to walk at some point and twisted an ankle or something. He could have shattered a bone, slipped and hit his head, fallen unconscious while the cold settled over him and slid him deep into hypothermia.

A hundred different outcomes all lead to the same place: Brent's not here and help's not here and we're running out of food and time and morale. I hate to ever side with Jeff, but I wish we had a drone so we could see what's happening out there in the woods. Not knowing makes me feel wildly out of control, and I want to bolt out into the darkness and prove to Jeff and Sydney and Caitlyn that they should have let me go in the first place, that I could have done the job. But it's too late for that. At least, tonight it is.

"So there's a problem," Sydney says. She glances outside and chews on her lower lip. "What do we do?"

"Nothing for now," Caitlyn says.

Jeff's face starts to go red. "We can't just sit here."

"Yes, we can," I say, hating that I'm agreeing with Caitlyn. "She's right." Jeff turns to scowl at me, so it's Sydney I look at instead. She's listening with rapt attention, and if it's not trust glimmering in her wide-eyed gaze, then it's at least a level of respect. "It wouldn't be safe to go after Brent right now. Not in the darkness. Our best chance is to go in the morning, when it's warmer and we have better visibility."

"So we just hold out a few more hours until dawn?" Syd asks.

"Exactly. We have enough food to last until then."

"What are we supposed to do in the meantime?"

"We sit tight. Maybe help will come. Maybe the internet will come back on. Either way, we wait. There are no shortcuts."

I'm no stranger to waiting. I've spent whole seasons watching time pass until I could return to the life I wanted to lead.

There's a letting go that happens when you've committed yourself to waiting. We all do it sometimes—put our fate in the hands of other people. College admissions officers, doctors, bosses. Sydney, Caitlyn, Jeff.

Brent.

Tonight I have to hope that everything I'm worried about is just anxious speculation and not the truth about why he's delayed. I need to trust that Brent will somehow come through, that the darkness won't prohibit help from getting to us. Still, there's a helplessness to waiting that makes me restless. I can't stay in this stifling lodge anymore, squirming under Jeff's angry glare. There are only so many phone games I can play to distract myself.

"I need a fucking drink," Jeff announces. "Where's that bottle of vodka?"

"Ooh," Caitlyn squeals. "Great idea."

I take it as my cue and rise, slinging my camera bag over my shoulder. "I'm going to head back to my cabin."

"Suit yourself," Caitlyn says. "More booze for the rest of us."

Sydney has the decency to wrap me in a hug before I go. "Be safe," she whispers in my ear. A wish and not a warning, I hope.

"Try to get some sleep," I tell the others before I slip out the door. "It's a great way to pass the time. We'll need the rest for whatever happens next."

50

LUCY

I don't take my own advice. I have every intention of heading back to my cabin, and I even hesitate outside my door with my fingers drifting over the shaft of my room key. But my restlessness follows me into the night, and I know I won't be able to rest if my mind's still whirling with fear. Instead, I wrap my sweater tighter around my body and melt into the forest, walking the path past the cabins and down the ridge.

It's tough going. The snow on the ground has crusted over, and each step feels like punching my feet through Styrofoam, unstable and unsupported. While the sky has stopped spitting out snow, a fresh wind has picked up. It knifes through my sweater and scrapes against my skin like teeth.

I walk until the cold stops feeling like a shock, until numbness slides into its place. If I were home right now, I'd be walking through the streets with a slice of hot pizza in my hand. Nick's arms would be around me—yes, Nick, because in this fantasy I haven't utterly destroyed my life—and I'd be marveling at the way the city lights glow. The darkness would be romantic, the hustle of the city sparkling and full of promise.

Here the darkness feels empty, like a gnawed-out stomach or a cave. The night feels absolute. It feels hungry.

Yet I don't turn back.

I walk until I've passed all the cabins and the night has swallowed me. Until I've disappeared.

At last, when my body reaches the point of exhaustion and my mind finally empties out, I stop beside a sole evergreen. Most of the trees here are deciduous, and this tree's prickly green foliage is the only marker to distinguish it from all the other trees. I reach around my body and slide the flare gun I found in the garage from the waistband of my jeans. It trembles in my palm, a plastic barrel that I can feel but not quite see.

I shouldn't be afraid of this gun, but I am. There's something that feels so irreparable about a gunshot, so final. In theory, this gun's loaded with flares instead of bullets, but touching it makes me want to crawl out of my skin. Still, I feel safer with it than without it. This deadly little tool is the only reason I feel remotely okay being outside right now. If help comes up the road to find us, I can signal to them. If a bear comes, the fire can scare it away.

Win-win.

I only wish I'd felt comfortable sharing my discovery with Syd. With everything thrown into chaos, it's hard to know how she would have reacted, and some tiny voice in my mind made me feel like the gun was a secret I needed to keep safe. Just in case.

I hate that I'm having thoughts like that, but as soon as someone dies, things get real.

Working by touch rather than sight, I open the flap of my camera bag and slide the gun inside. The gun and the camera together are a tight squeeze, but there's a reassuring weight to them. I can protect myself if it comes to that. I need to defend this body, broken as it may be. It's the only one I have.

Feeling like I can finally breathe, I turn back toward the cabins. I've come around a slight bend in my walk, and my new angle gives me a chance to see all the buildings at once—the cabins lit in a row, the shape of them like knobs on a spine. They perch at the edge of the cliff, casting a soft glow into the darkness, literal beacons in the night.

The cabins—and the image they'll make—are too tempting to resist. I'm exhausted and famished and on edge, but even now the artist in me stirs awake, a bear pulled out of hibernation by an early spring.

I make sure I'm nowhere near the edge of the cliff, then reach for my camera. My heart jolts when I brush against the gun. Ignoring the shivery sensation of danger, I take a few photographs of the landscape, those cabins shining in the dark. My cell and camera are still tethered, so the pictures will show up on my phone for safekeeping. I don't know if or when I'll look at them again, but the act of taking them steadies me enough for me to bear heading back.

By the time I reach my cabin, I'm frozen down to my bones, a chill I might never shake off. I fight it the only way I know how, by taking a shower that's hot enough to scald my skin. Then I tuck myself into bed and turn out the lights. The weight of everything that happened today is enough to press me into the mattress.

Out of habit, I open my phone to check my messages before I drift off to sleep, but there's just the infuriatingly blank glow of the screen. No new messages. No connection. Brent's not back, and there's no sign of anyone else coming to help. There hasn't even been word from Meghan, which makes me worry about her on top of everything else.

It hits me all at once how desperately bad this situation is. How little control I have.

The first sob comes like a thief, sneaking in on silent feet. I clamp my hands over my mouth, but it doesn't stop a second sob from racking my body. A hot trickle of tears slips to the corner of my lips, making the world taste like salt and sadness.

I know by now that life doesn't give you breaks. It hands you whatever it wants. Loss upon loss upon loss, grief welling up like a spring. But everything feels like so much—like too much. I've had a lifetime of being tested, and all I want is to rest.

Poor Nash, dead just as his star was beginning to shine. His cabin empty beside mine, his huge presence never again to fill that room.

Nick, distant because I pushed him away when all I should have done was hold him close. I miss him so much, the loneliness is an ache.

Nick, who's been steady and never judged me.

Nick, who stuck by me when my world almost ended.

Nick, who I miss like a limb.

The banging from next door starts as I finally calm myself. This time I recognize the noises right away. None of yesterday's moaning, but short bursts of a bed whacking against the wall. Guess Syd and Jeff made up.

A flush sweeps through my body without my permission, heat surging to my core. I press my thighs together, filled with shame. I cannot get turned on by Sydney and Jeff.

And yet.

The banging grows more desperate, and so do I.

Nick's name is on my lips, my body throbbing with need.

Without thinking, I slip my hands under the covers. Trail a finger up my thigh and between my legs.

I fool myself into thinking Nick's here with me and sink into the sensation of my own touch. Let myself get swept away.

The pressure mounts inside my body, my cheeks heating and my heart rate climbing higher and higher. My ragged breath covers the sounds from next door, so I don't know when they stop.

I'm single-minded in pursuit of my goal now: I just need a release.

A little more time.

A few more deft movements of my fingers.

No one ever needs to know.

51

CAITLYN

The knock comes as I'm sitting cross-legged on the bed for lack of better seating options, shoving an almond meal cracker into my mouth. I don't feel bad that when we were collecting food to share, I slipped a sleeve of the crackers into the lining of my suitcase before handing over the box, especially with Jeff's misunderstanding about gluten in his protein powder. But the knock reminds me that I *am* guilty.

My pulse spikes as I brush crumbs from my lips and return the crackers to their hiding place. Shortly after Lucy left the Lodge, the rest of us indulged in a round of vodka, then dispersed back to our own cabins for the night, so the knock is unexpected. I've got reasons to feel nervous no matter who's outside.

"Yeah?" I call through the thick metal door. With Nash dead, there's no way I'm opening up without knowing who to expect.

Sydney's muffled voice returns. "It's me."

I crack the door but don't let her in just yet. A sconce on the cabin's exterior wall illuminates Sydney's flawless skin and big eyes. The repentant, hesitant expression on her face.

I'm pleased to see she's showered, her hair still damp. I don't want to think about what she was doing before this.

"What a day," she says. It's a gentle test: *Are we okay?* "I came to check on you."

"You left Jeff?"

She shrugs. "He took a Benadryl so he could sleep better." A rush of satisfaction courses through me. She could have stayed with Jeff like a doting girlfriend, but instead she came to me. A quiet victory I want to savor.

Sydney looks up at me through her lashes. "Waiting for Brent is terrible."

I nudge the door wider with my hip. "We could wait together."

Sydney's eyes light up. She steps into the room with a rush of cold air that makes my skin come alive. She's wearing a pair of jeans and a sweatshirt that hangs off one shoulder. Nothing fancy, but I don't blame her for defaulting to her warmest clothes. It's fricking freezing out there.

"Are you okay?" She wraps her arms around herself. "I don't like how we left things."

The group dynamics at the end of the night certainly left a lot to be desired: Jeff's rippling anger, the awkward tension with Lucy. Syd might be here to be with me, but she's also come to smooth things over. Always the peacemaker who dreams big, she wants real life to be as ideal as she pretends it is online.

I realize now that I've tried to play this whole thing cool, unbothered and unflappable. But all it's doing is creating more distance between me and Sydney. I'm going to lose her if I don't open up and get vulnerable. She's already shown that she'll side with Lucy over even her boyfriend. Who's to say I'm any less disposable than him?

Over the years, I've built a fortress of defenses to protect myself. After Cole died, I never let anyone get too close to me lest they be taken from me the way he was. And then as my career grew, I could never let anyone see me sweat—my audience or my peers. It's a double-edged sword to have the kind of online presence that I do. You're supposed to be aspirational and human at the same time, and it's nearly impossible for those to coexist. Sydney manages it, but she also wears her heart on her sleeve like an open wound, absorbing the world's pain.

I have too much pain of my own to bear taking on more.

I've shut myself off—I see that now. Leaned in to being aspirational, because for that, I didn't have to crack open my soul. For Sydney to trust me, I'll have to be more.

"We're okay," I tell her. "You and me."

Her guard comes down, her smile sneaking open like I've unlocked a vault. "Well." She grabs the hem of her sweatshirt and tugs it over her head, revealing a snow-white bodysuit made of floral lace. The balconette bra hugs her small breasts, the boning of the corseted middle tailored to flatter her lean curves. My stomach swoops at the sight of it. "What if I want to be more than okay?"

She steps forward in that scandalous little scrap of fabric and traces my hip with her finger. I'm glad I packed these button-down silk pajamas. You can get knock-off versions at every big-box store, but the real deal feels exquisite against my skin. Every touch of Sydney's hands sends shivers through my body. Still, the pajamas pale in comparison to her outfit. She's always showing me up.

"I'm underdressed," I whisper, and Syd's grin widens.

"Not yet. But you will be."

My voice dries up in my throat, and I nod.

She reaches for me then, lips and tongue and teeth crashing against mine. We've been doing this in secret for almost six months, a familiar dance that somehow never gets less thrilling.

Her tongue swirls over the pulse in my neck, and I let my head tip back. Close my eyes and fall into the pleasure of the moment.

There will be time later to worry and mourn, to figure out how to get out of this place unscathed. But right now, none of that matters. Right now, Sydney's falling to her knees, her fingers hooking into the waistband of my pajamas and sliding them down my legs.

Right now, Sydney Kent is exactly where I want her.

52

CAITLYN

After sex with Sydney, I always feel the tiniest bit insecure. Getting naked with a model certainly checks your confidence, but it's not baring my body to her that makes me waver. She's definitely appreciative enough about what she likes, and she lets me know it, both in the way her body responds to mine like a lit match and the way she worships me with her words and her touch.

No, it's a feeling instead that my skin doesn't fit quite right, the way I have to second-guess all of her intentions. Does she want me for me, or am I a stand-in for a thousand other pretty girls who she wants but can't admit to wanting out loud?

In the moments when she closes her eyes in satisfaction, I always wonder who she imagines she's with. Frankly, I hate it. I don't want to have to compete with Sydney's ghosts.

She yawns now as we lie in bed, and her fingers trace lazy circles on the bare skin of my stomach. Sated, she says nothing more about what drove her into my bed, and if I tasted like almond meal crackers when she first kissed me tonight, she doesn't mention it.

I want to feel relaxed in her arms, yet I can't let down my guard. The little box of a cabin should feel cozy—it's certainly small enough that two bodies heat the interior just fine—but my skin's cooling and the stark decor fails to add any visual warmth.

I try not to look past the end of the bed to where the huge window wall lets in the darkness. Your imagination could take hold of you if you think about what waits outside. It's not the cliff so much that unsettles me. It's the drop.

I roll onto my stomach and press my face into the mattress. The better to hide what I feel.

When I settle, Sydney's hands return to my skin. This time swirling patterns over my back.

The first time she ever kissed me, I wasn't expecting it, but I also wasn't *not* expecting it. I'd had a theory about her for a while—the way she welcomed flirtation from anyone, the way her hungry eyes would drop to my lips every now and then—and I wanted to test it. Halloween was the perfect opportunity, a night to try out different personas without a long-term commitment. I figured if she was going to make a move, a night without inhibitions would be an ideal time to do it.

I dressed as a devil in cherry-red lingerie, and she was a fallen angel in all black. The perfect pair. Sin and redemption.

I didn't let her out of my sight even as the DJ whipped the crowd into a frenzy, and I reveled in the way she couldn't tear her eyes away from my curves.

I don't remember the party as much as I remember after. The way she stumbled into my apartment a little drunk, having dismissed Jeff hours before. The secret thrill of being alone with her and being so close to the real Sydney, the unstaged, unpolished one.

My heart hummed like it would burst out of my skin, nerves and anticipation. I asked if she was thirsty just to have something to do with my hands. When she nodded, I reached into my fridge to grab us some sparkling waters. Then I turned back, and there she was. Eyes luminous and unwavering, mouth parted.

She caught my gaze and that was it. This was happening. My stomach fluttered even as she was kissing me, her mouth all scotch and strawberries. Smoke and sweetness.

Time fell away, and when we finally parted, she rested her forehead against mine with a crazy, stupid grin on her face. Then she had the audacity to crush me as fast as she'd caught me.

"Don't tell," she whispered against my lips.

Stung, I reeled back. "Tell who? Jeff?"

She blinked at me unapologetically, that feline smile still on her lips. "I'm not going to leave him." And that was that.

Sydney kept calling, kept crawling into my bed at night when she got lonely or horny or drunk, when Jeff wasn't enough or just wasn't who she wanted. She brought me to photo shoots, flaunted our friendship, and I watched my social media following explode. But she never once dared to let it slip that I was the person she reached out to in her vulnerable moments. That I was the one she most wanted to kiss.

I hated that I had to come in second to anyone. I still do.

Tonight I wish I could wash it all away, but the old insecurity bubbles to the surface, and I can't help asking a variation of the question I've asked ever since she first kissed me. "Why are you still with him?"

The hand gliding over my skin stops for a beat. Then it keeps going. Sydney takes so long to respond that I'm not sure if she heard me fully. That, or she's ignoring the question again. But something seems to have changed out here in the woods. The circumstances forcing us to leave behind our tired dance of half-truths and excuses.

"I can't believe the OnlyFans thing," she says. "Can you?"

Ugh. That's what she's fixated on? I do not want to think about Jeff posting pictures of his schlong online. Still, it's a chance to test Syd again, to see how much she believes what he's been telling her. "He said he was hacked."

She sighs. "Come on, Cait. Jeff might be a model, but he's not an actor. Even if he was hacked, there's something else going on there too. I saw his face."

"Well, it clearly wasn't bad enough for you to break up with him," I mumble into the sheets, trying to keep the bitterness out of my voice. "So why are you so upset about it?"

She scoffs. "Don't you see? It delegitimizes what we have if he can just give it away to other people."

The words slip out before I can stop them. "What you have or what you're trying to show the world?"

All she's doing is using Jeff as a cover. Sure, the two of them look good together, and they sell a story that's palatable to the masses: a power couple in all their beauty. But when Sydney focuses only on the optics, it makes it all too easy for her to forget about everyone she hurts. I've overlooked a lot about her, because when she turns her attention on me, it's the best feeling in the world. But this part? It fucking sucks.

Sydney's hand skips a beat again, and I continue to press. "Why is it so important that you be in a relationship with him?" What I'm really asking is why it has to be a guy.

"I tried to be open about who I was once before." She lets out a hoarse, self-deprecating laugh. "It was a disaster."

"You mean about liking girls?" I turn my face to the side so I can gauge her reaction, and I catch the way she flinches.

"Yeah, that." She shifts away from me and draws her knees up to her chest. "It's not like I only like girls, but . . ."

"You realize what decade we're in, right? No one's going to judge you."

"You'd be surprised." She goes quiet for a moment, and I think that's it, that's all she's going to say. I'll forever be left in the shadow that her fears have cast over her life, unable to understand this core thing that shaped her. Her truth infuriatingly out of reach. But then a whoosh of air leaves her lungs and she continues. "I had a boyfriend once, back in college, who found out that being a guy didn't necessarily give him a leg up when it came to dating me." She shakes her head, sadness making her voice come out rough and thick. "Before that night, I thought he was going to have staying power. I mean, I really, really liked him. But he couldn't handle the truth. Me being me didn't change how I felt about him, but it changed how he felt about me. And he took it out on me."

My body goes tense. Maybe I'm just as bad as him, not wanting to hear the truth. But I've come this far for answers, and I know I need to ask. No cowards here. "Physically?"

Sydney wipes at her cheeks and nods. My heart tumbles. That can't be true. "So, yeah, maybe I keep Jeff around for a reason, even when he messes up. It's not to hurt you. It's to protect me."

I feel like I might be sick.

I can't unknow her history now, can't unfeel her pain. Maybe she kept it from me all this time because she knew it would hurt me.

Sydney's not going to change. There's not going to be some big moment when she tells the world about us. There was never a scenario in which she'd tell the truth.

I'm always going to come in second place.

Sydney bends down and presses a kiss between my shoulder blades. "Don't worry," she whispers against my skin. "You still have me."

It's not the consolation prize it used to be.

53

LUCY

A scream tears through the silent forest and jolts me awake in my bed. I bolt upright into the morning light, disoriented and afraid, my heart pounding so hard it squeezes the breath from my lungs. Ice in the air, ice in my veins.

What happened?

Another scream comes from right outside my cabin, and now I can place the sound. It's the scream that made Sydney famous in her college film debut. We joked about it then: terror porn. The joy of watching pretty girls scream.

Only there's nothing funny about it now.

I'm out of bed before I can think, shoving my feet into a pair of slippers with Reverie's logo on the toes. Outside within thirty seconds.

My teeth chatter as the air hits me. First the air, and then the sight: Sydney has dropped to her knees in the snow, wearing barely more than jeans and some lingerie. In front of her, the door to her cabin hangs open like an angry maw.

Something very, very bad must have happened in there for her to be shivering out here like she is.

I pelt across the snow to her, fear dripping down my back. "What's going on?"

She keeps shaking, her body racked by involuntary gasps.

I touch her shoulder and she flinches away, another ragged scream ripping from her throat. Her eyes don't move from the darkness beyond the door.

"Stay here," I tell her. "You're safe."

Footsteps crunch in the background, and Caitlyn's calling "Sydney!" from behind me, but I'm already moving toward the cabin. I need to protect Sydney from whatever's put that horrified expression on her face.

I pause in the doorway to listen, but it's eerily quiet inside. From here the room looks . . . brutalized. It's the only word for it. Clothes are strewn over the furniture and floor, and a tub of supplements has exploded, scattering dozens of shiny blue pills underfoot.

Sipping in some air, I step inside. "Hello?" I call out, which I then realize is utterly stupid because if someone in here wants to hurt me, I've just announced my exact location. I grab the nearest thing I can find for protection—a fifteen-pound kettlebell that Jeff must have brought with him. If I need to, maybe I can swing it at someone? My cheeks heat, but any embarrassment washes away when I take another step and come within view of the bed.

Oh god.

If I hadn't heard Sydney scream, I could have mistakenly thought Jeff's sleeping. He's sprawled on his back in the king-size bed with his eyes closed. But as I look closer, it's impossible not to miss all the things wrong with this picture. The twisted bedsheets, the fitted bottom sheet ripped up at the corners.

Marks on the wall where the headboard must have dug into the soft wood over and over. Jeff's dislodged sling, his arm wrenched at an impossible angle and the skin of his neck rubbed raw.

He's exceedingly still. Deathly still.

He's also stunningly naked.

Oh shit.

Hands land on my shoulders, and I shriek and drop the kettlebell. So much for that.

"Don't look," Caitlyn says. She spins me away from the bed. "It was bad enough you had to see Nash. You don't want to see this too."

I press a hand against my chest, trying to calm my racing heart. "I didn't hear you come in." I look over my shoulder toward Jeff, but she gently grabs my chin.

"Eyes on me."

"He's—" I start, but I can't finish. My breath's all tight and jerky, my lungs uncooperative.

Caitlyn nods, her face full of pity. "Looks like it. What the fuck is going on?"

I can feel my eyes grow wide. "He didn't smoke a joint too, did he?"

"After Nash? He wasn't that dumb."

"Then what happened?" Panic takes over my body. I think of Sydney, outside in the snow, and suddenly I need to hear it from her.

I rip out of Caitlyn's grasp and stumble back outside on shaky legs. Sydney's poised where I left her, tears shining on her cheeks. She must be freezing—it feels like the cold's settled into my bones. But she still sits there as if frozen in shock, the snow turning the knees of her jeans dark and wet.

"Syd?" I ask tentatively.

Strands of her dark hair are plastered against her forehead in disarray. Her skin so, so pale in contrast. "I found him like that," she whispers.

"When you woke up?" I ask.

She looks up at me with glazed eyes. "Just now."

That doesn't make sense. Unless Jeff had a silent heart attack last night, she would have heard whatever happened to him. So why would she say she just found him?

"But you were together last night." It's a question more than a statement.

Sydney softens her voice like she's delivering a blow. "I was with Caitlyn."

I don't know why it hurts. Sydney's a big girl, and she doesn't owe me anything. Last night, I was the one who left the Lodge first, on my own. But she could have come to me as easily as she could have found Caitlyn.

My chest feels like a raw wound that someone's poured rubbing alcohol into. "You weren't here?" I pinch the bridge of my nose, mostly so I can feel something and ground myself. Everything's spiraling out of control.

"I mean, for a minute, yes. After everyone left the Lodge. We came back here. I took a shower, Jeff passed out, and I left."

It sounds so simple, but there's so much missing. "What time?"

"I don't know!" Sydney bursts out. "I wasn't looking at a fucking clock!"

A possibility opens up in front of me, one that rattles me to my core. There's a period of time when Sydney was unaccounted for. She wasn't with me and she wasn't with Caitlyn. So she could have done this.

No. I fling the idea from my head like I'm shaking spiders off a rug. Don't dare say it out loud.

I have to believe Sydney's telling the truth and that when she left, Jeff was asleep but alive. I know for sure I heard banging, though. Which means what I overheard when I brought myself to that exquisite orgasm . . .

I wasn't listening to Jeff have sex with Sydney. I was listening to him die.

54

LUCY

He fought back." The words slip out before I can stop them, but now that my mind's putting the pieces together, it makes sense. The cabin showing signs of a struggle, the sounds I overheard. Jeff didn't smoke a joint or have a heart attack or accidentally mix the wrong supplements together.

He was murdered.

It takes everything in me not to throw up in the snow.

Nash is dead and Jeff is dead. We're being picked off like we're in one of Sydney's horror movies. One death could be a terrible accident. But two spell something far more sinister.

I want someone to tell me I'm wrong, that I imagined everything that happened last night. But the absolute revulsion on Sydney's face makes me realize how wrong my words came out. If you take them the wrong way, it could make it seem like I was there. Like I was responsible.

"I overheard . . . something," I hurry to add. The idea of recounting the specifics makes my cheeks burn with humiliation, but it doesn't matter anyway. They're drawing away from me,

Caitlyn placing a protective hand on Sydney's shoulder and guiding her to her feet. Horror on both their faces.

Oh shit.

We're in so far over our heads, and now they're starting to doubt me.

"We need to call someone," I say, trying to bring them to my side. Whatever happened to Jeff wasn't my doing. And if they were together, then it wasn't their doing either. I need to help them see there's something dangerous out there so we can work together to get ourselves out of this mess. "Do either of you have your phones?" In my rush when Syd screamed, I didn't grab anything other than my slippers.

Caitlyn's eyes narrow. "You know there's no signal," she says flatly.

"In the Lodge." I take a halting step toward my cabin, the snow reaching over the tops of my feet. Somehow it's gotten so deep. "We can see if Wi-Fi's working," I call over my shoulder.

"No."

"No?" I whip my head toward Caitlyn, who's put herself between me and Syd.

Sydney's eyes are huge and round as she looks at us.

"Clearly you misunderstood. Sydney was with me last night." An oil-slick shimmer of smugness floats on Caitlyn's words. "Our movements are accounted for."

The implication is obvious, and cold blooms inside my chest. "You don't think I did this?"

"Oh, Luce." Her face twists with a mix of pity and disgust, and I feel like I did when I woke up after dying—like everyone knew something about me I didn't. "We were together. Don't you see? It had to be you."

But that's impossible.

Panic rises, cold and sharp. "I didn't kill Jeff! What reason would I have?"

"I don't know, Luce." Caitlyn draws this out like she's enjoying it. "Maybe because you're clingy and pathetic and would do whatever it takes to keep poor Sydney protected from anyone who might hurt her. Jeff just messed up big-time, and maybe this was your way of setting things right." She flashes a cold grin. "Or maybe you're just jealous of everyone who's closer to Sydney than you, and you wanted her to yourself."

"Are you kidding me?" I look at Sydney for backup, but she drops her eyes, the corner of her mouth pulling to the side. It's a tell: she almost always looks like this when she's about to cry.

But why? Because she hates doubting me? Or because she knows what really happened?

The thought makes my stomach turn over, a tiny bit of doubt that I can't dismiss. Caitlyn can claim they were together all she wants, but they weren't together the entire night.

Just thinking that makes me feel like a traitor.

"There's someone else out there," I say, my voice wooden. That has to be it. The other possibility is too horrifying to contemplate.

"Who?" Caitlyn asks.

"I don't know! Maybe the person with the gun."

"If they had a gun," Caitlyn volleys back, "why not just shoot him?"

I reel back, unable to answer. I hate how she's so logical and dispassionate. Why can't she just say she's confused or that she's scared? Wouldn't that tiny show of weakness be better than pitting us all against one another?

No matter what I say or how I try to defend myself, arguing feels like an impossible task. I know how things look, how they add up. When it comes to me and Syd, Caitlyn's always going to believe Syd over me. I'm just the original best friend, the one who came along as part of a package deal when Caitlyn first started hanging out with Sydney.

I don't blame Caitlyn for where her imagination's taking her; I can't.

But Sydney . . .

Sydney's always had my back the way I had hers. But not now.

"This is the second of my boyfriends who died," Sydney intones, her gaze distant before she snaps it to me like a whip.

That look flays me open. Because there's doubt in there. Like I can't be trusted.

Right now, Syd's picking Caitlyn. Not me.

"I promise I didn't do this!" I cry, but it's not enough. I stand there gasping in pain, tears blurring my vision while Caitlyn wraps an arm around Sydney. My best friend, with her ribs pressed against the thin lace of her bodysuit. Her hair a cloud of disarray around her face.

And then Caitlyn smooths back that hair, sweeps it over one of Syd's shoulders. The bruise it's been hiding winks out to taunt me. Not a bruise—a hickey. One that wasn't there when we parted ways last night.

Caitlyn looks up and catches my eye, her face shifting into an expression of self-righteous satisfaction. She wanted me to see the marks she's left behind, to prove the claim she has on Sydney.

I spent the night with Caitlyn, Sydney said.

And this is how she meant.

It's enough to make my hope flag, my shoulders drop. I need to find another way to convince them I didn't hurt Jeff, but first, I need to regroup.

Stung and ashamed, I rush toward my cabin, snow spilling into my slippers as I go.

Sydney has every chance to stop me before I reach the door.

But she doesn't say a word.

55

CAITLYN

I turn Sydney in my arms, gathering her in a hug while I watch Lucy retreat behind Syd's back. She's hunched over against the wind, a pathetic little hitch in her breath as she races toward her cabin.

Fucking Lucy. Looking manic and desperate, with those big Cancer Girl eyes. We're all strung out and terrified, but she was making things worse for everyone. At least now she's gone.

"Cait," Sydney says, shivering against me. It's a question and a plea. She's so close I can still smell the sex on her skin. She tries to hide her reaction, but she's in my arms, so I feel her flinch when Lucy slams her cabin door closed.

"We need to get inside. Get you some dry clothes."

Syd nods and steps back, glancing warily at the door to her cabin, which yawns open against the wood siding.

I have no desire to be back in that room with Jeff's body, but we've already been outside for ages. The cold could be just as deadly as whoever killed Jeff. I've got to get Sydney warm.

I lead the way forward, trudging through drifts of snow that crunch and sigh under my feet. Sydney stiffens further with each approaching step until we're at the threshold of her cabin and her limbs have locked in fear.

"You know what?" I blow out a breath. "We're not going to do this. You have your phone?" Sydney nods. "Lucy might have been right about the Lodge. Let's see what we can find there. Maybe we can make a call."

Relief breaks over her face, which makes me feel the tiniest bit steadier. Nothing that's happened this weekend is okay, but at least we have a plan and some actions to take. If we can't get a phone call through, then we'll make a new plan. We'll just keep moving forward until we can't anymore. But it's better than sitting still and waiting for more terrible things to happen to us.

We make it all the way to the Lodge without hearing Lucy's door open again, which makes me think we have a little time to set things right.

The big building's dark when we step inside, the morning light barely lancing the deep shadows that have gathered in the corners of the room. I hit the light switch by the front door to no effect.

"Power's out," I announce. I tap the switch a few more times to be sure. "Fucking great."

The room's cold too. Not freezing enough for my breath to come out in little puffs, but cold enough to be uncomfortable. It's a huge space, and that wall of windows is doing nothing to keep in the heat. Just like everything in this place, it's been designed for looks and not function. I shouldn't have expected anything else.

"No power means no Wi-Fi," Sydney muses beside me. Her fingertips land on my arm, shockingly cold. I turn over my hand so she can nestle hers inside it. Then I tug her toward the windows and settle her in one of the sculpted wooden chairs.

This close to the glass, it's brighter and easier to see. Sydney perches there, beautiful and tragic, a line of light tracing her features. Even terrified, she's captivating.

If Lucy were here, she would want to take pictures. I wouldn't blame her. There's something ephemeral about this moment, like if I don't pin it down, it'll be lost. It's just me and Syd and a sliver of calm inside an unfolding tragedy. Still, as beguiling as Syd is, there's a part of me that hangs back and won't let myself fall into the chair with her. A whisper of a thought in the back of my mind.

Sydney said she wouldn't leave her relationship with Jeff, but what if those were empty words meant to throw me off? After all, with the OnlyFans account still running and Jeff's naked pictures splashed everywhere online, he had just outlived his usefulness.

I cringe internally.

Poor choice of words, but there's still a *there* there. I was alone last night until Sydney showed up, so what really happened in Jeff's room is a mystery.

"You shouldn't have done that," Sydney says. I'm still lost in the whirling vortex of my mind, trying to untangle last night, and for a brief moment, I think she means I shouldn't have doubted her. My heart stutters, wondering if she's going to turn against me. But then she says, "If the power's out, Lucy's going to get cold."

I hate that everything comes back to Lucy.

"You really want her here?" I ask, not hiding the skepticism in my voice.

Syd lifts her doe eyes to mine. "She'll freeze."

"It wouldn't be the worst thing," I huff out.

"Cait!" she gasps, but there's a hint of a laugh behind her surprise. Gallows humor at its finest.

"Look," I say, "you can't really believe her wild theories about someone else being out there. Even if someone wanted to risk getting caught in the snowstorm, we'd see them coming. There's a literal cliff on one side of us and limited ways to approach the Lodge. You'd see their footsteps in the snow."

"I still don't like the idea of her freezing out there."

I sigh. "She'll come in before it comes to that. She's got a goddamned key." The idea makes my stomach sink. She could be literally anywhere. Not exactly ideal for the person who probably killed Jeff.

I don't think Lucy would harm Sydney. There's too much history there, too much unchecked adoration between them. But who's to say she won't come for me?

I'm not going to let her hurt me. I've spent too much time creating this life, working my ass off to climb to the top—of my career, of this industry. To die here on this mountain with Nash and Jeff would be unspeakably grim. There's no way I'm going to let it happen.

If it's between me and Lucy, I'm always going to pick me. But I can't protect myself if I'm not prepared.

I drift away from Sydney, making a show of grabbing some food in the kitchen to bring back to her. Opening drawers, taking a casual assessment of the inventory.

I can't slide one of those sharp, shiny knives into my pocket without alarming Sydney. But I can make absolutely sure I know where they all are.

If it comes down to it, I'll be ready.

56

LUCY

Before I knew Sydney, back when we were just roommates and she was a stranger to me, it didn't matter what she thought of me. I'd watch this pretty girl come and go from her classes, draping herself dramatically over furniture or nodding along to music as she studied lines for the theater majors' next performance. She was enigmatic, sure, but I was equally unknown to her. If she was indifferent to me or, worse, didn't like me, so be it. We'd be able to pick new roommates sophomore year, when everyone had found their way and drifted into friend groups. But then, surprisingly, Sydney looked at my photos that night and befriended me like we were always going to find each other.

Once I was her friend, it mattered to me what she thought. I didn't care about the little stuff, of course—like when she teased me about my thrift-store finds or when it grossed her out that I like the anchovies in traditional Caesar salad dressing. But on the big topics, the ones that define what kind of person someone is, yeah. Her opinion meant something to me.

When I slump against my cabin door, a sob caught in my

chest, I'm terrified that Sydney's reaction outside—her lack of care, the way she turned to Caitlyn instead of me—means her opinion of me is wavering. It was bad enough for her to be mad at me for hiding my connection to Reverie, but at least that was something I actually did. I didn't kill Jeff, and I hate that she might think I did. I don't want to lose her. Maybe I should be more concerned about someone coming after me than about worrying what Syd thinks, and a small, simmering part of me is. But I need Sydney to believe me. Trust in each other is the only thing that's going to get us through.

I need to prove I didn't do this.

My mind whirls, searching for ways to absolve myself, catching time and again on the word *proof.*

Proof.

That's it.

Maybe I can uncover some evidence hiding in the crime scene that points at my innocence. I might not have forensic tools, but I do have one thing no one else here has: my camera.

I exchange my pajamas and slippers for a sweatshirt, jeans, two pairs of socks, and sneakers. Then I slip my camera strap over my head and stride back into the snow, being careful not to step too close to the perimeter of Jeff's cabin and wipe out any footprints already there.

The snow holds the memory of the disturbances, crystalized in clear footprints and shuffled sweeps of powder. There's where Sydney's knees landed on the ground a few feet past the cabin door. There are her handprints, small and crisp.

I take pictures of it all, just like I did with Nash.

Sydney's slick-soled flats tiptoeing into her cabin, the longer strides as she ran back out.

My footsteps stopping next to Sydney's knee prints, dancing side to side while I tried to help. Another trail where I pushed past her, a distinctive star print from the heel of each of my slippers.

Caitlyn's stupid booties, the heels making spiky points in the snow. Stepping right into my footsteps in some places, like a dagger plunged straight through a heart.

The footprints all converge by the front door, funneling inside the cabin so it becomes impossible to tell whose steps have landed where. The blurry edges make some footprints warp and grow. Underneath everything lie other, less distinct footprints that must be Jeff's. The idea that those were his last steps, his last marks on the world, makes a chill slide under my skin.

What happened to him? Did someone strangle him? Suffocate him? With his arm immobilized and vodka and Benadryl in his system, he would have had a harder time fighting back against an attack. In that state, killing Jeff wouldn't require a show of brute strength. Which means anyone could have done it.

The thought makes me snap pictures more quickly, a prickle of awareness rippling down my spine to remind me that I'm out here alone and defenseless. When I've photographed the scene from every angle I can, I approach the cabin. Walk up the front steps, rigid with fear. I want to make myself go inside and finish the job I started, but poised by the door, my heart pounds and pounds.

It's so chillingly silent.

Just inside, Jeff's lying there, his chest still, his heart refusing to beat.

I try to tell myself that I've seen his body already; surely I can steel myself to do it again.

But I don't want to.

Death's chased me for years, coming for me, for my fellow cancer patients. For Breaker and for Nash and now for Jeff.

How much trauma must I relive to prove my point? To show Sydney that this wasn't me? No. I'll leave this scene to the police, who will surely come after me. I can protect the fragile thing inside me that's had enough.

Shaking my head, I back away from the door. I don't want to be here anymore. Not this cabin, not this retreat. Hell, not the Catskills.

Before I knew what would unfold here, I stupidly craved this vacation. Ran toward it with open arms, trying to escape my life. But now all I want to do is go back, back, back. Pack myself onto the Bash Bus and cruise toward New York without another thought about this place. Slide back into my apartment and into my life.

I snap the lens cap back on and hurry toward my cabin. The forest is eerily quiet. Watching. Waiting. It's just my breath puffing out of me and my heartbeat in my ears.

Inside the cabin, I double-check that the door is locked behind me. Then I start to throw my bags together, packing away everything I unpacked over the past few days. My phone's not fully charged, but I tuck it into my pocket like a lifeline. I don't know how or when we're getting out of here, but I'm going to be ready to leave the moment I can.

When everything is packed, I sink onto the foot of my bed and stare out at the vast landscape of bare trees and white snow. Someone's out there, causing harm. If I left, just grabbed the essentials and walked on out of here, would I make it to town in one piece? Or would whatever happened to Brent befall me too?

I'm not ready to find out, and the invisible thread of loyalty that binds me to Sydney is still wrapped around my heart. Whatever misgivings I might have about her involvement—stupid ones, I tell myself, trying to tamp down the doubt—I can't abandon her. In all my toughest moments, she stuck with me. I don't have enough information yet to cut and run.

Shivering, I yank down the sleeves of my sweatshirt. The clothes I put on earlier protected me against the deep chill of being outside, shocked and afraid. But as the adrenaline wears off, I realize how cold it is in here. When I push off the bed and examine the thermostat, I find that it's dead. Just a blank screen, none of its previous reassuring electronic glow.

The power's out, and my growling stomach reminds me that all the food's in the Lodge.

I'm caught between waiting it out and going for help, but with a sigh, I stand and grab my camera bag, heading for the door.

The safety of the cabin's an illusion—I could freeze or starve before help comes. I'm not thrilled about leaving, but I can't stay here.

57

CAITLYN

Do you think Brent's coming back?" Sydney glances at me from her spot beside the windows, and I yank my hand back from underneath the kitchen tap.

The bread knife that Jeff was so busy carrying around lies in the bottom of the sink, glistening with promise. It's wet but otherwise pristine—someone must have tossed it there without thought. I can imagine the heft of it in my hands, the weight. A smooth, cool grip. The sharp serrated blade.

The desire to protect myself is so strong that my fingers ache to reach out for the knife, but instead I smooth my hands over my thighs and stride across the room to Syd.

I kneel gently beside her chair and ask, "Do you?"

Stifling a sniff, she shakes her head. "We're going to have to go for help."

I nod, because of course it was coming to this. But we're not ready yet. "You're soaking wet." I touch the hem of Sydney's jeans to make my point, the stiff fabric damp from the knees down. "You need to warm up first."

As if the concept of the cold is just catching up with her, she starts to shiver. "About that." A sad smile plays on her lips as she flicks her gaze to the overhead lights that are completely useless without power.

It's uncomfortable seeing her like this. Syd the optimist, finally struck down by the reality of how cruel life can be.

At points in our relationship, I've wanted her to be more grounded, to understand that she—that *we*—live in a bubble of privilege. Now I'm not so sure I like the effect.

"We can build a fire." I blow out a breath and nod toward the fireplace, which rises in the center of the room, a behemoth of rough-hewn stone. Nash mentioned it burned wood, and that's the hope I'm clinging to. If it's an electric one, we're shit outta luck.

Syd stays put while I examine the fireplace, circling around it a few times. While there are grates on both sides—one facing the Lodge's dining area, one the living space—only the dining side can be opened.

I pry the grate from the stone and snag a fingernail in the process.

Frowning, I mutter to Syd, "You owe me a manicure."

She just blinks at me, long tear-soaked lashes brushing her cheeks.

An irrational anger starts to buzz behind my ribs. I wish she'd do something other than sit there. I know she's in shock, but it's like she's waiting for me to rescue her instead of doing anything to help herself. From the time I was born, I've had to figure things out for myself so I could keep up with the rest of my family. If you couldn't adapt, you didn't get to join in.

It's not fair of me, but I'm disappointed in Sydney. Maybe this is what the whole world does to her—fits her into the image of who they think she should be instead of who she really is. You can't be everything to everybody, and, out of everyone, I should understand that no one could live up to those unreasonable expectations. But right now, when it counts, she's not living up to the flawless reputation she's built online. What hurts is that I want her to be competent. I want to imagine she could save herself—and save me too. That it's worth it to try. Her doing nothing feels like she's giving up on us.

A sour taste coats the back of my mouth as I turn away from her. I reach into the firebox to see if I can feel a breeze, but I can't quite tell if there's fresh air coming through.

Of course it wouldn't be that easy.

Since there's no hearth, I drop onto the ground and start to wriggle the upper half of my body into the firebox.

"What are you doing?" Syd calls.

Panting with effort, I lean my head back out. "Checking that the flue is open." A confused twist of her lips. "If the flue's closed, smoke can't get out the chimney, and it all comes back into the building."

"Oh."

Oh. I duck my head inside the firebox to hide the way I roll my eyes.

We might be Reverie's inaugural guests, but someone has definitely lit a fire in here before. The faint smell of smoke lingers in the cool stone chimney, and I can practically feel the ashes and soot sinking into my pores and ruining the clothes I tugged on when Syd left my bed this morning. "Scratch that—you owe me a new outfit too."

It doesn't matter that she can't hear me; it feels good to say the words anyway.

Craning my neck, I look up and see a patch of gray sky at the top of the chimney.

A hit of relief rushes through me.

Sliding out, I tell Sydney we're good to go. For that part, anyway.

"How'd you learn all this?"

The memories come fast and sharp: tents pitched under a blanket of stars, my brothers and my dad sitting beside me late at night when there was nothing else to do except roast marshmallows and go to bed. My father's guidance and the crackle of a fire that I built with my own hands. The sweet heat of flames on our faces while cool air caressed our backs. How wild I felt out there in nature. How free.

The first year after my dad remarried, we had to settle for a "glamping" trip with Susan and Cole. Something low-key to ease Susan in. Secretly, it wasn't terrible to have an actual bed to sleep in, but we forgot to check the flue in the cabin and ended up having smoke pour back into the room and choke us until we could smother the fire and open the flue again.

Big mistake. My eyes itched for days. That was the trip when I got close to Cole, though. He was near enough to me in age that he didn't exclude me like my older brothers sometimes did, and we quickly discovered we shared a sense of humor that made everything seem better, even hair that smelled like a campfire.

I don't tell Sydney any of that. It feels too private to share. Instead I fold the memories tinier and tinier, like a napkin balled in my fist and hidden out of sight.

"Camping" is all I say, but it was so much more than that. It was a lesson in survival.

It feels good to know I can take care of myself—that, at the very least, I can start this fire. I'm less confident, though, about what else might be thrown my way.

"We need to get wood," I announce, but I don't bother asking Syd to join me. She's useless right now.

I leave her there and creep down the stairs toward the garage, holding my breath to better hear if anyone's inside the Lodge with us. Because, god, how cruel would it be to find myself offed by someone lying in wait while I'm trying to be a hero.

That sour taste floods my mouth again, and I realize it's not disgust, it's fear.

I should have grabbed the knife when I had the chance.

Something creaks nearby, one of those sounds whose origins are impossible to pinpoint. It could be Sydney overhead.

It could be someone right beside me.

Fuck. I'm freaking myself out.

If I'm not careful, fear's going to immobilize me, so I squash the queasy dread deep inside me and bury it like a body.

I have to get through this—I *will.*

Heart racing, I wait for what feels like an eternity before I move on. I need to get to that stack of wood I saw in the garage, allergies be damned. Light a fire, heat Syd and myself up, and move on to the next plan.

But when I finally sneak past the meditation room and reach for the garage door handle, it doesn't budge.

The door is locked tight as a trap.

Mother. Fucker. We need Lucy after all.

58

LUCY

If they don't let me in, I don't know what I'm going to do.

I rap against the door again, the cold and the wood stinging my bare knuckles. I'm trying to let Sydney and Caitlyn come to me rather than barging in and scaring the shit out of them. For all I know, the door's already unlocked, but if I go in on my own, it'll be a violation of whatever tenuous trust we have left.

I need to be invited.

But no one's coming.

My insides roil with dread as the silence stretches out. What if something terrible's already happened inside?

I still don't understand how we've come to this—our party of six reduced to three. The three of us left pitted against one another while we run out of everything: food, hope, time.

I lift my hand to knock a third time and almost fall through the doorway when it cracks open.

Caitlyn stands on the other side, shifting warily on her feet. She looks strung out and terrified, her normally perfect hair rumpled and a smudge of something dark on her cheek.

Any words I had prepared dissolve before my mouth can shape them. What am I supposed to say? *Hi, it's me, I know you think I killed Jeff, but please let me in.*

I crane my neck to try to see around her, wanting to catch a glimpse of Sydney so I can confirm she's okay. Or as okay as one can be, given the circumstances.

I can't see anything over Caitlyn's shoulder, and she flinches as I accidentally step too close.

Trying to fill the awkward silence, I blurt out the first thing I can think of. "Power out here too?"

She gives me a tight nod to confirm. Hesitation flickers over her face, and she lets out a huff. "We need to build a fire. And the garage with all the wood is locked." Her mouth twists in displeasure. "You've got the key, right?"

"Yeah."

Caitlyn opens the door wider and waves me inside.

Shame burns my ears. The only reason she's letting me in is because she doesn't have another choice. She and Syd need me, so she'll take her chances with me. But it doesn't mean Cait's happy about it.

At least I know where I stand.

I find Sydney sitting by the window, her eyes glazed. "You okay?" I ask.

She shrugs and manages a weak smile. "Girl Scout Cait over here has the fireplace ready for us. We just need some wood."

The corner of my mouth slides halfway up in a grin. "That's what I hear. Shall we?" I offer her a hand and haul her to her feet. Then the three of us tiptoe toward the stairs.

We don't talk about the circumstances pushing us apart.

We just focus on what needs to be done.

The garage feels like an icebox, or an igloo. A chill's seeped into the room from outside, and it's even colder down here than upstairs. Not quite see-your-breath temperature, but close.

Across the room, my eye catches on the pegboard of wicked instruments. Seeing them makes me glad I have the skeleton key and that I locked up before I left last time. It's not that I was trying to withhold the wood, of course. But all those sharp objects frighten me—the idea that anyone could have access to them. That they could be used against me.

Tamping down a shiver, I grab the waxed-canvas firewood carrier that's pegged to the wall beside the stack of firewood. I throw it on the ground to start loading it, but it's only big enough to carry about six logs. Syd and Cait reach for some wood, but there's no good way to grab it. The logs are all splinters and peeling bark, awkward and dangerous to lift.

"Ouch!" Caitlyn hisses, sucking the pad of her thumb into her mouth.

"Splinter?"

When she confirms my suspicions, I suggest that we rotate who gets to carry the sling. It's heavy, slow going, but we all share the burden, making multiple trips to ferry stacks of wood upstairs. Even Syd helps, moving like a zombie.

"At least the exertion's warming me up," Caitlyn quips as we deposit our third load of wood beside the fireplace.

I shoot her a tentative, grateful smile. Even her complaints are better than the terse silence.

"This should be enough to get us started," I tell her.

She nods and goes to the bathroom, returning with a handful of toilet paper. Then she starts arranging the skinniest pieces of wood in the fireplace, building a triangle formation with the tissue tucked into the center.

"We need a way to start this," she calls over her shoulder.

"Right!" I sound all too eager to get back into her good graces, considering I don't trust her. She had as much motivation to kill Jeff as anyone else here. Sydney was mad at him because of the whole OnlyFans thing, but Jeff was the lover standing between Sydney and Caitlyn. What if Caitlyn got greedy and wanted Syd for herself? I know she technically didn't have an opportunity to hurt him and that my theory's baseless, but it's that little pinprick of *what if* that still needles me.

"What did you use to light those tea lights the other night, Syd?"

"Jeff's lighter." Her devastated expression confirms there's no way we're going back to her cabin to find it. Guess it's up to me.

I make sure she's sitting before the fireplace, toss a protein bar at her, and tell her to eat. Then I back away toward the line of closets to begin my search. I don't need the key anymore—I left everything except the garage unlocked last time—but it still feels reassuring in my pocket.

I start with the storage room beside the bathroom, where I remember seeing tea lights. We didn't find matches during our first search, but surely they'd be stored with the candles. At least, if it were following any sort of logic.

Come on, Meghan. Why'd you make this so hard? I love my cousin, but this place needs a ton of work before it'll actually be ready for guests. I'm the one who hurried along the timeline for this trip because I was so desperate for an escape from my life, suggesting Meghan host the weekend as a preview of the grounds. It's clear she could have used the extra time to get the retreat as polished as she planned. Another reason for me to feel guilty.

Slipping into the closet, I leave the door partially shut behind me. Opened wide enough that I can hear anyone coming, but also closed enough to feel like I can breathe. There are no helpful matches or fire starters among the soft folds of the linens or the curves of the plates and cups, although I suppose we could burn a towel or two if we could actually start a fire, and if it came to that.

There's nothing useful nestled between the glistening forks and spoons either, though when I bend down to examine their bin more closely, I accidentally bump into the shelving unit behind me. I grab the edge of a swaying shelf to steady it, and the whole unit groans in protest.

For the love of god, please don't let this thing collapse on me.

Spinning to assess the damage, my gaze snags on something on the top shelf. There's something out of place, half-hidden by a hand towel. It normally wouldn't have caught my eye, but I must have exposed it when I bumped the shelf. Now the broken line and bowed plastic stand out in the otherwise orderly space.

I rise onto my tiptoes, cursing my shortness while I stretch to reach it. My fingers scrabble against the plastic before I finally get purchase and can ease the item off the shelf.

It takes me a long minute of staring at the plastic box before I realize what it is. For one, it's not something I look at all the time. And two, its original shape has been mangled. But the moment I put the pieces together, understanding dawns on me, followed by the deepest sense of betrayal.

We've been waiting so desperately to make contact with the outside world, but there's no hope of the internet coming back. Not here.

The router in my hand's been smashed beyond repair.

59

STORY POST

Reverie Retreat—Day 3

The light has always loved Sydney Kent. It caresses her now, a warm, flickering glow that dances across her skin and catches red undertones in her dark hair.

She's sitting in profile, facing the light, while the rest of the room is bathed in silky darkness. The effect of her in these conditions is as dramatic and timeless as an oil painting, and you could get lost in the sheer beauty of the moment. The pillowy slope of her lips. The white lace she wears, offering alluring glimpses of her skin. The swell of her breasts, the curve of her collarbones.

This is why you flip to her stories over and over; you never know what you'll get, but it's always intriguing. You want to know what she eats and wears, the exercises she does, the skin care products she uses. So, yeah, maybe sometimes you want to borrow a little of what makes her *her.* It's kind of the point.

But when Sydney turns to face the camera, you almost recoil. Everything you thought you saw in profile was an illusion. Head-on, she looks shell-shocked, with tracks of tears down her cheeks. Her hair hasn't been carefully styled into waves; it's tangled and limp at the same time.

You can't look away, pinned in place by the vicious satisfaction of seeing someone so unattainable brought down a peg or two. *Welcome to the real world, Syd.*

The second you think it, guilt slinks in and you want to take it back. Despite it all, your heart tugs a bit because she's an absolute mess.

"What?" she asks hoarsely.

A tiny, metallic crunching sound issues from her right hand, and when you look, you notice she's holding the distinctive wrapper of one of those Zyng energy bars.

Huh. Even after her last tirade, she's still eating them, absentmindedly brushing crumbs from her fingertips. Does that mean she's accepted her fate? Was her other post just some twisted publicity stunt?

No one answers Sydney, and she scowls. A hard edge slides into her voice. "I couldn't care less about my audience. That's all make-believe. What's happening here feels too real."

Okay, ouch.

She does know that the entire reason she gets to show up online for a living is because of her audience support, right?

She's not stupid, and something about this isn't sitting right with you. Has the pressure of the spotlight finally reached her? Is she cracking à la Queen Britney Spears and the unfortunate umbrella incident (bless her heart)?

Clearly Sydney's going through something, so you'll offer her a sliver of compassion. But given how much she's always thanking her audience—like, literally, two days ago she went on that whole spiel—your trust in her is feeling a little strained. You can't tell if you should be worried or pissed or curious, because there's always the possibility that this is leading to something bigger, in that mystical Sydney Kent way.

You settle on all the feelings, making room for anger and pity and fascination to sit side by side in your chest.

Sydney's story ends, and you're left holding your phone, disgruntled. You can't believe that's it; that's the whole story.

Sighing, you wonder what games she might be playing. But, of course, you'll watch again.

You need to see what happens next.

60

LUCY

For once, I'm glad when Caitlyn ignores me. Ever since I returned to the living room ten minutes ago, bearing a glass apothecary jar filled with green-tipped matches, she's avoided my eyes, busying herself with lighting the fire and then staring at the flames as if daring them to sputter out.

I can't believe she hasn't noticed how much I'm shaking, but I'm glad nonetheless. Whoever smashed the router—and god, when did they do it?—didn't want anyone to know they'd stranded us here without hope. It's obvious from the way the fractured pieces were hidden. Someone meant to cut us off from the world. They meant for us to be vulnerable.

I've been trying to pretend that Nash's and Jeff's deaths could have been accidents, because it's an easier thought to swallow than murder. The more I try to see it that way, though, the less my excuse holds up. No one could have predicted the way the snow would strand us, but cutting off the Wi-Fi was deliberate and planned—an inside job. The problem is I don't know when the router was destroyed. We last had Wi-Fi right before Nash died, which means anyone except him could have done it.

But who?

If it was Brent or Jeff, it would be terrible, but it would also be less frightening than having it be one of the women sitting in this suffocating room with me. I want to be able to trust them, but I know I shouldn't.

I feel so desperately alone that I want to cry.

I've done a lot of things in my life on my own, whether by choice or by circumstance. There are some things you simply can't face with other people. I've sat isolated in radiation rooms, the environment too toxic for healthy people to survive but where the doctors promised that same toxicity would be the trick to healing me. I've willingly taken on a poison that would kill the cancer and only just spare my life.

Hell, death was the ultimate solo mission.

But through all those experiences, people who loved me waited in the wings. Sydney and my mother. Nick and Oboe and a whole community of fellow cancer patients.

Now, though, I've cut myself off from everyone who loves me. Nick's not waiting for me anymore because I pushed him away. Sydney's here, but impossible to talk to because there's that tiny *what if* about Jeff.

I tuck my hands beneath my legs and close my eyes, trying to force away tears. If I can't get it together, Caitlyn and Sydney are going to start asking questions about why it took me so long to get the matches and what I might have found that has me so shaken.

I went through the motions after I discovered the router—returning it to the top shelf and hiding it behind a stack of towels, continuing my search until I found matches in a separate closet with the cleaning supplies (of course not with the tea lights or taper candles; why should we be rational?)—because I didn't want to raise suspicion. But now that I'm sitting with everyone, my hands keep trembling and my pulse is wild. I should have locked those closets back up when I had the chance. None of this would have happened if the router were out of reach.

"Hey." I open my eyes and Sydney's right there, standing over me, her voice soft and cautious.

Eight years of friendship, and I've seen her in all her moods. I want to believe I know Sydney better than anyone, but when I try to read her, all I sense is nervous energy.

"Hi."

Caitlyn watches us, not trying to mask her curiosity. It makes me feel edgy and itchy to be studied so blatantly, but I'd do the same thing in her shoes.

Sydney nods toward the kitchen. "You were so busy feeding me that you didn't eat anything yet. Come with me and I'll fix you some food." She widens her eyes ever so slightly at me, a signal developed over years of silent conversations. *I'm onto you.*

She knows something's wrong.

It takes me a second to swallow the lump in my throat. "Yeah. Sure." All this tension I've been carrying makes my muscles ache. When I unfold myself from my chair, my body feels a hundred years old.

Caitlyn scowls at us as I follow Syd across the room, but I don't care. I'm grateful for the way Sydney's led us someplace out of earshot. If I'm going to fall apart, I'd rather have an audience of only one.

It's cold away from the warmth of the fire. The kitchen rests in shadows, the countertops frigid under my hands as I hold myself steady.

Sydney turns on her phone's flashlight and sweeps the beam over the pathetic pile of food, making a show of choosing the right thing.

"What's wrong?" she whispers.

"Everything?"

"No." She presses a stale muffin into my hand, the last of the pastries. "Something new's got you freaking out." She narrows her eyes at me, and my heart swells at being seen.

I shake my head because I made up my mind to not tell her about the router. The secret feels like it's eating me alive, little pieces of my soul being swallowed by hungry, slavish jaws.

"Luce." Sydney takes my free hand in hers. "I know I fell apart for a minute there, but I'm here now. Okay? You can tell me."

I want to. She's my best friend, and I want more than anything to unburden myself. To share this load and hope we can figure out a plan.

But. But. But.

If Sydney killed the Wi-Fi, who's to say she didn't kill Jeff and Nash too? If I tell her what I know, I lose any advantage against her.

Thinking about her this way—as a suspect, as my enemy—makes me feel so shamefully guilty.

"Oh, babe." She wipes a stray tear off my cheek, and that tiny move unravels me.

"I'm terrified," I admit.

"Because?"

My pulse rushes in my ears so loudly that it drowns out the sound of me betraying myself. "I found the router."

Sydney's eyes light. "Did you try to reset it?"

I shake my head, my jaws still locked over this last piece of the truth. "It was broken. Someone . . . broke it."

For a second, it feels good to not be the only one with this knowledge. Until Syd's eyes narrow. "You think someone messed with it?"

"I know they did."

"That doesn't make any sense. Everyone here depends on the internet to make a living. Why would someone do that?"

"Jeff didn't want you to find out about his leaked pictures because he knew you'd be furious. Maybe smashing the router was his twisted way of keeping everything secret from you."

"No," she says firmly. "If Jeff was hacked, he would have spent every possible moment trying to fix it or have Brent fix it."

I shrug. "So maybe it was someone else."

"Do you know how much money we all lost this weekend by not being able to post?"

I have no idea how much money each person in our group makes with a single social media post. Gobs of it, I expect. But I'm pretty sure it's a rhetorical question, so I keep my mouth shut.

Sydney shakes her head as if rolling a thought around. "Except you," she finally whispers, her conclusion reached at last.

My heart catches. "What?"

"You, Luce." She says it so sadly, you'd think she weren't skewering me alive. "You're the only one who doesn't need the internet to do your job. The only one who didn't lose something by coming here."

"What possible reason would I have for cutting us off from the world?"

She squeezes her eyes shut. When she opens them again,

there's a hard glaze to them. "You lied about why we came here. Maybe you just wanted us alone."

Shit. That one stupid lie's going to cost me everything.

"I just . . ." Sydney pinches the bridge of her nose. "I need time to think, okay?"

"Right. Sure. Just go back to the fire, and I'll be here when you're ready to talk."

Her eyes drop to the food, and my stomach sinks. She's wondering if I'm going to take it.

She doesn't trust me.

"Syd . . ."

She holds up her hands in a placating gesture. "Please, Luce. This whole thing is making me feel crazy."

Once upon a time, after Breaker died, she said those same words to me. We'd been helping each other through the terrible aftermath of his death, trying to outrun the guilt of being with him in those final moments but being unable to stop what happened.

His death was so fast—one minute he stood beside us on the sidewalk, and the next he was pinned under that car. The danger was there and gone before we knew it. So quick we couldn't fully process it or understand what we should have done differently. Going through trauma like that can do weird things to your head if you aren't careful. You start to lose touch with what's safe or not—what's *real* or not.

The difference is, this time, people are dying around us, but there's no snap of your fingers and it's over. We're in the thick of it, not sure when the danger will pass, when we can let ourselves relax. That tight, claustrophobic madness is building to a roar, violence pressing in from all sides.

I don't blame Sydney for running from it. I just hate that it's making her run from me.

"You should go," she whispers. Those three little words shouldn't be a line in the sand, but they are. I've been tamping down all my resentment for ages, and suddenly I just can't anymore. I'm so sick of her, I could scream.

"You know what? Screw you, Sydney." The words burn my throat like acid, but I can't take them back. I won't.

Her face pales. "Excuse me?"

I know I'm only making her more suspicious of me, but I can't stop everything from gushing out. I've been loyal to her for years, letting her be the center of my story, but it's been a mistake. One bad day and she's throwing it all away—literally pushing me out into the cold because she's insecure.

She has no idea how much I've done for her.

"You heard me," I spit, and it feels good to be in the driver's seat for once, even if I'm steering us toward a crash. "I've been so caught up in trying to be this perfect employee for you that I forgot how to be a good friend. Good friends tell each other the truth. And the truth is you're selfish, Syd. You've been walking all over us this entire trip. This is just the latest example."

She crosses her arms over her chest. "You've got to be kidding me."

I tick the examples off on my fingers. "You made Caitlyn use her dress for your shampoo shoot because you were more concerned with surprising everyone than doing what was right for us, and same for Brent—he's had to scramble to fix your sponsorship mess because you wouldn't just talk to him. And not to speak ill of the dead, but we all know Jeff was a prop, right? I mean, you've clearly been screwing Caitlyn behind his back for god knows how long, so he can't have mattered to you that much. We've all been trying to help you, and you've been too caught up in your own privileged life to notice how much we're suffering."

"*We?*" she challenges. "Or do you mean you?"

"All of us. But, sure, me too. You got so caught up in making me a character that I think you started seeing me as one even when the cameras were off. Someone you could push around because I've always been there for you. You assumed I'd say yes to whatever you suggested, and shame on me for playing right into your hands because I didn't want to disappoint you. But you never asked what I wanted. You built an idea in your head based on what was most convenient for you."

"Wow," she says. "Tell me how you really feel."

"You sound like Caitlyn."

"Yeah, well, out of the two of you, she's the one who's supporting me right now."

"And you're the one trying to send me out into danger." We stand there, panting at each other, my heart beating sickeningly fast. Fault lines rising beneath our feet. We've never fought like this before. "Tell me I'm wrong about you," I plead, reaching for her hand. I want her to show me I've been looking at everything the wrong way. That there's hope for us. But she snatches her hand away.

"You have no idea how much pressure I'm under." She glares at me and shoves her hair over her shoulders. "I have to do everything perfectly. Every campaign that goes well raises the bar and everything that doesn't jeopardizes my ability to get another chance. God forbid I get fewer views or say something controversial and lose followers. It impacts my future prospects. And don't forget, succeeding is necessary so *I* can pay *you*. Your career is dependent on me doing my job."

I hate that we're fighting, that I didn't have the courage to speak up sooner, gentler. But I'm also not going to be afraid to tell the truth, even if it hurts her. "Well maybe I don't want that anymore." There it is, out in the open. I didn't ever want it to come out like this, and the way she sucks in a breath lets me know it stings.

"No shit," Syd snaps, but it's a false bravado. Her lips quiver in the way that means she's close to a meltdown.

"You alright over there?" Caitlyn calls in a singsong voice. I hate that I've given her the satisfaction of acting just as unstable as she's made me out to be.

"We're fine," I grit out, and when I turn back and see the tears spilling down Syd's cheeks, I know it's over. I've lost.

This time when she tells me I should go, I'm expecting it. But it doesn't hurt any less.

61

CAITLYN

Lucy leaves much the way she came: desperate and alone. One minute, I'm staring at the fire, pretending to give her and Sydney some space. The next, she's out the door, letting in a blast of cold air so strong that the fire almost gutters out.

"Where the fuck is she going?" I ask.

In the kitchen area, Sydney stares at the ceiling for a long moment as if gathering herself, then lets out a sigh. "Out."

"Wait, what?" I sit up straighter in my chair, a heightened sense of alertness coming over me. "For how long?"

"Long enough." The damp hems of Sydney's jeans make tiny shuffling sounds as she pads her way back to me. She hovers at the edge of the glow cast by the fire. "I told her I needed some space to think."

Of all the dumb ideas. "So you let the person who killed your boyfriend just waltz off into the woods?" I'm too upset to soften my words for her, to pick the right ones like I always do, and the accusation lands like a grenade.

"She didn't kill him." Sydney's face crumples. "I don't think."

Um. Hello. Then who else would have?

I can't say that because then Syd'll think it was me.

Sometimes Sydney wants to believe the best in people so much that she overlooks logic. Jeff's dead, and all the evidence points to Lucy. If Syd isn't saying anything about it, it makes me wonder just how far Cancer Girl would need to go before Syd will call her on it.

I push out of my chair, unable to sit still any longer. "Weren't you just fighting?" In what world do you go from yelling at each other to "She didn't kill him"? I just don't get it. Lucy's the biggest red flag there is. How can Sydney not see that?

"I'm mean, yeah, but . . ."

"You know this is bad, right?" Lucy's been sneaky since the start of this trip, and having her loose out there makes me think of all the things that could go wrong. We're trapped here like sitting ducks while the world whirls on around us. Lucy could be making plans to hurt us or trap us or, god, even desert us, and we'd be none the wiser.

Sydney makes a face. "I thought you didn't want her here anyway."

"I mean, not for company. But I wanted her where I can see her. It's just . . ." I let out a frustrated growl. "Shit."

I know I'm being dramatic when I start pacing, but the theatrics are deserved. This is so like Syd. You finally get on board with one of her plans only for her to change her mind again. I know her audience loves all the guessing and spontaneity of watching from afar, but living with it in real life is exhausting.

"What was so important you needed to think about?" I ask Syd.

She hesitates. Not long, but just enough for the air to tighten and my chest to feel cold. "Everything," she whispers.

She's holding out on me.

"Sydney."

The strident ring of my voice makes her gaze snap to mine, and there's uncertainty there, mixed with guilt. Whatever she's processing must be important, but she's also unsure of what it means.

I hold her gaze until she buckles.

"Someone smashed the Wi-Fi router."

Her confession makes me draw up short. "On purpose?"

"That's what Lucy thinks."

"So there's no cell service and no Wi-Fi, and we're in the middle of a freak snowstorm with minimal supplies. No one's coming until tomorrow, and even if they arrive, we could all be dead by then."

"I think that covers it," she whispers, her eyes huge and luminous in the firelight.

Hysteria rises inside me. If I weren't so scared, I'd be comforted that Sydney told me the truth. She betrayed Lucy's trust, and that means something to me. But I can't appreciate it right now. I have to think.

"Did she take any food?"

Syd shrugs. "I gave her a muffin."

It's not like I could eat a damn gluten bomb anyway, but still. We're at the point where we need to look at everything as a resource. The fewer resources we have, the less we can wait around for rescue. Syd's generosity means one less meal for her.

"Okay." I resume my pacing, trying to absorb the news and recalibrate. I tell myself it's the woodsmoke that's making my eyes tear up, but the blurry, frustrating truth is that nothing's really okay. We need a plan.

I dart a glance at Sydney, but she won't meet my eyes, and it makes me spiral. If she's so sure Lucy didn't hurt Jeff, is that because she's responsible? I know Syd said she'd never leave Jeff, but what if that was just to throw me off?

Now that we're alone, it's not hard to dream up a thousand miserable possibilities. I'm not thinking clearly, and that strange hold Syd has on me frustrates everything. It's hard, when you look at the surface, to separate what you think you know about someone from who they really are.

I've spent a long time getting to know Sydney, first from afar when I was just getting into the influencing business, then up close as her friend. But despite the last six months, there are still so many times she's kept me at arm's length. Now, when it's so damn important, I can't have her shut me out.

"Someone's going to have to go for help," I tell her.

That, at least, gets her attention. "We can both go," she agrees.

I'm not sure I like where she's headed with this. "Don't you think that's riskier?" I look out the wall of windows to the eerie, waiting woods. Being out there with so many unexpected variables will stretch both of us. Frankly, being alone with her is a risk in itself. "Brent left, and"—my voice wavers—"so far no one's come back."

Sydney wraps her arms around herself but stays firm. "At this point, everything's a risk. You said it yourself. We're running out of food and time. Our best hope of getting off this mountain is to get ourselves off the damn mountain."

She trusts me enough to share her plan. Maybe she thinks I'll save her, or that we can save each other. It's a sweet, impractical thought. Our track record's shit right now.

I can't let her know how anxious I'm feeling or that I have any doubts about her, so I offer what I can: a path forward. The start of a plan. "Okay. We'll do it together. But no one's going anywhere until you're dry."

I walk to Nash's rolling rack of clothes to assess our options. Unfortunately it's all strappy gowns and useless shoes, nothing that'll help Sydney make this trek. I'm not much better off in my jeans and long-sleeve blouse, but at least I wasn't sitting in the snow getting soaked.

"I don't want to send you back into the cabin to get new clothes with Jeff there." I crook a grin at her, hoping a sense of humor will put her at ease. "So come on, babe. Take off your pants and put them near the fire to get warm."

She blushes fiercely, as if there's still a modicum of shame left in her after everything we did last night. "You trying to get me naked, CaityCat? Is that what you're really after?"

"Oh, honey." My grin slides wider, despite myself. "You have no idea."

62

LUCY

The cabin door shuts behind me with a muffled thud, leaving me sealed in a room that feels too much in every way. Too quiet. Too still. Too cold.

The window wall lets in barely enough light to see, but—*there*—when I turn to the shadowy bathroom, I can just make out the faint puff of my breath in the dark. I'm creating clouds with every exhale, but there's nothing romantic about it.

It's freezing in here.

I can't stay.

My heart sinks with the weight of it, but denying the truth would be stupid. Sydney's pushed me away, and even if we have a miraculous reconciliation, we're still targets for whoever's been picking off our party.

There's no happy outcome here.

I can wait and hope and barricade myself in my cabin with my one measly muffin. I can try to mend things with Sydney and Caitlyn, and find they're already hurt.

Whatever we do, we're in danger. It's a terrible lot, but it's not the worst I've faced before. And I'm not going to give up now.

It starts as a small tingling in my chest, an awareness that spreads and grows until it's a roar of determination. I *will* get through this. *I must.*

With cancer, I was just surviving, my body doing the work. I got pulled along in the undertow, and what was going to happen was going to happen no matter what outcome I hoped for.

They call it a fight with cancer, but it's like a battle with nature itself—something too large and unstoppable for something as flimsy as human will to overcome. With cancer, there's nothing you can do except hope and trust and pray. There's no outsmarting fate.

With this trip, everything's different. I'm not going to survive just by sitting tight and wishing the danger away. Not when people are dying like this. There's someone out there doing this, and if I'm smart and bold, I might have a chance to walk away.

For so long, I've avoided letting myself envision a future, not allowing myself to think I'm worthy because of everything I've done wrong in my life. But I'm tired of denying that I want a future for myself. I'm ready to let go of my guilt and believe there's something more out there waiting for me.

I know what I want, and now I need to choose it.

I want to go home and rub Oboe's soft, sweet nose and floppy ears. I want to hear my dog's tail thump on the floor while I wrap myself in Nick's arms and forget every reason I pushed him away. I want to kiss him and let myself love him and let him love me back, imperfect as I am. I've paid my penance for everything I've done wrong. I've existed in limbo for far too long. More than anything, I want to live. Which means I've got to fight for it—for myself.

And dammit, I want to win.

Fresh determination floods my body as I stride to my suitcase and yank out extra clothes to wear. The best thing I can do is get out of here and find us help. Syd and Caitlyn can hate me all they want, as long as I know they're safe. Down the mountain I go.

Brent had a golf cart, and all I have are my own two feet. But it's going to work. It has to.

To stay warm, I'm going to have to move fast. Which also means I'm going to have to travel light.

As soon as I've pulled on some more layers and shoved half the muffin into my mouth, I grab my camera bag to hold a few essentials.

I lift the flap to stow my cell phone and charger, but when I reach inside, something doesn't feel right. I know my camera by touch, and my body chills as I pull it from my bag for closer inspection.

My camera's taken a nasty blow, the body heavily dented and a spiderweb of cracks running through the shattered lens. The SD card's been ripped out and broken in two.

What the hell?

I left my bag unattended when we were gathering firewood and when I was searching for those matches, but why would someone do this?

Panic spikes through me, and I want to cry. It feels like someone's injured a friend. I know it's only a camera, but its destruction feels so targeted and malicious. If someone's trying to scare me, it's working.

My terrified breath saws in and out as I set the camera on my bed and load the rest of my supplies into the empty space in my bag. I'm rushing now, throwing things in thoughtlessly just to get the job done.

I catch sight of myself in the mirror, the trembling mess I've become.

None of this makes sense.

Sydney or Caitlyn? Cait or Syd? They're the only ones left now. One of them did this. But if they were sending a message, why target my camera and not something more obvious?

Another shuddering breath clears my mind enough for an idea to sneak through. Maybe it's not that someone's trying to scare me or warn me. Maybe there's something on my camera that they didn't want me to find.

My teeth start to chatter involuntarily, from cold or adrenaline or both, and I fumble for my phone. A snapped SD card won't help me, but no one else knows I tethered my camera to my phone. If there's something incriminating on the camera, I can find it on my cell.

I unlock my phone with stiff, shaky fingers. There's so little battery left—only 15 percent to get me through whatever comes next. I waste precious time looking for a signal that I know isn't there. Then I dive into my camera roll and flip through pictures.

Our weekend unfolds in a dreamy sequence: the Lodge from afar; Cait and Syd and Jeff at the falls; all of us dancing in our swimsuits beneath the first snowflakes. Then the ridge frosted with a layer of pristine snow. Patches of sky through bare trees. Me in the snow, freshly made over and brimming with hope.

I don't know what I'm looking for, so I force myself to study each picture, even as they grow more and more distressing.

Nash's body makes the bile rise in my throat.

The glowing cabins from last night, perched in a row overlooking the drop, come as a brief reprieve.

And then Jeff's cabin; a sheen of sweat slicks my skin.

I get all the way to this morning and don't find what I need.

I give myself a second to scream into my pillow, and then I go back.

Back to Jeff's cabin, a disaster of violence.

Back to the cabins, all lit in a row.

Back to the—*wait.*

What struck me as beautiful last night—the bright line of cabins shining against the dark ridge—makes something catch in my mind. We might have accidentally left Nash's light on when we left his cabin, but that doesn't explain what I'm seeing. Why would all six cabins be lit if we only ever used five rooms?

I zoom in, trying to make sense of the image. In post-photography, you can manipulate a thousand things. You can make a crowded beach look like a deserted honeymoon location. You can clear blemishes and make people lose weight and have fuller, thicker hair. But all that comes after the initial image, that first raw shot.

My camera doesn't lie.

There's something smudged against the window of the sixth cabin, the one closest to where I stood last night, the cabin that shouldn't be lit at all. A pink blur of something soft.

The pink coat Brent wore when he left to go for help.

The air leaves my lungs, and I don't even need to look to know a frosted cloud hangs before me. Ice cold, but not nearly as cold as my chest.

Brent's back.

Or maybe he never left.

63

LUCY

It's him, it's him, it's him. Panic surges through my body, making it impossible to sort through all the information in front of me. My mind is a sieve, only catching the big, obvious conclusions.

Unshiny, unspecial, unassuming Brent. He killed Jeff and Nash.

But why? Was he jealous of them and their bright careers? Jeff made money for Brent, so why hurt him? Surely the two of them would have gotten past this scandal and gone on to make money together again. Or was Brent worried Jeff was going to rake him through the coals for letting someone hack his account? I can't believe covering his own ass would really be worth murdering someone, not to mention, Nash had nothing to do with it, and he's dead too.

Has Brent just come unhinged?

None of it makes sense, and all the finer details rush past me. The things I'm not seeing are mounting, magnifying the overwhelming sense of foreboding in my body. I'm stiff and heavy with fear.

It wasn't Sydney.

I hated myself for doubting her, but now I know.

I'd feel relieved if I weren't so damn scared for her. She and Caitlyn are in the Lodge and they have no idea how much danger they're in. If something happens to them—to Syd—I won't be able to forgive myself. I can't let the last thing I say to her be an insult spit out in a fight.

How could I have let myself say such terrible things? I might have been frustrated, but part of that's on me. I didn't get to tell her how much I care about her or thank her for being the one constant in my life. For believing in me when I didn't always believe in myself.

Guilt twists in my gut like a knife, but I can't let it distract me. I need to warn her and Caitlyn. And I need to get there fast.

My camera's useless to me now, so I leave its mangled body on the bed. Then I make sure my phone's safely tucked in my pocket. There's 10 percent battery and no way to make a call, but it's all I can do. There are no other weapons here, no convenient ways to protect myself, so I race for the door.

It's only when my hand lands on the doorknob that I realize what I didn't find inside my bag: the flare gun.

It's gone. Could Brent have sneaked in and stolen that too?

My chest goes tight, my lungs struggling against the cage of my ribs. There's no time to let the thought crush me, so I heave in one ragged breath and bolt out into the snow.

The sun's bled from the sky, leaving a smear of gray clouds hanging low across the landscape. The Lodge waits in the distance, a slick, modern monstrosity among all this rugged beauty.

I hurtle toward the building, cursing myself with every

footstep. Each disturbance in the snow feels accusing, like clues I might have missed. Are those Brent's footprints leading to the Lodge's front door? Am I already too late? And how could I have not known he was here?

At the last minute, I duck toward the back door, grateful that the wall facing the path is made of wood and not that enormous stretch of windows. Using the downstairs entrance might still put me right into danger, but at least whoever's inside won't see me coming.

Silence presses in around me the second I slip through the back door. I strain to catch any sign of life, but my pounding heart makes it hard to hear anything. When no one attacks me, I creep forward through the darkened corridor. For all the rushing I did to get here, now I need to be smart and evaluate the situation.

I slowly make my way toward the staircase, pausing every few steps to listen. The murmur of voices drifts down from upstairs, the noise centered along the hallway. I can't make out what they're saying, but the tone seems calm. With any luck, Sydney and Caitlyn are right by the fire where I left them.

Picking up the pace, I slip past the glow from the pool area and past the darkened meditation room. The staircase rises in front of me, solid and dark. I'm so intent on my destination that I don't see it coming when I kick something hard and plastic on the ground.

Shit!

The object skitters away into the shadows, the sound brutally loud in the near silence.

I freeze as the voices pause and then resume overhead.

What was that? I was down here not that long ago hauling

wood, and there was nothing in the way before. This sleek, minimal space is the antithesis of clutter.

I can't spare any phone battery to light the hall, so I feel my way through the darkness until my toes tap the object again and I can grab it. I find it's not one piece, but two connected by a cable, and my mind whirls as I carry them back to the entry to the pool. When the dim light from the window in the pool room illuminates the objects in my hands, I'm even more confused.

The router I'm holding isn't the damaged one I discovered before, but a new one plugged in to a battery backup and marked with the branding of a satellite internet company.

What the hell?

Has there been a way to reach the outside world right under my nose this whole time? And if so, who's been hiding it?

I flip over the router and discover a network name and password written on the back.

Holy shit. This just might work.

I juggle the hotspot in my hands so I can pull my phone from my pocket. Help is right there, so close I could cry.

The ceiling creaks overhead, the noise coming from the side of the room opposite from where Caitlyn and Sydney have been talking.

The realization jolts through me: someone else is here.

I need to get to my friends; there's no time to connect to the internet.

I drop everything, and then I run.

64

CAITLYN

The fire's crackling softly, its glow dancing across Sydney's half-naked body, when Lucy bursts upstairs looking stricken. Her face is pale, her form lumpy with too many sweaters and layers of socks.

Mother. Fucker.

She's been sneaking around yet again; she must have used the skeleton key to let herself in. If only Syd had listened to me when I told her this could happen.

"No!" Lucy's eyes narrow, and before I realize what's happening, she's charging right at me.

"What the fuck?" My heart trips with terror, and I jump from the chair, trying to scramble out of her reach. Beside me, Syd bolts upright, but she's too slow to help.

Lucy's hands connect with my upper back before Syd can reach me, and she shoves me, hard.

"Ouch!" I howl, tripping as I fall sideways against the chair Syd just abandoned.

But Lucy's not looking at me at all.

"Brent," she pants. She stares into the darkness just beyond my chair, fear glazing her eyes. "I told you someone else was here."

I follow her gaze, and my fingers go numb at the low, rumbling laugh that gathers in the gloom.

Brent materializes from the shadows wearing the same disheveled outfit he left us in. His right eye gleams in strange contrast to the dark bruise marring the side of his face. His jaw is spiky with stubble, and even though he took food with him, he looks haunted and hungry.

Oh shit. Lucy wasn't rushing at me to hurt me, she was knocking me out of Brent's reach. Protecting me.

Look at you, Lucy girl. Good time to grow a backbone.

Brent tries for casual. "Hey, guys." No mention of the fact that he was in the room all along, that he didn't come in through the front door.

A shiver of revulsion churns my stomach.

"You're back?" Sydney asks. She's so pretty and hopeful, standing before the flickering fire in only that thin lace bodysuit. She has no idea what's happening.

"He never left," Lucy explains. Slowly but surely she's been edging backward toward us, keeping Brent in her sights. She doesn't see the confusion on Syd's face like I do, but she has to hear it in Syd's voice.

"What?" Then understanding dawns, and Syd gasps like the star in all of her horror movies. "It was you."

"What was me?" Brent asks. "What's going on?"

But we've all wised up to him, and we shrink toward the front door as a collective unit.

No one answers.

"Guys?" Brent tries. "I don't know what's going on, but you're freaking me out." He scrubs a hand over his face.

"Where have you been?" Lucy demands.

Exasperated, Brent shakes his head. "I headed for town, but a few miles in, a tree came down on the golf cart. I took a branch to the fucking eye."

"You should have returned way before now," Lucy says.

"Yeah," Sydney agrees. "Why didn't you come back as soon as it happened?"

"It knocked me out. I woke up in the dark and was afraid I'd get lost if I tried to move. You can't see the road for shit. Figured it was safest to head back in the light." Brent takes a heavy step toward us, his face clouding. "I spent last night outside, freezing my fucking ass off. And now that I'm here, you're getting all paranoid on me?"

"So where's your coat?" Lucy asks, her voice firm and accusing.

"Wha—?"

"You say you waited outside all night, but where's your coat?"

Brent makes a scoffing sound in the back of his throat, unamused.

"The pink coat," Lucy snaps. She breaks eye contact with him long enough to glance at me and Syd, her face taut with fear. And then she drops the bomb: "The one that's in the spare cabin right now."

Oh shiiiit.

I don't know how she could know that, but her accusation destroys any last pretense of Brent being a nice, normal guy.

The change that comes over him is swift and shocking. It's like he . . . snaps. The real Brent cleaving the one we thought we knew in two.

He draws himself up, everything about him transforming from sand into stone. Gone is the talent manager who was comfortable taking a back seat to everyone else's antics. His soft posture melts away, leaving his body radiating with tension, all hard, aggressive lines. Anger and a touch of madness.

I can imagine how this version of him might have killed Jeff. This isn't the Brent I know.

"Stupid bitch," he snarls at Lucy.

He takes another step toward us, his eyes cold and hard.

And now I see it: something bright beside him, a glint of light reflecting off the knife in his hands.

"Fuck you!" Lucy shrieks, and Brent lunges.

Chaos erupts as we all burst into action.

Sydney grabs my hand and yanks me toward the front door. Her grip is so tight that the skin on my hand burns, but I don't let go.

I don't catch which direction Lucy runs in or whether she's escaped. All I know is that Brent's chasing after us, and we're scrambling through the darkness, trying to stay out of his grasp.

Sydney reaches the front door and throws it open with a bang. We stumble out into the gaspingly cold snow, the trees dotting the landscape far too sparse to offer much cover.

The uneven layer of trampled snow makes us stumble, but we hold on to each other until the jarring force of our gait breaks our hands apart.

A desperate terror folds over me. Sydney doesn't have shoes on, and I don't know how far she'll make it like this. My heart cracks in two.

"Go!" I shout at her.

And then we run.

65

LUCY

Help. We need help.

I run blindly in the dark, shins slamming into the legs of furniture until I'm half limping toward the back stairs. I glance wildly around the room as I go, looking for escape and protection, for help.

I dropped my phone downstairs, and now I feel horribly disconnected from anyone who can rescue us. When I see the glint of a cell phone left by the fire, I grab it and keep running.

Behind me, the Lodge goes strangely silent, and I look over my shoulder for the briefest moment to confirm: Brent followed Caitlyn and Sydney out into the snow.

For now I'm alone, but I'm not safe. And neither are my friends.

I think of the missing flare gun, and fear rushes through me. I can't stop Brent with my bare hands. I need a weapon.

I pound downstairs toward the garage, the one place no one else has access to. Those shiny tools wait for me, fortifying and strong.

Before I reach the garage door, the plastic brick of the router catches my eye. A connection to the outside world. Someone's had access the whole time.

Making a split-second decision, I skid to a stop and drop to the floor beside the hotspot. There's no lock on the home screen of the phone I grabbed, and a teeth-clenching burst of adrenaline rushes through me as I take precious seconds to try to connect to the Wi-Fi.

When the Wi-Fi signal on the phone lights up, I shove to my feet and rush for the garage, dialing 911 as I go.

The call rings in my ear as I yank a garden knife from the rack in the garage, the heft of sharp metal reassuring in my hand.

Come on, come on.

"Nine-one-one, what's your emergency?"

I almost sob. I've never been so relieved to hear another voice.

"He's killing people," I choke out, my voice garbled and panicked. "Two people are dead."

"Are you safe right now?"

"Y-yes," I say, though of course I'm not. None of us are safe anymore.

"Can you tell us where you are, miss?"

Where am I? In the darkened hallway, below ground, dead bodies all around me.

I open my mouth to answer, but a scream from outside shatters the silence.

It's Syd. Syd in pain.

No, no, no.

She's going to die thinking I hate her.

I can't let that happen.

My fingers slip on the keyboard of the unfamiliar phone, hanging up by accident, but I barely notice because I'm running again toward the darkness at the end of the hall. Toward what I hope is the exit.

I burst through the back door, and a fist of cold air pounds against my chest and steals the breath from my lungs. After all the darkness, I blink against the gray haze from outside, disoriented and terrified.

Another scream, this time from the edge of the ridge.

I lift the phone to dial the police again, but I realize the police are just a single group of people, and they already know I need help. What if there's someone closer?

Sydney's voice in my mind supplies an alternate option. *You always have to smile*, she reminds me. *Your fans could be everywhere. The delivery guy, the person who cleans your hotel room, whatever. There's always someone watching you.*

Maybe she's right. Sydney and Caitlyn and Jeff have millions of fans between them. If any of them are watching, even a few who can call for help, it's better than the single phone call I could make. Maybe there's another person on this godforsaken patch of land who can come for us.

It's a knee-jerk reaction to tap the glowing screen and lift the phone to my face.

I start talking into the phone as I run. "This is Lucy, I'm at the Reverie retreat in the Catskills. This is an emergency and I need your help. If anyone is out there, please, please help."

The snow drags at my feet as I run, slowing me down. The exertion of lifting each foot high enough to clear the drifts makes my breath come in ragged pants. I don't know if I'm being coherent as I run; I just keep babbling, terror taking hold of me and turning everything into a stream-of-consciousness plea for help.

I clear the side of the Lodge and look toward where the last scream came from. Everything's a shade of gray—the snow, the trees, the sky—but there's motion bursting between the trees. Syd and Caitlyn and Brent, a trio of bodies hurtling through the woods. Syd in front in bare feet and lingerie that's staining red, Cait to the side, and Brent in the rear, following relentlessly while the blade of that shiny knife runs dark with blood.

No.

Desperation floods through me, and thick, acidic bile rises on my tongue.

I glance down at the phone, and my heart plunges at the black screen. I must not have hit the button to stream my begging appeal.

I need help—I need the world to see this and to come to our aid. I might envy Sydney and Caitlyn sometimes and fight with them at others. I've felt betrayed when their attention has strayed, and we've misunderstood each other more than once. But none of that has ever changed how much I care. I need them to be okay.

I hit the streaming button again. I can't talk into the phone anymore or risk drawing attention to myself, but I can show the world the truth. When I'm sure my feed is truly live, I bolt from the cover of the Lodge and race toward the tree line, running at an angle toward Sydney with the hopes that I can intercept her.

If I can get to her first, maybe I can throw myself between her and Brent. Sydney's done so much for me; it's time I do the same for her.

Maybe I can stop this madness once and for all.

66

LUCY

Sydney's running the wrong way. She must have fled the Lodge on pure adrenaline, and the speed of the chase didn't give her time to catch her bearings. Instead of heading downhill toward the winding road to town, she's cutting closer to the ridge, aiming toward the waterfall, driven by the blind instinct to keep moving.

I want to shout at her to course correct, but don't dare risk distracting her. All her attention should be focused on escaping and surviving. Getting the fuck out of Brent's clutches.

I keep the phone camera recording as I run, and even with the awkward position of one hand in the air and the other holding the knife, I'm faster than Sydney and her poor, unprotected feet.

She's not going to make it much longer.

The farther we run, the thicker the forest grows, until I lose sight of the rest of them. I can only hear Sydney crashing through the underbrush, snapping branches as she runs, the roar of the waterfall in the background.

Another scream makes me stumble, and I land hard against a tree trunk, dropping the knife. Air slams from my lungs, and the tree bark rips at the skin on my hands. More red, more blood.

It's as good a place as any to intercept Sydney, so I crouch down behind the tree to catch my breath. As Sydney draws closer, the bright stain of blood gushing from her arm grows bigger. Darkness slicks down her arm and drips onto her lacy white corset. Her face twists in pure terror.

It's nothing like the movies, where pretty girls run and it's all slow-motion shots with bouncing boobs and shiny hair. Sydney's been in those movies; she's got the posters to prove it.

No, this is animal and raw. Watching makes a hole open up inside my chest. I didn't know it could hurt this much to watch someone else in pain, but I can't look away.

Sydney squeezes through two tree trunks, leaving a smear of blood behind her.

"Syd!" I shout, and her head snaps toward me. She's glazed with terror; just a hint of relief breaks through when she recognizes me.

I wave frantically, trying to catch her attention and guide her to a spot where we can make a stand.

But that one moment of carelessness costs her. She keeps running, but her hair catches in the branches of a nearby tree. One moment she's running, the next she's yanked from her feet.

She lands in the snow, still yards away from me, so hard I can hear the air get knocked from her lungs, her breathless grunt of pain.

Sydney kicks at the ground, scrambling to get to her feet.

But there's something wrong with her ankle, which flops uselessly as it slides for purchase. Her frantic motion kicks up the top layer of snow, exposing a layer of leaves and rot that spackles her legs and mixes with her blood to form a grimy paste.

I can't live behind a camera and just watch anymore. I prop the phone against the tree trunk and stand to grab her. When I lean out from the protection of the tree, my shadow falls across her face, casting her in darkness.

Sydney stares at me with wide eyes. For a second there's hope in there, but it snuffs out as something new catches her eye and she starts to scream again.

Every nerve in my body burns with the sensation. I am noise and pain and icy air.

With renewed energy, Sydney surges to her feet, but it's too late.

Brent emerges from between two trees beside Sydney, like the woods have parted just for him. Grim determination mars his face and transforms him into someone I don't know. I can't believe we ever thought he was one of us, that he was safe.

Right now, that knife hangs at his side, not something he's holding, but an extension of his arm. He's on her in just a few steps, the rigid span of his shoulders tight with malice.

Sydney can't run, but she twists away, and—god—I can see everything unfolding. I've spent so much time looking at things people would rather not examine: pain and cancer, loss and heartbreak. But I'll never be able to unsee this, and for the rest of my life, I'll regret that I didn't close my eyes.

Brent drags his knife down Sydney's back, the blade so sharp, it parts her skin like cutting through snow, exposing a red line of muscle and sinew and blood.

Like a seam unraveling.

I am unraveling. A scream builds inside my mind, inside my chest, and the swelling noise of my own internal horror folds over me and I am lost, I'm lost, I'm shattering apart.

Sydney makes a wet choking sound as she falls. The ground welcomes her with open arms, the snow catching her in its miserable embrace.

The forest goes quiet again. Waiting.

I keep begging for Sydney to move, to moan, to . . . something, but she's so terribly, permanently still.

I thought if I could only save her, I'd fix everything between us. But she's gone, and now I'll never have a chance.

"Bitch," Brent sneers. He looms over her with his knife at the ready, his focus entirely on her.

I'm braced for him to strike again, to drive that horrible blade home inside her soft, defenseless frame, but he toes her with his shoe and grunts, satisfied when she doesn't move again.

I'm rooted still with shock and horror, and it takes me a second to come back to myself and realize how exposed I am out here. I try to press into the trees and melt in their shadows, but they're much too thin to hide me for long, and if Brent glances up, he'll spot me.

Quietly and quickly, I step backward on trembling feet until something slams into my back and I trip. Someone's hands are there to catch me. Then they haul me up under my armpits.

Panic spears through me and I thrash wildly in their grip.

"Calm down," the voice snaps, annoyed.

It takes me a second to understand it's not Brent.

Caitlyn.

A burst of relief fills my mouth, the shaky solace that I'm not alone in this. I look to her for confirmation, for support, but she's not looking at me at all.

"Brent!" Caitlyn calls, and my world implodes. "She's over here."

67

LUCY

Caitlyn's face hovers before mine, haughty and gleeful, and now I see it: it was both of them. Brent and Caitlyn. Caitlyn and Brent.

Brent paces across the forest floor toward us, each heavy footstep full of menace. A cold rush of dread sweeps through me.

He killed Sydney. Sydney and Jeff and Nash. Their names repeat in a nonsensical babble through my mind, buzzing together in a high-pitched whine of fear.

I jerk in Caitlyn's arms like a terrified rabbit. Her grip is surprisingly strong.

Brent comes to a stop at Caitlyn's shoulder, so close I can smell the blood on him. When I whimper, I can taste it.

"LuckyLens," Brent muses, cocking his head to the side to study me coldly. "I guess you are lucky, aren't you? The last one standing." He grins. "For now."

"Tell me why," I beg. If I'm going to die, I need to understand the cosmic justice of it.

Brent wipes a hand across his jaw, wincing as he touches a tender spot. Sydney must have gotten a hit in.

He spits blood on the ground, confirming my suspicion. "Fucking bitch." Blood stains his teeth when he opens his mouth to speak. "She was going to ruin us in so many ways."

"What?" Sydney, who brought us all here? Sydney, who connected every single person at this retreat?

"Do you know how much income her launching Plentifol was going to cost me?" Brent shakes his head, his eyes hard.

"Because of lost partnerships?" I need to keep him talking. Every second he's speaking to me is a second I'm still alive.

"Of course," he snaps.

What he's saying makes sense, in its own twisted way. As Sydney's manager, Brent got a percentage of the sponsorships he helped her book. For Sydney to launch Plentifol, she'd have to cancel dozens of sponsorships for other brands' hair care products, not to mention affiliate commissions. With her reach and her influence, it could have been . . . a lot.

"But if you"—I can't make myself say the word *killed*—"hurt her, you're not making money either."

Another vicious grin that's not quite a grin. A sneer. "No one's irreplaceable, Lucy. You used to be Sydney's best friend; you should know that better than anyone."

I hate that it hurts. A tear leaks down my cheek, and Brent reaches out a red-slicked finger to wipe it away. The trail of blood I can feel him leave behind makes me want to crawl out of my skin.

"I already have a new It Girl," Brent says. "Someone who will work with me." He lifts his gaze and meets Caitlyn's eye over my shoulder. Her hair brushes against my cheek as she nods, but she removes her hands from my arms and comes to stand beside him.

This new development scares me almost more than anything. If Caitlyn's letting me go, she must be confident I'm not getting out of here.

They're going to kill me too.

It shouldn't come as a surprise, but it does. This whole twisted, surreal trip plays like a nightmare that's really happening. I'm terrified that this life will be over before I've learned how to live it. That I'll have had two chances to live and have squandered them both.

Another whimper escapes the trap of my throat, and the aftershocks of it vibrate all the way to my core.

"Sydney got too big," Brent continues, ignoring my distress. "Thought she didn't need people. But she forgot who made her, who put her in the spotlight and got her all those hair care sponsors to begin with."

I force myself to speak, my voice a whisper rubbed raw. "You did all this just so you could replace her? It was worth killing everyone instead of having a conversation with her?"

"It doesn't sound flattering when you say it like that," Brent snaps. "Let's not forget we got some great content out of it too." His mirthless chuckle makes goose bumps rise along my arms. "You weren't wrong about me taking videos. It's all part of the story we're selling."

"Speaking of which, great job with Jeff," Caitlyn tells him. "You really left me in suspense with how you were going to do it. The nudity was a nice touch."

A look of disgust crosses Brent's face. "I can't take credit for that part. That was all him. Bastard never could keep his pants on."

"But I'm sure you'll make it part of your story, won't you?" I choke out.

"Come on, you're a photographer," Caitlyn says. "Storytelling's what gets an audience invested. And it's a fucking spectacular story." She beams at me. "Think of it, Luce. I'll be the sole survivor of the Reverie Retreat Massacre. Not sure I love the name, but there's time to think of something better." She shakes her head as if impressed by her own brilliance. "I'm going to be more famous than God."

"The sole *female* survivor," Brent corrects.

His eyes are locked on me, wide with pleasure at my fear, so he doesn't see Caitlyn step back and draw the flare gun from the waistband of her pants.

I do, though, and I throw my hands up to protect myself. *This is it.* I wish I'd never found that gun. I wish I'd never come here.

I wish.

I wish.

But Caitlyn doesn't aim the gun at me. With straight arms, she confidently sweeps the barrel to just a foot away from the side of Brent's head. A lethal distance, and he doesn't see it coming. He doesn't flinch.

"No!" I scream.

Then she shoots.

68

CAITLYN

Brent falls, as they say, like a sack of potatoes. I hate to use a cliché, but it's true. His body hits the ground with a thud, and he just kind of slumps over in the snow.

Lucy positively quakes with fear.

"Oh, don't look so surprised," I snap at her. I'm still a little shaky after what I've done, but I can't let her know it's gotten to me. Killing Brent was a rush: half terror, pure power. The afterglow is a high like I've never known. "He heard me say 'sole survivor.' He just didn't want to listen."

"But he listened to you when you planned this?" she whispers, understanding that of course Brent didn't come up with this on his own. As soon as he started bitching to me about lost contracts and Syd betraying him, I saw an opening I could work to my advantage. Brent might have pointed out the problem, but the solution was all mine.

I'm proud that Lucy can see the work that went into this weekend, the planning and painstaking strategy. Even the disappearing drone was a mastermind touch—a way to ensure no one would catch Brent as he executed my vision.

"Of course Brent listened to me." I shrug. "Obviously I didn't tell him about the dying part, but otherwise, yeah." It's not my fault Brent didn't realize how expendable he'd be in this equation. He wanted to be the management, but I'm the fucking talent.

Irreplaceable.

"You're going to blame this whole thing on him," Lucy realizes.

"Wouldn't you? He killed everyone else. He planted the drugs, which could have very easily killed Nash or Jeff. And when that didn't take Jeff down, he strangled him." I stare pointedly at her. "I should say, he killed everyone but you." A wry twist of my mouth. "I guess that part's on me. No witnesses, I'm sorry to say."

"But, Sydney," she pleads, and the mention of her name makes my spine go stiff. Poor Sydney has not been having a good week on social media. Brent and I have been filming damaging videos all weekend, and Brent's been posting them to her account using his satellite router. To everyone watching, she's having a breakdown of the most epic degree. It's been fun showing the world who Sydney is when she thinks the cameras are off. Not to mention, the implosion of Jeff's account—nicely executed by Brent—gave Syd a smashing reason to want Jeff out of her life. It makes her a perfect scapegoat if things with Brent fall through. "You were her friend."

I told myself I was going to stay calm, that I needed to be controlled and in charge for this whole thing. But rage surges through me, blacking out the edges of my vision. "I was never her friend," I spit out, the last of my secrets slipping from me. "Not a single second of a goddamned day. Sydney Kent deserved to die alone and in pain, the way my brother did. When she killed him."

There are moments when your life cracks open and everything that comes after can be traced back to the second things changed. For me, it was the moment I got the phone call about Cole.

DOA was the code the doctors used, as if three little letters—a fucking acronym—can sum up someone's life. Dead on arrival. His body broken beyond repair by the car that smashed into him. Vertebrae pulverized, lungs crushed, life bled out of him.

They couldn't promise me that it didn't hurt.

The day Cole died sent everything into a spiral. Susan's stroke came just a year later, my brothers drifted away, and my dad fell back into survival mode.

The police told us Cole's girlfriend was with him at the time of the accident. A street with no witnesses and no cameras. She told them that he'd tripped just as the car came by. The driver had their head turned, looking into the intersection to come, and they couldn't refute her claim.

I wasn't there at the police station with my family that night. They'd squeezed onto an earlier flight, while mine was delayed because of bad weather at La Guardia. All I had was my family's story of how Cole's girlfriend came up to them after she gave her statement. The thing is, she kept apologizing, but she didn't look all that broken up about his death. And I knew then that there was more to the story.

There was no evidence of foul play, so my family never pushed it further, never pressed charges or asked questions after his death was ruled an accident. Forgive and forget. Part of their process of letting Cole go.

But what can I say? I don't forgive so easily, and I sure as hell don't forget. I'm not that kind of girl.

"Breaker?" Lucy asks. Her eyebrows draw together and her mouth has flopped open. I forgot that she met Sydney in college; she must have known Cole too.

"Cole Keller," I tell her. "My stepbrother. Breaker was just a nickname he used to make himself sound cooler."

I watch the realization wash over her: this weekend wasn't about me becoming the next big thing. That was just a story I sold to Brent to get him to go along with it, a bonus outcome of a bigger plan. This weekend has only ever been about one thing: revenge.

For a minute, back in my cabin, when Syd was naked in my arms, I allowed myself to wonder if it might be enough just to displace her from her throne. If I could stop there. I've overlooked a lot about her since we met, because when her attention is turned on me, it's the best feeling in the world. Despite what I told Lucy, I *do* care about Syd, however twisted that makes me, and hearing that Cole got violent with her made me reconsider everything I thought I knew. But I gave her a chance last night to commit to me, and she chose to bury what she really wanted. To stay with Jeff. If she could have just owned up to who she really wanted to be with, maybe I could have let her keep her other secrets. I could have let the thing with Cole go, told Brent it was time to stop going after Sydney.

She could have walked away.

Instead all she did was lie, and it made her lies about Cole that much more unforgivable. If she was going to double down on her deceptions, then so was I. I've gone too far—witnessed too much—to turn back now. I need to see this through.

"But Break—Cole—died years ago," Lucy whispers. Her face is terribly pale against the shock of her red hair.

"Sweetheart, I can play the long game better than anyone."

Everyone always thinks of Sydney as this great actress, but if they knew everything I've been working on for the last few years, it would put her performances to shame. It takes talent—lots of it—to transform into someone new and make the world believe the new version was you all along. And that's exactly what I did. Brick by brick, building myself up from the ground to be just who Sydney Kent wanted.

A social media star she could relate to on a personal level.

A fellow creative who could keep up with her endless enthusiasm and hunger for new projects.

A flirt who could catch her attention and keep it.

A girl next door from the family that only-child Sydney never had.

I worked my ass off, stepping out of my past and into Sydney's world, putting myself in her orbit to get closer to the truth. I scrubbed the accent from my voice, leveled up my wardrobe and my clothes and my hair. I lost the ten pounds holding me back from a truly enviable body. I figured out how to put myself in front of the right people at the right times to catch their attention and really shine.

I did that, and the world warmed to me.

Lucy thinks she got a makeover? *Pssht.* I'm the motherfucking queen of them.

"So you planned all this to get back at Sydney." I don't need to answer for her to know it's true. Lucy nods, contemplating, but the fear isn't quite so strong on her face anymore and she sounds . . . amused. "That's a lot of effort. But you did it all for nothing."

Her unflappable act is getting under my skin, and I can't help screeching, "She killed him!"

"Poor, mistaken Caitlyn."

I take a step closer to her, but she doesn't shrink away this time. "What the fuck are you talking about?"

Lucy levels a twisted grin at me. "You got it all wrong."

69

LUCY

"What. Do. You. Know?" Caitlyn demands, her face a mask of fury.

My eyes drop to the flare gun in her hand for a fleeting second. Is there another shot in there? I hope to god I never find out.

"About what?" I ask innocently, trying to buy myself time.

Caitlyn's furious, but she wants answers now. When I sway backward, in the same direction Sydney was running, she follows me. I take a step back; she takes a step forward. The gun remains mercifully at her side.

"Cole!" she shouts, and the memories I've suppressed for so long flood in. The sharp angle of his cheekbones, the husky grit of his laugh. If he could have only loved Syd well, it would have been enough for me. Eventually I would have gotten over feeling like a third wheel and found peace in whatever friendship he could offer. But he didn't love her well. Couldn't keep his hands off her, first in passion, then in anger.

I shudder under the weight of the memories, the flashes coming stronger and faster now. The bruises on Sydney's skin, the way she retreated inward until she was barely more than a husk.

The only thing tethering me to my body is the cold shock of snow against my ankles, quickly seeping through my shoes and soaking my socks. The woods around the Lodge have gone deathly silent, and the hush only amplifies the distant roar of the waterfall.

I take another step backward, and when the ever-present shadows from the trees drop away, I realize I've broken the tree line. There's a dizzying expanse of nothing at my back.

We've reached the edge of the cliff.

"Answer me!" Caitlyn growls.

Movement comes at the corner of my eye, motion over Caitlyn's shoulder. A bubble of relief swells in my chest, and I want to cry. It's Sydney, hauling herself along the ground. Alive. Living. Sydney.

I need to keep Caitlyn talking, but her patience is wearing thin. She aims the gun at my face, and my terror ripens to a fever pitch. "You can't be stupid enough to think Cole's death was an accident," she spits.

It's time to stop running from myself. I've pushed people away for years, shut down their affections so they couldn't get close to me. All in protection of this one truth, the secret that's shaped me and that I shaped my life around.

"No," I whisper.

Caitlyn's eyes go wide with surprise and vindication, but I'm expecting that response. It's only fair.

Sydney's close enough to hear me now, and it feels good to let this last truth go. To set myself free. After this, if she hates me, then at least she hates all of me, the *real* me.

I'm hoping, though, that she doesn't hate me at all.

I tilt my chin up, letting a cold breeze wash over my face, cleansing me of these last sins. "But Sydney didn't kill him." My hands flex with the memory of it. The texture of Breaker's jacket against my fingertips, the firm weight of his muscles beneath my palms.

It only took a simple push.

"*I* did."

I hold Caitlyn's gaze and watch the rage take over. Before she can move, Sydney's there, behind her back, rising to her feet. Her lace outfit's plastered to her body, red with blood. But she's standing.

"You want to know what?" I ask without dropping Caitlyn's gaze, knowing she's so hungry for answers that I have her whole focus. I'm onto her. I watch people, get to know them from afar. That's what I do. "I'm glad the bastard's dead."

Sydney meets my eye and nods, and an understanding passes between us. It's her turn to make the push. "I'm glad too."

She slams into Caitlyn from behind, catching the other woman by surprise. Sydney's body is weak and unsteady, but the momentum of the impact is enough to knock Caitlyn from her feet near the treacherous cliff.

For a second before she drops over the edge, Caitlyn's eyes go wide with shock. Then she's falling, arms windmilling as she plummets toward the unyielding earth far below.

We listen until we can no longer hear her scream.

70

LUCY

Sydney sags into my arms, her breath ragged. I catch her against my chest and squeeze her tight as she whispers, "Is she . . . ?"

There's no way Caitlyn could have survived that fall. "It's over."

Syd's whole body trembles with cold or pain or the shaky aftershocks of adrenaline wearing off. "We're okay," she says, and I repeat the same thing back to her. We did what we needed to do.

I press a kiss to the side of her head, her long hair tickling my face. "You saved me."

"Everyone wants to think I'm a terrible actress, but I did okay when it counted. Playing dead." She shakes her head, and her voice turns sad. "You saved me a long time ago," she admits. Her words are a kind of forgiveness, and I can finally let myself breathe. "If you hadn't stopped Cole . . ."

She doesn't continue, but we can both imagine what she's left unsaid. She's the kind of person who believes in the inherent goodness of the world, who believes in second chances. She would have stayed with him. He could have broken her.

If she stayed, I might have buried her instead of him.

I'd make the choice I made that night a thousand times over if it meant Syd and I would come through the challenge together. The thing Caitlyn didn't understand is that there doesn't have to be a final girl, a single winner against a vicious world. There can be final girls. Ones who help each other through the darkest times. Who walk out of the forest hand in hand.

"Syd?" When I saw her with Brent's knife in her back, I thought I'd lost the chance to apologize. But she's here and I can't waste another second. I need to make things right. "I'm so sorry for what I said before. It wasn't true."

She shakes her head, and my stomach sinks until she explains: "But it was. I mean, I hope you don't think I'm a categorically terrible person. But what you said was true. You have every right to feel burned-out and upset. Sometimes I get too caught up in trying to be who everyone expects me to be. This career is sort of unprecedented, and I don't always know how to do it right. But I do know that I haven't done a good job listening, and I want to change that."

"And I haven't done a good job being honest." The confession feels like a bubble in my chest. "I think I'm done taking influencer pictures."

She manages a watery laugh. "Fair enough."

I squeeze her gently. "It's not because of this weekend, though that definitely didn't help. It's just that you're my best friend, Syd. I don't want you to be my boss."

"Okay, then, you're fired," she tries to joke. "I'll have to put together your severance package and—"

"It's okay," I promise. "I'm going to be fine." This time, I know that it's true. I can get through whatever comes next as long as I'm honest about what I need.

Syd's faint with blood loss, so I loop my arms under hers, careful to avoid the carnage of her back, and help her hobble toward the Lodge. We follow the trail blazed through the snow during our escape, guided by splatters of blood. It's a slow march, marked by plenty of stops to rest, but her bare feet can barely hold her. They're mangled beyond belief.

Around us, the forest returns to life. A bird carries a song across the sky. The waterfall hushes in the distance.

As we round the Lodge, the sounds change, a new rumbling layered on top of the breeze. I can't see the source of the noise around the looming building, but it sounds like a car chugging up the hill.

Syd's been staring at her feet, careful not to trip on our journey, but now she lifts her eyes to mine in wonder. "Is that—?"

My heartbeat speeds up, and I nod. Someone's coming for us. It makes me want to cry. "An engine." And then a car door slams.

It's the police, I think, but a bark rings out through the forest, and then there's a dog bounding to us through the snow.

Sweet brown eyes, long, soft ears. Velvet snout.

"Oboe?"

He snuffles his wet nose into my palm, his tail whipping against my leg. So happy, happy, happy to see me.

It takes me a minute to understand, to look past him and see Nick clear the corner of the Lodge, and then my whole body hums with hope.

"Good boy," I whisper as my dog trots back to the man I never stopped loving.

Nick breaks into a run at the sight of us, coming to prop up Sydney from the other side and take some of her weight from me. Together we make slow progress toward the front of the Lodge.

"You're here," I croak. "You beat the police."

Nick's eyes catch mine, warm and worried. "What the hell happened?"

Sydney lets out a wet cough, halfway to a bitter laugh. "How much time do you have?"

There'll be time later to talk, to detail Caitlyn and Brent's murder spree. But for now he lets it go so we can catch our breath. Nick, who's never been anything but patient and kind. "I could tell something was wrong, Luce. You didn't answer your texts. So I started watching everyone's social media stories." It does something funny to my heart to know he checked up on me even after I pushed him away. He wanted to see me; he still cared.

"I don't understand," I tell him. "We lost Wi-Fi. There were no stories."

He flicks his eyes toward Sydney. "But there were." He sighs and delivers the news that Sydney's been having the worst weekend of her life on social media. Half of her fans think she's planning a publicity stunt and the other half think she's gone crazy, but they can all agree the optics aren't good.

Caitlyn must have had backup plans upon backup plans to destroy us all. If Sydney survived, she was never going to live it down.

Caitlyn might have been unhinged, but she was also undeniably clever. Evil fucking genius–level smart.

Too bad for her that we were smarter.

"I heard about the storm," Nick tells us, "and I came as soon as I could. I left yesterday, but it took me until this morning to get around a downed tree." He looks at Sydney, slumped between us, not enough blood in her body. "God, if only I'd gotten here sooner."

"All that matters is you came."

Silence folds over us as we make our way to the four-wheel drive Nick must have rented, complete with snow chains. Nick hates to drive, and yet he came.

Careful not to disturb her injured back, we load Sydney into the car and wrap blankets around her feet.

"You're going to be okay," I tell her, heat from the vents blasting my face.

She squeezes my hand and offers me the ghost of her signature smile. "We both are." She aims a pointed glance out the window toward where Nick is standing in the snow. "Now go get him," she mouths.

I whisper back, "I will."

Sydney's forgiven me for everything that happened in the past. I've taken a life and I've saved a life, and maybe there's balance in that. It's time to forgive myself. To let myself have the things I want. And there's nothing I want more in the world than Nick.

I want a home with him and Oboe.

I want to get out of my own way and truly live.

Sydney shuts the car door, trapping the heat around her. As sirens start to wail in the distance, I make my way toward the man I love.

"Sounds like the cavalry is coming," Nick tells me.

I look up at him with an exhausted smile. "I might have made some calls."

"I'm so glad you did." And then I'm in his arms, my face crushed against his chest, the spicy, comforting smell of his cologne enveloping me.

It feels like the start of everything, and my chest fills with the best kind of hope. Nick draws his arms closer around me, and I snuggle in. For the first time in ages, I let myself be held.

Epilogue

STORY POST

August

The start of August is as good a time as any to launch a new brand, and even though you're not there at the party, you can tell the ambiance is just right. The SoHo loft hums with noise, the crowd large enough to celebrate the hard work Sydney's put into building a company, but edited enough to feel exclusive.

Draped in thousands of twinkling white lights, the room shines almost as bright as the gems in Sydney's hair. That hair—that famous hair—is styled in loose, gleaming waves, and when she brushes it over her shoulder, you can fully appreciate the open-backed dress she wears in defiance of the long pink scar that traces her spine.

What happened to Sydney and Lucy out in the woods didn't just cause a buzz online—it made the actual news. First there were the headlines splashed across the broadcast networks, and then, when Syd was healed enough to leave the hospital, a series of interviews on the late-night talk shows. Caitlyn might have wanted to wipe out Syd and take her place, but the attack had the opposite effect: the world's not getting rid of Sydney Kent.

She's slated to star in two movies next year, and, of course, there's tonight's launch. Plentifol is ready for purchase at last.

If something so horrible was going to happen, you're glad something good came out of it. The world needs something to believe in.

You watch the screen expectantly, drinking the same little Aperol Spritz that's being served at the party. Syd provided the recipe in advance to make you feel like you were part of the celebration too. The bubbles fill your chest pleasantly, a bit like hope.

Tonight Sydney isn't talking directly into the camera; instead, she's handed off her phone for someone else to capture the event. It makes her appear to be part of the party instead of the whole of it. Still a star, of course, but also a link to something bigger.

Ever since she and Lucy crawled out of that death-trap retreat, there's been something different about her, a humility that wasn't always there before. In the past, Sydney preached the virtues of gratitude, but now she truly lives it. She and Lucy even teamed up to pay off medical debt for Caitlyn's stepmom, saying that the woman deserved proper treatments no matter how heinously Caitlyn might have behaved. The act raised Syd and Lucy to practically saint status.

Speaking of Lucy, she's here too, tucked among the shifting bodies, that red hair impossible to miss. There's no camera looped around her neck anymore. Instead, an engagement ring glitters on her left hand, while her other hand is tucked into her handsome fiancé's. Her smile is wide and easy. It looks good on her, and you don't see Cancer Girl when you look at her; you see a woman full of life.

Spoons clink against glasses, and someone cries, "Speech!," dragging your attention away from Lucy.

In front of a wall covered in the same flowers that appeared in Plentifol's inaugural advertising campaign, a blushing Sydney accepts the microphone that's thrust into her hands. The room hushes; the lights glow on her skin.

"Thank you so much for being here," Sydney begins. "I've said it before, but I truly wouldn't have had the confidence to go after this dream without your support."

She holds up a bottle of Plentifol shampoo. Unlike the ones sold at retail, this one's jewel-encrusted, the entire shape flawlessly covered in tiny crystals. Sparks of light dance off the surface, a disco ball reflection flickering on her skin.

She goes on to tell you that before his tragic murder, her friend Nash commissioned this custom bottle for her to mark the occasion of the launch. They'd worked on Plentifol together, and while he's not here tonight to celebrate, Sydney wishes desperately that he were. In the middle of the horror in the woods, she thought she couldn't trust anyone, but this gift of Nash's proved her wrong. There's still some good in the world.

To honor Nash's memory, Sydney announces that Plentifol will be creating an annual scholarship awarded to a worthy recipient who wants to pursue a career as a fashion or beauty stylist. Not only will they earn funding toward the education program of their choice, they'll also get a six-week internship with Sydney herself.

You were paying attention before, but now you're really paying attention.

Everyone wants a chance to be the next It Girl, but you can

see the opportunity for what it is: a way to get close to Sydney and have her sparkle rub off on you.

People want to achieve greatness, but not everyone has what it takes.

You could be different, though, you think. There might be something *there* there, and Sydney makes you believe that anything is possible. Interning with her is a benediction and a validation and a test.

You're not sure if this path is for you, if you can cut it, but a smile crosses your face.

You're going to apply anyway.

You'd like to find out.

Acknowledgments

Caitlyn and Lucy talk a lot about how much work goes into creating content—and how challenging it is to make anything look effortless—and in many ways, writing a book is no different. *Made You Look* would not have been possible without the hard work and dedication of so many people, and I can't say enough how grateful I am.

To my amazing agent, Samantha Fabien, thank you for believing in me and this story. Your enthusiasm, support, and willingness to always talk strategy make my writer heart sing. I'm endlessly grateful that this publishing journey brought us together.

To my incredible editor, Carly James, I'm so glad this story found a home with you—I couldn't imagine a better champion. Your keen eye, your sense of humor, and your spot-on editorial vision have helped this book become its best self. Thank you for your partnership and encouragement every step of the way.

To the rest of the team at Berkley, thank you for taking a pile of words and turning it into this gorgeous book—and for helping it find readers. I'm indebted to Alaina Christensen, Jenni

Surasky, Katheryn Gao, Abby Graves, Nicole Wayland, Heidi Ward, Lauren Burnstein, Kaila Mundell-Hill, and Kalie Barnes-Young. And thank you to Sarah Oberrender for creating such a stunning cover.

I'm a better writer and person because of the writers around me. I owe so much to my critique partners, Sheila Masterson and Jennifer Skogen, whose invaluable feedback has helped shape early drafts of this story. Thank you for helping me grow, cheering me on, and recklessly following me down each writing rabbit hole. Your friendship is the biggest gift.

To Faith Allington, Kirsten Rue, Nicole Comforto, Elizabeth Crouch, Victoria Brown, Laurel Bard, Cade Roach, Patricia Eddy, #TeamSamantha, and the Berkletes, thank you for welcoming me with open arms. You're fantastic writers and all-around amazing humans, and I'm so lucky to have found community with you. Thanks also to Carolina Beltran and Nicole Weinroth for helping me dream big and envision what this story could be.

To every writer, book blogger, librarian, and book seller that I've connected with in person and online, thank you for screaming about stories with me and for doing the important work of getting books into readers' hands. I'm not being even a little bit biased when I say the book community is the best corner of the internet. The world is warmer and kinder because of you. And to my non-writing friends who've supported me and this book along the way, thank you for being there with hugs, memes, and reminders to hydrate.

Thanks also to my parents, who have always spoiled me with books, as well as to the rest of my family for your encouragement. In particular, thanks to my brother Ben, who is an incredible journalist and storyteller, and who inspires me daily.

To my husband, Ian, you make me laugh like no one else and have supported my writing from the start. Thank you for understanding when I need to disappear into a story, and for being there with open arms and snacks when I reemerge. To my tremendous kids, I love you so, so much. Thank you for being so strong and kind and funny and wise, and for reminding me to always stay curious.

And to you. Yes, you. Thank you for picking up this book and spending time between its pages. I'm so grateful you're here.

Author photo by Seattle Headshots

Tanya Grant writes twisty thrillers full of secrets, murder, and gossipy group dynamics. When not conducting highly suspicious web searches (for research!), she also writes romances. Her essays have appeared on HelloGiggles.com and Bust.com, and she's spoken about creativity on various podcasts. When she's not writing, you can find Tanya listening to the coyotes howl outside her Seattle-area home, drinking cinnamon tea, and chasing her two children.

Visit Tanya Grant Online

TanyaGrantBooks.com

TanyaGrantBooks